DAEMON'S MARK

CAITLIN KITTREDGE

St. Martin's Paperbacks

This is a work of fiction. All of the characters, organizations, and events portrayed in this novel are either products of the author's imagination or are used fictitiously.

DAEMON'S MARK

Copyright © 2010 by Caitlin Kittredge.

All rights reserved.

For information address St. Martin's Press, 175 Fifth Avenue, New York, NY 10010.

ISBN: 978-0-312-94366-0

Printed in the United States of America

St. Martin's Paperbacks edition / June 2010

St. Martin's Paperbacks are published by St. Martin's Press, 175 Fifth Avenue, New York, NY 10010.

10 9 8 7 6 5 4 3 2 1

CHAPTER 1

When you're a cop, you learn fast that any attempt at a nice evening out can and will be spoiled by a dead body.

The restaurant was Macpherson's, an upscale steakhouse with medium-rare walls and décor made of antlers, and my dining partner was Agent Will Fagin, Bureau of Alcohol, Tobacco, and Firearms. More than just my dining partner, really . . . I guessed that William Fagin was, after six months of steady dating, my boyfriend.

I don't do well with the boyfriend/girlfriend designation, but we went out on too many dates to be friends with benefits and stayed in too often to be friends, period.

Will smiled at me over his porterhouse. He had a great smile. Great everything, if you wanted to quantify it—forty years ago he would have been staring back at me from a movie-house poster. Thick blond hair, dancing black eyes, a long skinny frame that belied strength and manly prowess and all of that stuff that women supposedly swoon over in a boyfriend.

"I get something on my face?" he asked, running a hand along his mouth.

"No," I said. "Sorry."

Will's eyes gleamed. "You were staring at me like you're thinking hard. That never bodes well for me."

"I was just thinking about what this is," I said, gesturing with my napkin at the table, the near-empty wineglasses and the remains of my New York strip, the crumbs in the bread basket. Will held up his hand.

"Say no more. That *what is this* talk never ends in anything except me sleeping on a sofa, so I'm going to ask for the check and we're going to head back to your apartment and have great sex until we forget about this conversation."

I laughed, pulling Will's hand down and covering it with mine. "If you let me finish, I was going to say that for me, this is good. It's the first time it's been good—calm—since I was in high school, and I like it. Gods, you're neurotic sometimes."

Will turned my hand over, running his thumb along my palm. "The offer to go back to your apartment still stands, Lieutenant Wilder."

I was about to tell him that sounded like a fine idea when my BlackBerry chirped from inside my purse. As the lieutenant in charge of the Supernatural Crime Squad for the Nocturne City Police Department, I was never really *off* call. The brass liked me to show up at crime scenes, wave to the news cameras, prove to the plain humans of Nocturne City that their pet werewolf detective was on the job.

"Hold that thought," I told Fagin, praying it would just be a text message from my cousin Sunny and not an emergency call.

My luck is never that good. *Code 187, Pier 16, Port of Nocturne,* the message read. It came from Javier

Batista, one of my detectives who had started picking up overtime and doing night shifts a few days a week.

"What's the word?" Fagin said, forkful of steak poised halfway to his mouth.

"Homicide down at the port," I said. "Batista wants me at the scene."

Will shrugged. "It happens. Don't take all night, doll." He leaned across the table and kissed my cheek, then turned around and called for our check. One of the benefits of having a man who has the same job you do—he may not like it, but he can't very well complain about the odd hours and the rushing off and the constant low background noise of the job in your everyday life.

I was already jogging out of the restaurant when he pulled out his credit card to pay. I got my 1971 Chevy Nova out of hock from the valet, who looked at the car like it personally offended him when it rumbled up at the curb. He did not receive a tip. My baby might not be pretty, but it had a decent amount of power under the hood and a roomy, boxy interior that I favored for things like changing out of a couture dress into jeans and a blouse in the front seat.

I pulled around the corner into the alley, wriggled into a pair of battered jeans that had seen more than one washing to take blood, fingerprint ink or plain grime out of them already and a plain black blouse. I was a lieutenant now—torn T-shirts and leather jackets were a thing of the past. Sadly. I kicked off my Chanel pumps—vintage, like most designer clothes worth wearing—and slipped on a pair of motorcycle boots that I kept on the passenger seat. Another thing you learn fast as a cop—have a change of clothes handy.

You never know what will get spattered on you at a crime scene. Wardrobe change accomplished, I put the Nova in gear and drove.

The Port of Nocturne is a sagging, rusting collection of warehouses, piers and cargo containers stacked like a dystopian labyrinth along the broad main avenue that stretches like a skeletal finger into the dark water of Siren Bay.

I rumbled up to the gate, flashing my bronze shield at the gatehouse guard. He waved me on. "Your people are down at Pier 16. Hell of thing."

Well, wasn't he a ray of sunshine. I drove through the stacks of cargo containers, the sodium lights spitting in the light mist rolling off Siren Bay. It was mid-March, that dank, chill time when even sunny California hunkers down and hibernates until spring. Nocturne City, poking out into the Pacific, felt the chill more than most.

Batista's unmarked car and a pair of patrol units were at the entrance to the pier, and a small cluster of officers milled around, staring at something in the water.

I reached over and grabbed my tub of VapoRub out of the glove compartment. As a werewolf, I have the heightened sense of smell to go with the temper, the strength and the once-a-month bloodlust, and floaters never smell all that great even if you're a plain human.

"LT," Batista called to me, waving me over. I met him at the edge of the pier. Batista looked tired, rings under his eyes and his normally tanned and healthy face sallow. "It's a bad one. My wife is gonna kill me when I don't come home at six."

"How's Marisol?" I asked. His wife was the reason he was working nights.

"Pregnant, as is usual these past few months," he said. "Morning sickness, and I'm still pulling double shifts to pay for the kid's nursery, and his college fund, and God knows what else."

I patted him on the shoulder. "I'll make sure you clock out on time, Javier."

"I appreciate it, *jefe*." He gestured to the water. "She's caught up against the pilings. I called the ME and he's en route, but it's definitely a homicide."

"And the SCS caught this how?"

"One of the first responders, Natchez, says he recognizes her. Says she's a were."

Freaking fantastic. "All right," I said, taking out my penlight and walking to the edge. The water was black and oil-slick, the weak lighting catching the detritus and spills floating on the surface.

The girl's face floated up at me on the gentle swell of the waves, caught just below the surface of the water. She had pale hair that drifted in the current like sea life, wide staring eyes and an open mouth, everything pale and bleached by her time underwater.

I saw a gaping stab wound in her sternum, dark against the translucent skin. It was ugly and broad, nothing clean or surgical about it. The girl was wearing a black miniskirt, mesh top and bra. Club clothes. She'd been having a good time somewhere, and ended up here, suspended in the filthy water of the port.

"Call the rest of the team, will you, Javier?" I said, standing up from my crouch. "Once we get her out of the bay, I want this wrapped up quick."

"Sure thing, LT," he said, pulling out his cell phone.

The rest of the detectives in the SCS wouldn't be happy about getting rousted out of bed, but a dead were girl warranted it. Were packs are territorial and hostile on a good day, and when one of their number is killed, they close ranks faster than a bunch of bad cops facing an Internal Affairs investigation.

I walked over to the knot of uniforms and found Officer Natchez, tall as a beanpole and curly-haired. "You told Detective Batista you recognized the victim?"

"Yes, ma'am," he said. "I worked private security before I joined the force and her family hired me for a few events." He pushed a hand through his hair. "This is pretty awful. She was a nice kid."

"And this nice kid's name would be?"

"The family is Dubois. The girl was named . . . Lila or Lisa or something. I'm sorry, ma'am. I can't recall."

Dubois didn't ring any immediate alarm bells as bad-ass pack members, but at least we didn't have to faff around with dental records or DNA for an identification. Unless Natchez was wrong, which was entirely possible, judging from his shell-shocked expression.

"This your first floater?" I said gently. He nodded.

"We don't catch much worse than junkie ODs or bar fights, ma'am. I was going off shift and I heard the call."

"Take a break," I said. "I'm sure my detectives and the CSU team could use some coffee."

"Okay," he said, and got into his patrol car, backing away from the pier. It's all about delegating at the crime scene—an officer who's losing his shit is worse than worthless for actual police work. Plus, everyone needs coffee.

"Sawbones is here," Batista said. "And I've called in."

"Great," I said absently. I was watching the second car behind the ME's black city Lincoln. It was a pale green hybrid, the sort of thing that Will—and me, too, I freely admit—would have dismissed as a "chick car." Sure enough, a chick was driving it, and she got out from behind the wheel in a swirl of Columbo-esque tan trenchcoat.

"Lieutenant Wilder?" she called. I sized her up as she came over. Brown hair, carrying about twenty over her ideal weight, flattering, flaw-minimizing pantsuit, makeup that was way too good for this time of night.

"Help you with something?" I said.

"I'm Detective Lane, with Special Victims," she said. "You can call me Natalie, though."

I cocked my eyebrow at her. "Right. Good to know. Was there something you wanted?"

"Oh, yes, actually. I got the call that there was a minor homicide."

"I appreciate you coming down," I said perfunctorily, "but we've got it under control."

"If the victim is under eighteen that makes it SVU jurisdiction," she said. "The rules are in place for a very specific reason, mostly to prevent cross-contamination of sensitive investigations . . ."

"Detective Lane." I held up my hands. "I appreciate that your captain yelled at you and made you drive down here, but the dead girl is a were. That makes it an SCS case."

"Actually," she said, "it was Deputy Chief Beck. Your boss? He requested someone from Special Victims liaise this case to cover all of the bases."

I shut my eyes for a second, praying for self-control. Beck never did a thing with the SCS unless he was haranguing me for something he figured I'd done the wrong way. He preferred to cozy up to the lieutenants and captains in Vice and Narcotics, who were men and didn't turn fuzzy on the full moon.

I hated the guy, but if he'd set this perky soccer mom with a badge on me, there wasn't much I could do except act bitchy and complain a lot.

"All right," I snapped, since complaining never did anything for me. "If I'm stuck with you, hang back and don't expect a warm, friendly group hug from the rest of my squad."

Lane—sorry, *Natalie*—blinked. I got the feeling she was used to her sweet round face and perky demeanor making people nice and cooperative. "I . . . All right. You're the ranking officer."

"What do you know. You can recite protocol." I was probably being nastier than I strictly had to be, but I resented Chief Beck sending some white-bread kiddie cop to babysit me. I was good at my job—two years on the street, five in Homicide and nearly a year heading up the SCS.

Ignoring for the moment the suspensions, write-ups and general chaos that had categorized my time as a detective, I went to meet Bart Kronen, the night-shift medical examiner.

"Only the good die young," he greeted me. "I'll wait for CSU to take a few scene photos and then we'll get her out of the water."

The techs showed up in short order and once they'd documented the scene, Kronen laid out a body bag and then got one of the patrol officers to lend him a rope from his prowler car.

"A bit of help, if you please," he said to the scene at large. No one moved, so I came over.

"We will attempt to slip the rope around her torso to avoid unnecessary damage to the skin," he said. We laid down on our stomachs, the girl's face staring back at us. The rope looped around her skinny torso, and Kronen drew it tight. "Pull, Lieutenant Wilder. If you please." We got to our feet and drew the girl up and out of the dark water. Even waterlogged as she was, she weighed barely enough to strain my arms.

I'm stronger than a human, but even Kronen only gave a slight wheeze as we lowered her into the body bag. He crouched, unzipping his portable kit. Lane crowded at my shoulder.

"Poor girl. She can't be more than seventeen." She bent down to examine the body and Kronen cleared his throat loudly. I reached out and pulled Lane back by the shoulder of her coat.

"Let the doc work. Save the Oprah moment for later."

"Cause of death appears to be mutilation to the left upper chest," Kronen said. "She most likely bled out, accounting for the lack of lividity in her skin."

He took a pair of tweezers and plucked at the edges of the wound. The top layer of skin sloughed off, with a sound like wet paper bunching. Lane's face lost color and she let out a small, choked sound. Kronen had the grace to pretend not to notice. "By the condition of her dermis, I would estimate that she's been in the water at least twelve hours. Time of death will be difficult to fix because of the condition of the body."

He probed the wound further, and his forehead furrowed. "Hmm. That's odd."

"What?" I said. Kronen finding things "odd" was never good. After twenty years as a Nocturne City ME, he was about as hard to rattle as an android.

"Her heart," he said. "It appears to be missing."

"You mean it's hacked up?" Lane said. "That wound looks pretty severe. Maybe she got impaled on something."

"No," Kronen said. "Her ribs have been cracked. Her heart is not damaged. Her heart is gone."

I cocked my head. "*Gone?*" Just when you think you've seen everything.

"That's what I said," Kronen agreed mildly. "I think we're done here. Zip her up and I'll get her back to the morgue."

"I want her autopsied ASAP," Lane said. "This isn't some hooker we're dealing with. This is somebody's daughter."

Kronen gave a stiff nod and gestured for the coroner's assistant to zip up the body bag.

Lane noticed me glaring at her after a second. "What?"

I crossed my arms. "A hooker is somebody's daughter, too."

"You know what I meant," Lane said. She at least had the grace to turn colors under the sodium lights.

Just because the body leaves the scene doesn't mean there isn't still a crapton of work to do. The rest of the SCS trickled in, and I assigned them each to a sector of the scene to process it.

David Bryson, whom I'd known in Homicide, looked rumpled and red-eyed from lack of sleep. Andy

Zacharias, a rookie detective who'd been initiated into my squad by being the hostage of a bunch of off-the-reservation Thelemite cultists, looked like he'd either been awake waiting for my call or mainlined a whole lot of caffeine.

"Andy." I corralled him, as Bryson and Batista started looking for tire tracks along with a CSU tech.

"You look nice, ma'am," he said, gesturing to my upswept hair and makeup. "Date interrupted?"

"None of your damn business, Andy," I said cheerfully. "I need you to find the security office and pull their footage for this part of the port. If we're lucky, everything is on tape and we can wrap this up before the weekend."

Hunter Kelly was the last to arrive, and with Andy shooed away from anything that would actually get him into trouble, I caught him at the yellow tape. "I need to ask you something."

Kelly, who's built like a surly Irish tree trunk and about as expressive, grunted. "Shoot."

"Is there something that a witch would need a human heart for?" I said. Kelly was a warlock, a battle witch, and I figured if anyone would know about the icky, slasher-film stuff he would.

Kelly shrugged. "Lots of things. You can eat your enemy's heart for prowess in battle. You can preserve it to bind someone to you in spirit for eternity. And it's a punishment."

"That, I agree on," I said. "Losing internal organs usually isn't a fun, lighthearted romp through the park."

"It's a punishment for betrayal," Kelly said. "Cut out the heart of the one who broke yours. That sort of poetic bullshit. Never put much stock in it, myself."

That I'd buy. Kelly was many things, but he wasn't a romantic. "Okay, thanks," I said. "I have to head to the morgue for a body ID. Have Batista call me when you're finished here, and keep an eye on that bright-eyed moron from SVU. She's way too eager."

"Got it," Kelly rumbled. I took one last look at the pier and the black water beyond as I walked back to my car. What had brought the girl here?

And with her missing heart, who the hell was I chasing for her murder?

CHAPTER 2

The morgue at night is the sort of place you'd expect zombies to congregate, or maybe a pack of particularly lame Goth vampires, if such a thing existed. In a city where Wendigo, werewolves, magick-users and trolls all shared space, it was sort of refreshing to know I didn't have to worry about Dracula sneaking up and making me into a Slurpee.

I found Kronen in scrubs, washing his hands in the steel sink off of the autopsy bay. "Before you cut her open, I need to notify her parents. Can you give me an hour?"

Kronen kicked off the water and nodded. "It would be prudent, I think. She's very young—I checked her mouth for trace and her wisdom teeth aren't even close to erupting. I'd put her age at perhaps fifteen."

Even with my job, there were times I wondered what the world was coming to, when magick-users ripped out a teenage girl's heart and left her for the sea to take.

"Mind if I use your computer?" I asked Kronen. He graciously pretended not to notice my grim expression.

"Please. I'll ask an attendant to take our poor girl to the viewing bay, shall I?"

"Do that," I said, pulling up the department search utility. The Dubois family wasn't hard to find—Nathaniel and Petra. A Cedar Hill address and no criminal records. The slick, pretty faces on the DMV photos didn't look like they even had a daughter, never mind one who would end up dead on a city pier.

I picked up the phone on the morgue wall, anyway. Looks weren't everything—to the casual eye I was a too-tall, dark-haired, reasonably pretty thirty-something woman. There was no clue to what was lurking under my skin, until the monster came out, in my eyes or my teeth or my claws.

"Hello?" A groggy answer, with a Latino accent. I looked at my watch. It was almost one A.M. I worked nights when I was in Homicide, and time has always been fluid for me, anyway.

"Hello. This is Luna Wilder, with the Nocturne City police. I need to speak to the Dubois family."

"Okay, okay. Hold, please." The phone was set down with a clunk and a moment later a male voice came over the line.

"You people better have a damn good excuse for calling me in the middle of the night."

"Mr. Dubois?"

"Who else would it be?"

Oh, he was leaving himself wide open there. The gravity of the news I had to deliver stopped me from saying anything grossly unprofessional, but I can't say it wasn't tempting. "Mr. Dubois, I'm afraid I have some bad news. I need you and your wife to come down to the city morgue as soon as possible."

A slow breath on the other end of the line. When

Nathaniel Dubois spoke again, he was subdued, almost scared. "Could you tell me what this is regarding?"

I was going to tear Natchez a new windpipe if he was wrong about this. "It's about your daughter, sir."

"Lily? What? What's happened to Lily?"

So that was her name. Not Lisa or Lila. Lily.

"Sir, I think it's best if I speak to you and your wife in person."

Dubois was numb now, and I could hear him panting into the phone. "We'll be right there."

I headed out to the waiting room, the public face of the morgue, where doors and curtains hid the procession of the dead from unsuspecting eyes. A familiar form was sitting in one of the butt-deadening institutional chairs, and I looked again, surprised, even though I shouldn't be. He always knew how to be in the right place at the right time. "Will?"

"Hey, doll," he said, sliding to his feet. "I figured you weren't going to come home to me, so I came to you."

"I was going to call," I said. Will smiled.

"Yeah, but this is so much better." He came over and planted a slow kiss, and I let myself relax into him, for just a second. I don't like dead children. There's something so unnatural about seeing a small body, still and lifeless, that makes you want to rush home and reclaim life any way you can.

"Bad one?" Will whispered into my neck.

"About as bad as they come," I said. He stroked my cheek with the back of his knuckles and stepped away, holding me at arm's length.

"Don't let it eat at you. Think you'll be home for breakfast?"

"I don't know," I said, truthfully. Will stroked the back of his fingers along my cheekbone.

"I'll go to the market and get the stuff for omelets. I'm an optimist."

The elevator from the lobby groaned its ancient way toward us, and my guts went cold. "That's got to be my ID, Will."

He nodded. "I'll leave you to it, then." Dropping a quick peck on my cheek, he headed for the loading bay and the street exit.

I watched him go, avoiding thinking about the Duboises until they actually appeared. Will was a damn near perfect guy—considerate, funny, handsome, great in bed. I wasn't used to perfect and it freaked me out a little bit. I kept expecting to find out that this was all an elaborate cosmic prank.

Or get bored. I tend to go for men who are so heavily broken they might as well be on the scrap heap. Will was a conscious effort to break the pattern. Even though he carried a curse in his veins the way I carried the were in my DNA—a curse worked on him by a vengeful witch almost four hundred years ago—aside from his pesky immortality, he might as well have hopped out of a cheesy romance movie.

"Excuse me." The gravity in the voice was the same from the phone. I turned and faced the Duboises. They were less polished than the DMV photos, but only marginally. Petra was blonde, probably originally closer to my blue-black brunette if her coloring was any indication. Nathaniel was tall, boxy, brown hair swept back into a playboy wave.

Both of them scented of were. I knew it was coming, but it still sent a faint quiver of unease through me. I'm an Insoli, a packless were, and the Duboises most certainly ranked higher in the natural order than I did.

I tried not to let it bother me overmuch. I belonged here, doing my job. This was my territory. "Mr. Dubois, Mrs. Dubois," I said. "Thank you for coming down."

"Are you Lieutenant Wilder?" Petra asked. "What's happened to Lily?"

"I am," I said, reaching out my hand. She looked at it, her nostrils flaring, and didn't offer her own. The push-pull for dominance had already started. Great. "There's no easy way to say this," I told the Duboises. "A person we believe to be your daughter was discovered earlier tonight in the water, in the Port of Nocturne."

Nathaniel passed a hand over his face. "Discovered? What does that mean?"

"It means we have a body," I said softly. "And we need you to take a look at it and identify your daughter."

Petra fell against Nathaniel's considerable chest with a sob. "No," she whispered. "No, no, no. It's not Lily."

"Sweetie," he said, stroking her hair. "Sweetie, we have to look."

"*No.*" Petra shoved away from him and wrapped her arms around herself.

"Are you sure, Lieutenant?" Nathaniel said to me, a quiver just evident in his hands, his voice. He was trying to be strong, be the husband and the alpha male, but he'd shattered from the inside and his eyes were empty.

"We're fairly sure, yes," I said quietly.

"What does that gutterwolf know?" Petra spat. "The police make mistakes all the time!"

I ignored the slur for the moment and gestured to the viewing room. "If you'll both come this way?" I hated body IDs with every fiber of my being. I hated being the one to spread the bad news, hated to be there in someone's worst and most private moment of grief.

But it was my job, so I buzzed the viewing bay to make sure the morgue attendant was ready and then pulled the curtain back.

The girl was under a sterile sheet that covered the gaping wound in her chest. Her lank, light hair, like dead seaweed, spread around her on the steel table. Kronen had closed her eyes. He was a lot better at this sort of thing than I would ever be.

Petra Dubois let out a strangled sound, her knees buckling. Her husband caught one side and I caught the other. "Mrs. Dubois?" I asked softly.

She looked up at me, fresh makeup streaked with tears, black runnels in her perfect mask. "That's her. That's my little girl."

"Thank you," I said, suddenly very tired. "I'm so sorry for your loss." I should have been sound asleep right now, Will's body curled around mine. I shouldn't have been here, in the stuffy viewing room. I pulled the curtain and ushered the Duboises out.

"How did this happen?" Nathaniel asked me. "Who did it?" His jaw was jumping, the muscles knotting in a rage I recognized too well. It was the same one that boiled out of the pit of my animal brain when my were recognized a threat or predator.

"That's what we're all trying to find out," I said. "Mr. Dubois, given your . . . status in the community, the Supernatural Crime Squad is handling your daughter's homicide."

"So it was murder." Petra's voice was deathly cold, colder than the freezers waiting for me back in the morgue. "My pack will tear him to shreds. He'll see death coming and he'll have time to scream."

"Let's not be hasty," said Nathaniel.

"If you don't mind right now, there are some questions . . ." I said, trying to stall the inevitable "pack justice" track Petra Dubois's mind was taking. Weres don't tolerate outsiders dealing with violence against one of their own. They have a cockeyed vigilante system dating back to the time before police, when villagers were likely to pick up pitchforks and go after any were they met.

"Can't it wait?" Petra cried. "Can't we have just one night for our little girl?"

"I'm very, very sorry," I said, so softly I was worried I'd have to repeat myself. "But the faster we can get our investigation moving, the better the chance of us catching your daughter's killer." Most homicides are solved within the forty-eight hours immediately following the crime, and I was already an entire day behind schedule.

"All right," said Nathaniel. "Go ahead. Ask your questions."

"Who had a reason to hurt Lily?" I said. Direct approach works best with weres. Most don't appreciate beating around the bush.

"No one," Petra said. "She was a wonderful girl. Star of the choir at her prep school, got excellent grades . . ."

"Petra." Her husband's voice was heavy. "You know and I know that's not the whole truth. Not anymore."

She turned on him with a snarl. "I am not discussing this right now, Nate."

"The detective wants to know if someone could have hurt Lily," Nathaniel hissed. "Someone *did* hurt Lily. Are you honestly going to keep her in the dark?"

I didn't correct him that I was actually a lieutenant. "What do you mean, Mr. Dubois?"

"Lily was having problems in school and problems with us," he snapped. "She was a handful, even for a fourteen-year-old girl."

Fourteen. Even younger than Kronen and I had suspected. "A handful how?" I said.

"We found pills in her bedroom," Nathaniel said. "It's my fault. I didn't pay attention when her grades started slipping. She had to leave Alder Bay Prep and go to public school, here in the city." His words tumbled out like cars rushing by on the freeway, fast and blurred, trying to make up for lost time.

"Stop it," Petra whispered. "Stop making this about you, and stop blaming Lily."

Nathaniel bared his teeth. "Then what the hell do you want me to say, Petra?"

"Lay the blame where it belongs!" she shouted. "For once in your fucking life. Lily had a boyfriend," she said to me. "A much older, scumbag boyfriend."

"Russ wasn't to blame for everything . . ." Nathaniel started. "Lily only met him after she flunked out and came back home."

"The drugs started after she met him," Petra said, cold enough to shatter. "The partying, and the lies. He's a wretched, ugly piece of trash and we forbid her to see him."

"Did she listen?" I asked.

Petra snorted. "Did you listen to your mother at fourteen?" She had a point. At fourteen I'd been sneaking my father's cheap scotch and smoking pot. The inappropriate boyfriends, too. One of them was the reason I had a monster in me now. A beach bonfire, a bite on the shoulder and a month later, the moon had pulled it free.

"One more thing," I said. "Our preliminary findings indicate that magick may have been a factor in your daughter's death. Was she associating with any magick-users that you knew about?"

The parents traded looks. Dating a witch was tantamount to spitting on your parents' shoes in were packs. "No," Petra said. "Just that son of a bitch, Russ. Russell Meyer. He lives somewhere over in Highland Park."

"Thank you," I said, making a note of the boyfriend's name on my BlackBerry. "You can go home now . . . I'll have the medical examiner call you as soon as your daughter's body is released so you can make funeral arrangements. I also have the name of a departmental grief counselor . . ."

"We don't need a counselor," Petra snapped. "We need the bastard's head."

Petra started for the elevator, looking like she'd rather be anywhere else. Nathaniel followed her, and then turned back to me, halfway between the doors and where I stood in the entrance of the viewing room.

"You have to find who did this," he said. "You're a were. You find him and you give him to us. It's your duty."

"I have to find who killed Lily," I said. "I have to give her justice for what happened. I don't have to do a gods-damned thing for your pack."

"I'd rethink that attitude, Insoli," Nathaniel said with

a sad smile. "Before you become a bigger problem then you're worth."

"Mr. Dubois, it's been my experience that people under intense strain or grief say things that they don't mean. I'd take that to heart, if I were you."

Petra came and plucked at his sleeve. "Can we please just go home, Nate? I don't want to be here anymore."

"You remember what I said," Nate Dubois said as the elevator doors closed on them.

"Oh," I told the empty morgue. "I will."

CHAPTER 3

I couldn't interview Russ Meyer in the middle of the night, so I went to Fagin's loft instead, slipping into bed next to him and wrapping my arms around his slim, strong frame. "Hey, gorgeous," he murmured, and fell back to sleep almost instantly.

Sleeping next to Will wasn't hard, but every time I shut my eyes I saw Lily's face under the water, skin translucent, suspended in time.

I kept hoping that the visions of the dead would go away, get less, as I spent more time among them, but it didn't work that way. My were sensory input made sure that I remembered everything in diamond-sharp detail, and rarely forgot. The victims and I entered into a pact when I stood over their body, and they stayed with me whether or not I was able to fulfill it.

I was still awake when Will's alarm went off at 5:30 A.M., and I got up with him, although I could sleep until seven and still make it to work on time.

Will went out for his run and I dressed in some clothes I'd left at his place, gray suit trousers and a red blouse, nothing fancy. I didn't want to freak out Russ Meyer.

I called Bryson once I was caffeinated and dressed.

"David, can you pull an address for Russell Meyer in Highland Park and meet me there?"

Bryson grumbled. "Do you have any idea how early it is? I'm barely out of my tighty-whities from the night before, Wilder."

"Just don't show up naked and we'll be in good shape," I said. I wanted to get the jump on Russ, shake him up, try to spook something out of him. A hugely disproportionate number of homicides involving women and girls are the work of pissed-off boyfriends or husbands.

Plus, he was the only lead I had.

Bryson texted me back with the address, and I drove to the run-down section of Highland Park, which was becoming more gentrified every day. There was a Java Jones on the corner of Meyer's street, and an organic market, but the bum sleeping just down the sidewalk shattered a little bit of the ambiance.

Bryson's grimy Taurus was parked at the curb in front of a pool hall, and I knocked on his passenger window.

"Yo, Wilder," he said, thrusting a white bag at me. "Got you a cruller. Those hippies down the block do a pastry that ain't half bad."

"This is the address?" I said, pointing at the pool hall. Bryson nodded, brushing crumbs off his tie. Bryson was handsome, in a pugilistic way, if you could get past his blocky neck and his appalling taste in fashion, music, women and just about everything else.

Still, he was an honest cop, and a stand-up guy once you peeled away the layers ingrained by Charles Bronson movies and too much time in strip clubs.

"Apartments above the tavern," he said. "Guy shacks up in one of 'em. Credit is for shit—he owes about a grand in back rent from what I could see."

"He got a sheet?" I said, starting for the back stairs to the apartments above the closed-up bar.

"Minor stuff," said Bryson. "Underage DUI, vandalism, drunk stupid misdemeanors. The kind we all got hiding behind our eighteenth birthday."

"Speak for yourself," I said, mounting the rickety stairs. Paint flaked off the brick wall under my palm and a dog snarled from behind one of the doors we passed.

"You mean to tell me that you never raised any hell?" Bryson snorted.

"I raised plenty," I said, giving him a grin. "I just never got caught."

"Guess that's why you're the lieutenant, then," Bryson muttered. "All brass is good at being slippery."

"David, you keep talking like that and I'm gonna think you don't love me anymore." I raised my fist and pounded on Russ Meyer's door. After a few moments, a lock clicked and a pale, scruffy goatee with a pale, scruffy face behind it peered out.

"Yeah?"

"Russ Meyer?" I said. He squinted, looking me up and down. His eyes were glassy and bloodshot with the tiny roadmaps of veins particular to stoners. Stoned on what was the real question.

"Maybe. You asking in a personal or professional capacity?"

I showed him my shield, and a large, predatory smile. "That, Mr. Meyer, is entirely up to you."

"Wow," he said, blinking. "Uh, you wanna come in?"

"That's a start," I said. He stepped back, ushering us in. He was clad only in boxers and a ratty robe, and I could see a tattoo crawling across his stomach, concave where the rest of his skinny body was convex. Oh, yeah, the ladies must drop into a dead faint when this guy came calling.

We stepped inside, Bryson straight ahead and me to the side, clearing his line of fire. Neither of us was going to take Russ's laid-back stoner-dude act at face value.

Nothing sinister happened when I entered the dim apartment. I felt cobwebs brush my face and dust go up my nose, and I sneezed. Bryson stopped inside the door, wrinkling his nose.

"Uh, you want some coffee, Officers? Maybe a donut?" His mouth twitched, trying to hide his smile unsuccessfully.

"You think that's funny?" Bryson demanded, sucking in his waistline. I held up my hand.

"It's fine, David. Mr. Meyer should laugh while he can."

Russ slumped down on his plaid sofa, eliciting a shriek of springs, and fumbled a cigarette out of the crushed pack on the coffee table. "What's that supposed to mean?"

"It means that Lily Dubois is dead, Russell, and her parents fingered you as the asshole boyfriend interfering with their baby girl."

He choked on his first drag. "Lily's *dead?* You're messing with me."

I grabbed the cigarette from his hand. "I am so far from messing with you, you don't even want to know. How old are you, Russell?"

He glared at me, floppy strawberry blond hair hanging in his pimply face. A rat skittered in the kitchen area, and I caught a whiff of rot. "I'm waiting," I told him. I was going to need a dozen showers when I left this filthy craphole.

"Seventeen," he said, finally. I gave David the nod, and he rummaged on the tabletops and the Murphy bed in the corner until he found a chain wallet, stamped with the Diesel logo. High-end clothes, shitty apartment. Either Russ was a heavy-duty user or he was even more of a poser than he looked.

"Hey, that's mine!" Russ said, jolting off the sofa. I pushed him back down.

"Well, will you look at this horseshit," Bryson said. "Our boy is twenty-one."

I looked back at Russ. "Well?"

"It's a fake ID," he muttered. "She had one, too."

Bryson shook his head, tilting the license back and forth under the bedside light. "Not unless they got their hands on a state hologram stamp. This baby's real as they come."

"You cops will do anything to pin a rap on a kid. You're all facists." With that pronouncement, Russ reached for a fresh cigarette.

"You know," I said, standing over him, backing him into the sofa. "A few things occur to me here: First, you're a liar. Second, a twenty-one-year-old guy with a fourteen-year-old girl is statutory rape, and third, you don't seem that broken up about her being *dead*."

Russ snorted wetly, a snort of the deeply asthmatic or the deeply coked-up. "For all I know that's a lie. Lily and I talked last night. She sent me a text right after I left late night at the Belladonna."

I knew the Belladonna bar. I'd caught a homicide there eighteen months ago. It was a dive, a haven for dealers and burnout students from Nocturne University.

"So after you were done snorting your daddy's allowance up your nose, you got a text?" I said. "Show me."

He glared. "Show me a warrant."

Great, the one connection to Lily's death was a *Law & Order* fan. I reached out and grabbed the front of his robe, pulling him halfway off the sofa. "You got any syringes on you, Russell?"

"Hell no," he snorted. "Not all kids who like to have fun are junkies, 5-0."

"You're twenty-one," I said. "You're not a kid." I felt around in his pockets until my fingers closed around a high-end cell phone. I checked the message history. Sure enough, LilyGrrl was the last text. *C u at tha spot cnt wait 2 tayste u baby.*

I showed it to Bryson, who wrinkled his nose. "Look at that fucking grammar. This country's going all to hell."

"You lied to me again, Russ," I said, snapping the phone shut. "You and Lily were together last night. You're 0 for 2 here and I'm not a patient woman. You have one more chance to tell me the truth or I'm going to lay your skinny ass out for rape and obstruction, and that's just off the top of my head."

Meyer opened his mouth, but I held up a finger. "Think before you answer. The next smart-ass comment is getting you tossed down those stairs out there."

He was silent for a moment, the rats in the kitchen scrabbling and squeaking. Something thin and black tickled the back of my neck.

"Okay," he said finally, getting up and thrusting out his chest in the same way young tigers show their teeth. "Yeah, Lily and I hooked up. She loved what I did for her. She was only young in years. More mature than any of those spoiled college bitches I met. We had a great time."

"You're a real class act," said Bryson. "Her father should have kicked your skinny little ass."

Russ snorted. "That puppy couldn't touch me. He knew better."

In close proximity, underneath the scent of body odor, pot and some bitter drug on his sweat, Russ had the distinctive charred scent that always made my stomach drop. He had the blood.

"You're a witch," I said out loud, using the feminine noun on purpose.

"I have talents that frighten the narrow-minded, yeah," Russ said. "Including those rich pig parents of Lily's."

I gave him my most predatory smile. "Too bad for you that Lily was killed in a magick ritual," I said. "You're under arrest. Turn around and put your hands behind you. Thumbs up." I reached for my cuffs.

Russ smirked at me. "I don't answer to the police."

"No," I said, moving my hands from my cuffs to my gun. "You answer to me. Turn. Now."

"I'm not going away," Russ said. "I'm not going to be framed. I know what they do to kiddie fiddlers in prison."

"Wilder . . ." Bryson said, and then choked off, going to his knees. I drew my Sig Sauer P226 and aimed it between Russell's eyes.

"Don't you move." I turned my head toward Bryson,

trying to quiet the panic that flamed up in my brain. The scrabbling of the rats grew unbearably loud, and I saw a black shadow creep across the floor, overtaking Bryson, who gave a yelp and tried to swat it away.

"Ambient magick, pig," said Russ. "Wardings. Can't wipe that off."

I flipped the safety off of my Sig. "Call it off."

"No can do," said Russ. "My boundary ward doesn't take kindly to uninvited guests."

I stepped closer and pressed the gun into his forehead. "I'm willing to bet that blowing your skull a new skylight will take care of any workings you control just fine."

"Wilder . . ." Bryson choked. "Wilder, I can't breathe . . ."

I felt the working crawl over my feet, my legs, and my own breath got short. I'd encountered boundary wards that caused pain, or those that simply paralyzed, but this was new, and I'd walked right into it.

"He has about another minute before he suffocates," Russ said, boring into me with his bleary gaze. "Your call, pork sausage."

"I take the gun off if you let my detective go," I said. Russ nodded.

"Do it."

I put the gun up, and Russ exhaled. I felt the prickles on my neck recede, the sound, and the smothering feeling of magick on my skin. I've never liked being that close to magick, even though most of my family has the blood. Maybe it comes from feeling left out.

Bryson wheezed, and stumbled to his feet, his thick face near purple. "I'll kill you, you little son of a bitch . . ."

"David, no," I started, but it was too late. Russ slammed into me with his whole weight, spinning me around and into Bryson. He was out the door, robe flapping, before I could recover.

"Go," Bryson said, righting me. "I'll call it in."

I was already moving, out the door and straight over the railing to the alley a story below. Russ's orange robe flickered out of the corner of my eye as he rounded the front of the building.

My ankle twisted when I landed, but I shook it off and kept running. It would heal by the time I caught up with Russ, and if it was sprained, I could at least make him hurt as much as I was.

Russ had made it across the street, into the alley between a bodega and a handbag boutique. I darted into traffic, nearly clipping the bumper of a late-model Lexus. The driver cursed at me.

I drew my Sig, aiming at Russ's skinny back. He fetched up against the blank wall of the building on the next street, rattling the emergency door fruitlessly.

"Nowhere to go, Russ," I said. "Now, let's try this again, with the knowledge that if you try any more magick tricks I'm going to put two in your head. Sound good?"

He turned around, his lip curling. "I didn't kill her."

"At this point," I said, grabbing his arms and cuffing them behind his back, "I don't even care. You're under arrest." I Mirandized him while Bryson got the car and helped me load Meyer into the back seat.

"Get Pete down here to search his apartment," I said. "If there's any hard evidence he was with Lily last night, we'll find it."

Bryson rubbed his throat, glaring at Russ in the

rearview mirror. "What I wouldn't do for five minutes alone with you, you little shit."

"You know, Russ," I said. "If you just give us an alibi, I can probably save you from having Detective Bryson here accidentally ram your head into your cell door on the way in."

"Go piss up a rope, cop," Russ said. "I want a lawyer."

"Have it your way," I sighed, and drove toward the SCS offices.

CHAPTER 4

The SCS doesn't get a real office. Like most of the unpleasant things that normal people like to keep out of sight, we're hidden in the basement of the main administrative building in downtown Nocturne City. The top floors of the Justice Plaza are full of Narcotics, Vice, SWAT and other noble pursuits.

The freak squad is in the old bomb shelter. In a way, it's appropriate.

I walked Russ Meyer to an interview room and cuffed him to a chair. He smirked at me. "You think these will hold a witch?"

"They've done pretty well so far," I said. "And if you get cute, look up." Russ blinked, staring at the ward drawn on the ceiling of the interview room. "Think of yourself as a cell phone," I said. "This is a dead spot. That ward mark makes sure of it."

Bryson knocked on the observation mirror, and I stuck my head out the door. "Bright boy here doesn't have a lawyer. I called the public defender's office. Couple of hours."

I gave Russ a smile. "Make yourself at home, Mr. Meyer." Ducking out, I walked into the bullpen with

Bryson. "Let's use the time we have and dig deep on Russ's no doubt sad and inadequate life. If he's got a sealed juvenile record, find a judge who will unseal it. Look at his financials. See where he's getting his drugs from. Everything."

My detectives bent their heads over their computers. I tapped Kelly on the shoulder. "Hunter, do me a favor."

Kelly raised his eyebrows. He was about as strong and silent as they came. I said, "Go offer our suspect a coffee and see if you can get a read on what kind of magick he's messing with, and more importantly, if it involves pulling hearts out of little girls' chests."

Hunter nodded. "My pleasure." He lumbered up, like a landslide in reverse, and headed for the interview room.

I went into my office, settling down with a cup of microwave coffee and the overnight dispatches that had come in. Two assaults at were bars, one drunk and disorderly, a domestic dispute between a witch and her live-in boyfriend.

I shoved the dispatches into my outbox for Norris, our unit's civilian assistant, to distribute to the detectives and put on the board, and was about to call Kronen for the autopsy results on Lily Dubois when my office door opened and Detective Just-Call-Me Natalie Lane came in.

"I know SVU is one big happy commune, but around here we knock," I told her without looking up from my email.

"The desk by the coffee machine was empty," Lane said. "I put my things there. Hope that's okay."

"I can't imagine you'd care if it wasn't," I said. Lane spread her hands.

"Is there some problem I'm not aware of?"

"The squad might not be too happy with you," I said, gesturing at Andy and Javier, who were looking at Lane's box of things and her potted fern with frowns. "Lot of baggage comes with that desk."

Lane raised her eyebrows. "Oh?"

"Annemarie Marceaux used to sit there," I said.

"Really. That detective who went bad?"

"The same," I said. Lane shook her head.

"That was a real shame. Whatever happened to her?"

"I shot her in the stomach after she tried to kill me." I closed out my email in-box and stood up. "Was there anything else I could help you with, Detective? A welcoming fruit basket, maybe?"

Lane shook her head and backed out of my office, giving me a twitchy look over her shoulder. I smiled. I was having a crappy morning and I didn't feel bad at all about taking it out on Lane. She sat down at her desk and started to arrange her knickknacks.

I took a minute to dispel the memory of Annemarie, the detective who had sold me out to the Thelemites and almost gotten Will, Bryson and me killed. I'd trusted Annemarie. She'd been a friend. Lane's cutesy framed photographs and ceramic figurines wouldn't change that.

Kelly came out of the interrogation room and stalked across the bullpen, beckoning me. "He's a warlock, like me, and a piss-poor one. You believe he had the nerve to give me attitude?"

I snorted. "I know biker gangs that wouldn't give you attitude, Kelly."

"No call for cutting out the heart," Kelly said. "Warlocks don't use fetishes for their workings. You're looking for some low-down, dirty blood magick."

"Great," I muttered. There was nothing to do but wait for the public defender to show up. "Andy." I snapped my fingers at him. "What's going on with the security footage from the port?"

"No joy, ma'am," he said. "They cycle the tapes every twelve hours and they'd already been erased."

"Fucking perfect," I muttered. Andy gave me his sad-puppy look, and I waved him off. I hate waiting for a case to break when there's nothing I, personally, can do to dispense justice. I looked at Russ Meyer, sitting in the interrogation room staring at the ceiling, drumming discordantly on the tabletop.

Pete Anderson, our CSU investigator, was still collecting evidence in the scuzzball's apartment, but I had Russ's cell phone, bagged and tagged. I slipped on gloves and took it out of the evidence baggie, scrolling through the call history.

There were a series of photos from the night before, and I perched myself on the edge of Lane's desk to look through them, just to be a pain in her ass.

Lane cleared her throat, and I turned the screen toward her. A waitress's ample bosom filled the screen, poured into a black lace top with a nametag that read, improbably, TROUBLE. "There're about twenty of these," I said. "Looks like a bar-hop."

"I can't believe what passes for a night out these days," Lane sniffed.

"Yeah," I said, scrolling past three more rack shots,

"it's sure a far cry from a wholesome outing at the roller disco with the musical stylings of Andy Gibb and Leif Garrett."

Lane slammed her hands down on her keyboard. "How much older am I than you, Lieutenant? Five years? Seven? What gives you the right to judge me, just because you batted your eyes and got into a desk job early instead of being stuck on the streets because you didn't suck the right cock?"

"You don't want to go there with me," I said, still looking at Russ's cell phone. "I worked my ass off on the streets. I didn't sleep my way into this job and if I did, that would just mean you were jealous of my good looks and charm."

A long stretch of quiet. I deliberately kept my eyes on my work, not giving Lane the satisfaction of a re-action. I wasn't losing control of my squad because of some self-righteous sex detective.

"Maybe I was mistaken," Lane said stiffly, looking back at Lily's autopsy report.

"Maybe you were indeed," I said. The next photo in the text history was a self-portrait of Russ and the type of bar skank who thinks that a shredded denim skirt and a cowboy hat are a look.

Lane opened her mouth, but I shushed her. "Hex me." The timestamp of the photo was 2:23 A.M.

"What?" Lane demanded. I flipped through my notes from the scene, finding Kronen's estimate of how long Lily had been in the water.

"Time of death was between one and three A.M., best guess. You know how hard it is when a body goes in the water . . ."

Lane lifted her shoulders. "So?"

"Look," I said, showing her the phone. Lane sat back, her plump face folding into lines of displeasure.

"Shit. You just gave him an alibi."

"That I did," I said. "Let's figure out where this is so we can confirm it."

Bryson came over and looked at the screen. "That's the OK Corral," he said. I cocked an eyebrow at him.

"Do a lot of clubbing on your off nights, David?"

He smirked. "I'd recognize those cute little cowboy hats anywhere. They do a line-dancing contest on the bar Saturday nights . . ."

I held up my hand. "I got it. You and I are going down there. Lane, Meyer is all yours when the lawyer shows up. Maybe you can irritate something else out of him about Lily."

"My pleasure," Lane said, pushing back from her desk with a glare and going toward the elevators and the bathroom.

"You're being kinda hard on her, aren't you?" Bryson said as I grabbed my jacket from my office.

"I don't like some overgrown honor student foisted on me," I said. "She's way too eager and she's a pain in the ass."

"That's fair," said Bryson. "But you were a way bigger pain when you came to Homicide."

"David, don't go making sense. It goes against the natural order of things."

We took the Nova down Devere, to the wasteland of cheap bars, biker hangouts and piercing parlors behind Nocturne University. The OK Corral was on the outskirts, beyond the safety zone that college students populated, out in tweaker, hooker and bad-guy territory.

I automatically noted a few road bikes parked at the curb, flying gang colors, and shrugged out of my suit jacket, unbuttoning the top button of my shirt and pulling it loose to hide my badge and waist rig. I didn't want to look threatening if I didn't have to.

"It's not as bad as it looks," Bryson said, shoving the metal fire door open like he owned the place. The smell of stale beer, sawdust, vomit and sex slapped me across the face along with a loud blast of Brooks & Dunn.

"Clearly," I told Bryson.

A blonde girl was winding herself around a pole on one of the raised platforms at the rear of the bar, apathetic as if she were waiting for a bus. The décor, a few token hay bales, longhorns and strands of barbed wire crisscrossing the ceiling, was about as sad as the rest of the place.

I tapped on the bar and motioned the bartender over, showing him the cell phone picture. "You see a skinny tweaker kid in here last night snapping these?"

He shrugged one thin shoulder, his bones poking against the skin. "Maybe. What you want him for?"

Bryson and I showed our shields and the bartender's eyes darted around, taking inventory of his scant customers. Probably trying to remember any outstanding warrants.

"We're not looking to bust you," I said. "Just tell us if the kid was in here or not."

"Yeah," the bartender sighed. "Threw him out at last call. Drunk off his ass."

Last call was 4 A.M. in the city limits. Assuming that the barkeep wasn't covering for Russ, he had an even more rock-solid alibi than we thought. I pulled a folded picture of Lily Dubois on the autopsy table from my hip pocket and showed it. "How about her?"

"Lemme see . . ." He took it with fingers black on the tips from holding a glass smoke bowl. After he squinted for a second, he recoiled. "Is she dead?"

"Nah, she's napping," Bryson snorted. "Just tell us: You seen her, yes or no?"

The bartender grimaced. "I knew she looked young."

"Meaning?" I prompted.

"Look, I tell you what I know and you don't bust me for serving a minor, right?"

"We're not Vice, you twitchy little freak," Bryson said. "Just spill it."

"She was in here," said the bartender, going to the register and digging around under the cash tray. "She ordered a gin and tonic. Not a gin and tonic sort of place, you feel me?"

I looked at the gyrating girl again. She was having a hard time staying upright. "I get it."

"Anyway, her ID was sketchy but we were slammed, so I took it to start a tab and she never came back for it. Never paid her fucking tab, neither." He passed me the small laminate square, and I ran my thumb over Lily Dubois's face. The ID wasn't obviously a fake, but it gave her age as twenty-two, so it had to be.

"You didn't think she looked maybe a little *youthful* to be in this shithole?" Bryson asked the bartender. He spread his hands.

"Man, this place has dancers twenty-five years old that look younger than that chickie. She had the cleavage, she had the attitude, and I didn't look too hard. My mistake."

"Yes," I agreed pleasantly. "Your mistake that

allowed her to be killed and dumped in the bay. Who did she leave with?"

The bartender didn't appear remorseful in the least. "I don't keep track of the skirts in here, lady. I did my civic duty and talked to you cops. Now I got work to do." He retreated to polish glasses. At least until we left, and he returned to dealing meth to his customers.

"You have *got* to find a new place to hang out," I told Bryson. "This is just sad."

"Dead end, too," he said. "No cameras, no witnesses."

"Don't be too sure," I said. "Give me fifty bucks."

Bryson frowned. "You make more than I do. Pay scale for lieutenants is a whole gods-damned galaxy away from us grunts."

"You want results, David? Give me the fifty bucks."

He counted out two twenties and two fives and passed them to me. I crossed the sawdust, peanut shells and broken glass crunching under my boots. The dancer perked up when I approached. "You want a private session?"

I gave her a peek at my shield. "I want to talk to you. You working last night?"

She stopped moving and tottered to the edge of the platform in her hot-pink platform heels. "Yeah. Usually I'm days but I took a double. I was here until closing. Napped in the back."

"What's your name?"

"Dakota."

"Original." I fanned the photograph of Lily and the money under her nose. "You see this girl leave with anyone, Dakota?"

The dancer bit her lip. "Money first." I passed her the bills and she tucked them into her bra, disappearing the green folds like a magic trick. "She left around the beginning of my shift with Johnny Boy. I was glad, too—she was dancing like a tramp and cutting into my tips."

"Johnny Boy?" I said. The dancer shrugged.

"Well, it's not, like, his *real* name. That's something all long and foreign and stuff."

"Of course," I said. "Silly me."

"He comes in every night," she said, starting to gyrate again as the song changed. "Around nine. Stays until two or so. Unless he meets a girl he likes, then it's earlier."

"Thanks," I said, pocketing Lily's photo. "We'll be back."

CHAPTER 5

It was getting near lunch time, and the hole in my stomach told me I'd only had coffee since my abruptly interrupted supper the night before. I have a were metabolism, and when it demands food it's hard to ignore.

"Hey, I'm starving," I said as we passed my favorite burrito stand. "Let's stop and pick up lunch for the squad."

I cut across traffic, garnering an angry chorus of horns that I returned with a finger. Some people have no respect for the police and their lunch.

Bryson stayed in the passenger seat. "Hey. Get me a churro."

"Do I look like your waitress?" I asked as I climbed out.

"No, but I did give you fifty bucks. Make sure it's fresh. I don't want one that's been sitting out for half an hour."

"Bitch, bitch, bitch," I told him before I headed across the sidewalk to the open-air taco truck.

The guys who worked the truck knew me, and I put in an order for one of everything that the squad liked to eat. Lane would just have to fend for herself.

I dug my wallet out and paid in cash—I had more than enough on me to bribe Dakota, but I liked letting Bryson do my dirty work for me. A perk of being a lieutenant.

Turning to head back to the Nova, I found my way blocked by a very tall, very thin gentleman in an all-black suit and aviator sunglasses that reflected my own tired, makeup-free face back at me. "Can I help you?" I asked.

The taco truck driver tapped me on the shoulder. "Miss? You forgot your extra habanero salsa." That was for Andy—he liked his food nuclear, contrary to all outward appearances.

"Thanks," I said, palming the plastic bucket. "And I ask again, sir . . . can I help you?"

Skinny looked me over, head to toe. I wasn't un-used to the reaction from straight men, but there was something about him that set me off. I opened my nostrils, over the scent of frying beef and chilies. He was a were.

"The Duboises sent me," he said. Just that, no explanation, as if I could read minds.

"How nice for you," I said. "They like the tacos here, too?"

"They sent me to look in on you," he said. "Make sure progress was being made on the case. On Russ Meyer."

I shut my eyes. The Duboises had found out my former suspect's name. Crap. "I'm sorry," I said, smiling mightily at Skinny. "I can't confirm or deny any rumors about an open case, Mr. . . . ?"

"Teddy will do for now, Lieutenant."

"Teddy. Is that supposed to be one of those ironic

nicknames? Never mind, I don't care. You can tell the Duboises that I'm sorry for their loss, but this case is none of your business, *Teddy*, so why don't you toddle on back to 1987, where those shades came from?"

He showed some teeth, fangs at the ready. Great, he was in a bad mood as well as a bad dresser. I gently set down the two paper bags of food on the bench at the trolley stop by the curb. No sense in my lunch getting mangled.

"I'm here to ensure that nothing is overlooked," Teddy said. "And that the police give Russ Meyer the strongest justice possible. If they fail, I'll report that back to the Duboises, too."

"Listen," I said. "I don't know where you're getting your intel from, but it's old. Russ Meyer has an alibi, and I don't like being harassed while I'm just trying to buy a gods-damned beef burrito."

"Well," said Teddy. "If you were doing your job instead of stuffing your face, maybe it wouldn't be necessary for the pack to check up on your progress."

He just had to go there. I grabbed Teddy by his string tie and pulled him down so our faces were even. "You know what else I don't like, Miami Vice? Pack thugs sticking their snouts into my police work."

I heard a click and saw the sheen of a switchblade in Teddy's hand. He was fast, even for a were. "Let go of me," he warned. "You don't, you're going against the pack."

You can tell a lot about a man by how far he's willing to go against a cop, especially a lady cop like myself. If they back off and don't get into trouble, it means they're sane, or at least reasonable. If they pull a weapon without a flinch, they're either a psychopath or they think they're untouchable. I was betting Big Teddy figured on the latter.

Oh, well. He wouldn't be the first to make that mistake.

"Hex you," I told Teddy, "and Hex your pack." I flicked the top off the habanero salsa with my thumb and tossed the contents of the tub into his face. Chilies burn plain humans—in a were's eyes and soft tissue, they're worse than taking a Taser jolt straight up the nose.

Teddy let out a scream and dropped the knife, falling on the sidewalk and clawing at his face in what I thought, perhaps uncharitably, was an overdramatic and hysterical manner. I pocketed the switchblade, which was black enamel with bone inlay—very James Dean—and turned to the taco truck clerk, who was watching the whole proceeding with interest. "*Agua, por favor,*" I said. He passed me a bottle and I doused Teddy's head with it, washing away the peppers and specks of cilantro.

"You tell Nate Dubois that I'm doing my job," I said, bending over him.

"Bitch," he moaned. "I'm blind."

"And yet, your mouth still works," I said. "So you can also tell him that I resent being muscled like some cheap gutterwolf whore and if he sends one of his thugs after me again, I'm going to forget that he's just lost his daughter and get real damn pissy."

Bryson came to my elbow, looking down at Teddy. To his credit, he didn't seem the least bit surprised. "You okay, Wilder?" he said, picking up the food from the trolley bench.

I looked at Teddy. "Are we?"

After a long moment he glared at me, and nodded once. "Fine. But you can't find the killer, we find you."

"Don't threaten me while you're lying on the ground with salsa all over your face," I said. "It's not effective." I turned and left him there. Once I was in the car, my hands started to shake, a delayed reaction from my body letting me know how close to bleeding I'd come.

The Duboises were leaning hard, and I knew that if I didn't produce results soon, their pack would take its pound of flesh out of me first and the killer second. I really hoped this Johnny Boy was good for it.

I parked in the employee lot at the Plaza and let Bryson take lunch to the SCS while I went into Pete's office. "What do you know about fake IDs?" I said, passing him an enchilada and extra cheese.

"I know that I got kicked out of a bar in college using one my buddy and I made with Photoshop," he said. "Never had much use for them since."

"You got kicked out of a bar in this city?" I said, raising my eyebrows. I didn't know there were any college taverns that actually enforced ID laws in my town.

"Not here," Pete said. "I was at Stanford for my undergrad."

I sat down on his rolling stool, fishing Lily's bogus license out of my pocket. "Don't take this the wrong way, Pete, but if that's the case, then what the hell are you doing working for the police?"

"I like the work and the coffee is better than at a research lab," Pete said, solemn. "What've you got there?"

"Lily Dubois's fake ID," I said. "I was hoping we

could find out who made it, trace her descent into the tawdry nightlife, that sort of thing."

"I can't," Pete said. "But I'm sure one of my buddies from the ID Bureau can. I keep in touch with those guys."

"Great," I said, taking it back. "Come on." I walked us down to the fire door and through a dank stairwell into the lower floor of the old bomb shelter, a tunnel that ran between the morgue and Justice Plaza. It was a handy shortcut, but I didn't come down here if I could help it.

Not fifty yards away, I'd shot Annemarie Marceaux to death. They'd washed away the blood and the chalk outline from the Internal Affairs investigation, but the memory was as strong as ever. I swore I could still smell the gunpowder from my .38 revolver, hear the hollow *boom* of my holdout weapon, my last resort after Annemarie took my Sig.

"Spooky down here," Pete commented. "I'd rather walk aboveground, even when the weather is crap."

"You aren't the only one," I murmured, breathing again, finally, as we climbed the stairs to the emergency entrance in the morgue.

Annemarie's ghost stayed where it was, just breathing a cold sigh onto the back of my neck as the door swung shut. If I believed in ghosts. These days, I tried as hard as I could not to.

Pete and I rode the elevator to the ID division, which handled fingerprinting and dental identifications as well as ID fraud. A guy with a bushy Moses beard hiding a young face jumped up and pumped Pete's hand. "How the hell are you, Anderson?"

"Fine, fine," Pete said. "CSU keeps me busy."

The tech grinned approvingly. "You look slick, Anderson. What brings you back here to slum with the lab rats?"

Pete jerked his thumb at me. "She does. This is Lieutenant Wilder."

The tech eyed me. "We've met."

I checked his nametag, since he didn't sound happy. His badge read D. Dellarocco. *Oh, shit.* I remembered the guy, and I'd been rude to him the single time we'd met. Maybe I could blame it on bad shellfish . . .

"Hi," I said with a large smile. Dellarocco crossed his arms.

"What can I help you with, ma'am? Or do you just want to yell and threaten me again?"

People were looking now, techs turning away from their light tables and their AFIS computers to watch. I felt my cheeks turning pink. "Listen," I said to Dellarocco, low, "you don't be a dick and make a big deal out of this and I will apologize by buying you and Pete a very, very good meal at some future date. Deal?"

Dellarocco pursed his lips and considered for a whole two seconds. When it comes to lab geeks and free food, food wins every time. "Fine, deal. What've you got for me?"

I handed over Lily's ID. "Fake license for a fourteen-year-old murder victim. I need to know who made it."

Dellarocco took it and whistled. "Nice work. Usually the fakes have frayed edges and a grainy scan of the state seal under some shitty Photoshopping. This was professionally laminated."

He rolled a stool over to a tubular light and flicked

it on. "You see the hologram? It's old. They changed it to the state seal surrounded by the state motto a few years ago, and this license is brand new. So they not only have a laminating machine, they got their hands on surplus equipment from the Department of Licensing, which is theoretically destroyed when it becomes obsolete. The felonies are racking up." Dellarocco sounded pleased.

"Okay, so any idea who made this with their fancy machines?" I said.

"Hmm," said Dellarocco. "Something this state-of-the-art is usually organized crime. The Chinese are big into fake IDs for the workers the snakeheads bring over, and the various other mobs—Vietnamese, Russian, the Colombians . . . it's a profitable sideline for them."

"If I'm a poor little rich girl," I said, "where am I gonna go to get a decent ID?"

Dellarocco spread his hands. "Guys who sell IDs usually hang out at clubs, troll on college campuses. The pro outfits use stringers to insulate themselves from the cops."

"Like drug dealers," Pete said.

"Don't kid yourself," said Dellarocco. "A fake ID that will pass muster can be worth two or three grand to the right customer. Five times that for a fake passport, especially after 9/11."

"Can you put together a list of names and email it to my desk?" I asked. "Your usual suspects?"

Dellarocco cocked his eyebrow. "You buy us food *and* a round of beers."

Demanding little nerd. "Done. Soon as you can."

Dellarocco threw me a salute and rolled over to his computer, pulling up the department database.

"Now what?" Pete said.

I sighed. "Now I go home, put on a skimpy outfit and drag my boyfriend out to a titty bar."

"Damn, LT." Pete whistled. "Your home life is sure different from mine. I'm lucky if we get to cuddle on the couch while the lady watches her *CSI*."

"She makes you watch *CSI*?"

"Yeah." Pete grimaced. "I got in trouble for yelling at the TV."

I patted him on the shoulder. "Good luck, Pete. Don't wake your neighbors."

"Sometimes I wish I were still a geek with no social life," he muttered before we parted.

Sometimes I wished I were still an overworked homicide detective, hiding the fact that I was a were from everyone except my old lieutenant. Things seemed easier back then, even though my personal life was in the toilet and I lived in constant fear of exposure.

We don't always get what we want. I'd lost my anonymity but I'd gotten Will, and I'd done something to actually help my city by heading up the SCS.

At least, that was what I told myself as I drove home.

My apartment was in an old building at the edge of Waterfront, the neighborhood bad enough to be cheap and good enough that me being a cop kept the worst of the street kids and home-grown pot dealers out of my immediate eyeline. I used to have a cottage— secluded, run-down and homey, but the Thelemites had burned it down in an attempt to burn me right along with it.

The apartment wasn't ideal for when the phase came—if I broke out of my self-imposed cage, which was currently taking up most of the closet space in my handkerchief-sized bedroom, it would be a straight shot through the flimsy wall into my next-door neighbor's apartment.

Running through my workout with the heavy bag in the corner of my living room, I tried to clear my mind of the day's unpleasantness. I needed to find out what pack the Duboises ran and what their pull in the city was like. I'd reacted on instinct when the thug had grabbed me in the street, and I had to find out how bad of a hole I'd dug.

But first, I had a date with Johnny Boy.

I called Will and got him on his cell. "Hey, beautiful. You feel like Chinese?"

"Actually," I said, sifting through my closet, "how do you feel about line dancing?"

"It's freakish and unnatural and should be banned from the civilized world?"

"What if a bunch of drunk college girls in cowboy hats are doing it on a bar?" I used to have a collection of vintage clothes worth more than my yearly salary, but they had burned up along with my cottage. I was replacing it, but slowly. I pulled a stretchy black alligator-skin tank out of the closet and decided it would do.

"I'm listening," Will said. "You're getting my attention."

"I need to stake out a witness and I'm looking for a strong, silent Eastwood type to do it with," I said, pairing the tank with the trashiest skirt I own, a flippy red plaid schoolgirl number.

"Ah, I see how it is," Will said. "You only want me for my body."

"Pretty much." I threw in thigh-highs and my motorcycle boots and called the undercover outfit complete. Sure, I was closer to thirty-one than twenty-one, but if the lights were dim and Johnny Boy was a few beers in, I could pass.

"I can't say I've ever turned down an offer like that," Will said. "Meet you when and where? And should I bring my .44 Magnum, the most powerful handgun in the world?"

"The OK Corral, off of Devere, around nine. And no, I think we're going to get more out of Johnny Boy with breasts than bullets."

"Your breasts, I hope. I have a hard time filling out my training bra."

"I'm hanging up," I said, and did so, but not without a smile. Will could usually make me smile. Another unique quality that he possessed, unlike all of my former boyfriends.

I dressed myself in my trampy outfit and shoved my .38 holdout pistol into the waistband of my skirt, puffing the tank over it. I wasn't planning for things to get messy, but you never know when you're dealing with men, their egos and booze.

Driving from my respectable, if seedy, neighborhood into the dangerous territory behind the university caused a shiver down my spine from the cool, misty air. The were in me thrived on danger, ate adrenaline, but the human in me was getting more and more cautious. I had a good life, for the first time—I had Will, I had the job. I had stability.

For the first time, I found myself unwilling to rock the boat. I wasn't sure how I felt about that.

The OK Corral was hopping when I pulled up, far from the lackluster crowd of the morning. Smokers crowded the sidewalk, and a few prostitutes wound sinuously through the civilians like brassy sharks on the prowl in a school of bright tropical fish. I caught the smell of a few weres in the crowd, a few blood witches that stood out among the humans like bright copper pennies.

I parked in the side lot, under good light, and locked the car. Not that anyone would be keen to steal a pea-green '71 Nova, but you never know what sort of freaks are out there.

Will was waiting for me in front of the club, twirling the keys to his vintage Mustang around his finger.

"You trusted the valet?" I said by way of greeting. "In this neighborhood?"

"I live dangerously, doll," he said, sliding his arm around my waist. "Damn, look at you. I could get used to this."

"You'll get used to nothing," I said with a grin, pulling his hand up from my rear end. "We're here to work."

"Nuts," Will said, giving me a quick kiss. "Come on, then. Let's find this numbskull and get down to the real business of the night."

"That would be?" I said, as we pushed through the swinging doors to the honking of Garth Brooks. Nine P.M. and they were already playing *Friends in Low Places*. That should have been a warning right there.

"That's for me to know, and you to find out, doll." Will grinned at me lasciviously.

No one carded us, ironically. Will could look practically any age he chose with a change of wardrobe and hair—the perks of being immortal—and I was hanging off him like a sorority sister three shots to the wind.

A different bartender was working, a muscular girl with spiked black hair and a riot of tattoos, full sleeves up either arm. Will steered me toward her and I fell against the bar with a giggle. "Hey, Joanie. You seen Johnny Boy tonight?"

The bartender cocked her eyebrow. "Joanie?"

"Joanie as in Jett? 'Cuz of the hair? And then . . ."

Will cut me off. "Is Johnny Boy here?"

"Yeah," said the bartender. "Over there fixated on the tits, like he always is."

I reached over the bar and patted her arm. "You're cute. Hang loose, Joanie."

Will guided me away before the poor bartender could slug me. "You're unbelievable," he murmured in my ear. "Truly."

"Hey, you gotta sell it," I muttered. "I'm just doing my part."

Johnny Boy wasn't hard to spot once we left the bar and plunged into the cluster of horny frat boys and drunken cowboys surrounding the dancers' platforms. He was the only one sitting back, calmly smoking a thin cigar and swirling a glass of vodka while a brunette in a black bustier and little else gyrated on his lap.

I waded through the crowd and tapped her on the shoulder. "Mind if I cut in?"

She turned around and bared her teeth at me. "Get lost, skank."

Oh, irony. I grabbed her by the laces of her bustier and jerked her off Johnny Boy's lap, taking her place, my thighs straddling his, rubbing against the cheap polyester of his suit.

He glared up at me through the haze of cigar smoke. "I know you?"

"Not yet," I cooed, running a finger down his cheek. "I heard a girl could get a good fake ID off of Johnny Boy. I've got cash. I'll pay."

Johnny Boy snorted, looking me over. "Lady, you need a fake license about as much as my grandmother's Pomeranian does."

Will shook his head. "Of all the things you could have said, my man . . . that one wasn't the right choice."

JB cut Will a look that would have taken his nose off, *Chinatown* style. "She want to get carded? Make her feel young again?" He started to stand up. "I don't have time for your *Desperate Housewives* bullshit."

I shoved him back, rocking his chair against the table, spilling his drink. "Sit your ass down, tough guy."

He took a second look at me, his expression shifting from boredom to rage inside of a bass beat of the tinny Carrie Underwood number that had replaced Garth. "What is this?" JB demanded.

"This is a dead teenage girl," I said. I had the photo tucked into my top, and I shoved it in JB's face with no small amount of relish.

He didn't react, except to twitch his lips in disgust. "I've never seen her. I'm very busy." Up again, and I shoved him back again. He gave me a smile that was the same smile a tiger gives a side of beef right before it pounces.

"I take it you're a cop. If so, you obviously don't know me." He reached out one hand and ran it down the bare thigh between my skirt and my stocking. "I'd change that if you're up for it, miss cop. What are you? Vice? Those are my favorite. They know how to moan and squeal—part of the job, when they're chasing johns."

Will stepped in. "That's far enough, John Boy."

JB slid his hand from my thigh to my ass and squeezed, hard. "This your piece? You should keep her on a leash."

I needed to get control back, and the fastest way to do that is usually with violence. I balled up my fist and punched JB in the eye, pulling the jab so I didn't break his orbital bone. I'm a lot stronger than a human, and you have to be careful about those things.

JB let out a yelp and I switched out my fist for my .38, pressing it between his eyes. If anyone in the crowd noticed or cared, they hinted not one whit. Beer and country music will do that to a person.

"I hate repeating myself, Johnny," I said. "Did you sell Lily Dubois her fake license?"

He drew his lips back in a snarl that rivaled my own. "Fuck you, bitch. I don't answer to the police."

"Okay," I said, putting the hammer up on the .38. "Then let's find out who you do answer to." I felt inside his suit jacket, the silk lining tickling my fingers. The ID business was good. JB's wallet was a soft leather that felt alive under my fingers. I tossed it to Will and stepped back. "I'll be in touch, John. You may want to find a new watering hole, too." I jerked my thumb at a college student wearing a Nocturne University Theta Theta shirt, doubled over and vomiting Jagermeister-colored bile into the sawdust. "This one is about to be violated for about ten different health codes. That, and the music sucks."

I waggled a hand at JB as Will and I walked away. "Don't get too comfortable. I'll be seeing you again."

"You can count on it!" JB stood up, his face red. "I'm not finished with you, bitch! You don't get to mess with me like this, in my place of business!"

I looked at Will, who rolled his eyes. "Well, at least he admits it," I said.

"What do you think all of those threats were about?" Will asked. "There's a lot of brave sons of bitches running around the city lately. Meyer, this jackass . . ."

I stopped at my car, leaning against the hood and rifling through the wallet. "Let's see what he thinks he has over somebody who's authorized to carry a gun and shoot mouthy people with it."

The wallet was devoid of everything except a balance-carrying credit card, one of the types that were just glorified gift cards and could be refilled with cash. Speaking of cash, there was a fat pack of it, five hundred-dollar bills fresh from the ATM.

"And here we have a bona-fide California state driver's license," I said, pulling it out of plastic. "John Black." I looked at the squinty-eyed photo of Johnny Boy.

"The only way that gets faker is if you replace 'Black' with 'Smith,'" said Will.

"He'd have to give an address," I said. "Two-seven-two-seven Winchester, apartment eighteen."

"I'm game for driving over there if you are," Will

said. "I can even wake a judge up if you want to make it legal."

"Do it," I said. I pulled out my cell and dialed Dellarocco. "Hey, it's Lieutenant Wilder. If I drop something by, can I get an AFIS report by morning?"

Dellarocco masterfully hid a yawn before he spoke. "Sure. What's a few hours of REM sleep?"

"I touched it," I said, slipping the wallet into a evidence baggie from my glove compartment. "My exclusionary prints are on file from the Holly Street shooting about five years back. The prints you want are from a guy calling himself John Black."

"Good enough," said Dellarocco. "Although would it kill you pavement-pounders to wear gloves?"

"Sorry," I said. "Carrie Underwood makes me very distracted."

"What?"

"Trust me, Dellarocco, you're better off not knowing."

Will shut his own phone. "Judge Hannity is calling in a warrant to the SCS. We're good to go."

"You and your federal connections," I said, hopping in the car. "Very sexy."

Will stroked the same spot on my thigh that JB had touched, no perverse intent behind it, but as if he was reassuring himself I was still there. "I try my best, doll."

I reached over and patted his knee as we drove toward the ID lab. "So far, so good."

CHAPTER 6

The apartment building on Winchester Drive was a brick turn-of-the-century firetrap, common to the old part of the city. There was no doorman, no elevator, and no one to care what went on in the dank, half-lit halls.

I climbed up two flights to 18, trying the door. It was locked, with a shiny new deadbolt that was top of the line. I snarled under my breath. "I can't pick this."

"We can wake the super up," Will said. "Assuming this place has one . . ."

I braced myself against the jamb and gave the door a kick. The deadbolt ripped clean out of the frame and the door rocketed back into the apartment, hinges and all.

". . . Or we could do that," Will finished. I shrugged.

"Didn't mean to kick it quite so hard." I'd have to watch that—even with fifteen years of being a were, sometimes I miscalculated.

Will slipped on a pair of gloves and hit the lights, while I cleared the front room, the small kitchen and the bedroom. No one home. JB was probably still frothing at the mouth back at the club.

"Neat in here," Will said. "For a single guy."

I gestured at the front room, which managed to hold a leather sofa and a plasma-screen home-theater system, small though it was. "Does this look like the apartment of some club rat to you?"

Will shook his head. "It looks like he's got some money stashed and doesn't want to broadcast it with his address."

"Okay, John Black," I said, stealing a pair of gloves from Will. "What have you got to hide?"

I searched the kitchen, which held a lot of booze but no food beyond a suspicious container of Thai takeout, and the bathroom. John was fond of his products, as any metrosexual mobster would be. "He's got to be in with an outfit," I told Will as I rifled through the papers on the small desk, next to a high-end laptop. "Otherwise this apartment would be stripped clean the first time he stepped out to grab a bag of groceries."

I ran my hands along the underside of the bed frame, trying to ignore the crimson satin sheets. Single guys have the worst taste.

"Looking for a gun?" Will said.

"Finding one." I pulled at the small-frame pistol duct-taped to the frame, finding a small Ruger automatic in my hand. Will whistled.

"That's some serious hardware. Pricey, too."

"Think he's got a permit for this?" I said, getting on my knees and peering under the bed. A shoebox greeted me, also taped.

"I dunno. You think that I could click my heels and take us all to Oz?" Will said. I drew the shoebox out and tore the lid off.

"Good point." The box was full of Polaroids and

a few creased documents, bills of lading from a shipping company. The photographs were of girls, many of them grinning against the backdrop of a club or a bar, a few posed against a blank white-painted brick wall with vacant expressions on their faces and glazed eyes.

"Not sexy," Will said. "What does he do, document his conquests?"

I unfolded the bills and looked at the contents—electronics, souvenirs, party supplies. The destinations were all cities in the Ukraine, the shipping company listing an import/export house as the receiver. I chewed on my lip. "I don't think these are conquests, Will. I think these are business partners."

Will looked over my shoulder. "Prostitutes?"

"Looks that way," I said. All of the girls were like Lily, older than their years, perfectly blonde, perfectly tempting to any man with a taste for younger flesh.

"Let's bag this and get it out of here," I said softly. "I don't want to look at it anymore."

Had Lily been lured to her death with the promise of a party she'd never experienced before? Had John Black been the one to do it? And who were the other girls?

Will and I bagged the evidence and sealed it, and I locked it in the trunk of the Nova for Pete to examine tomorrow. For now, I just wanted to go home and curl up in my own bed.

"Want me to stay?" Will said when we pulled up at my apartment. "I can. It's closer to my work, anyway."

"Yeah," I said. I was tired, suddenly, all of my limbs heavy. Lily Dubois's face wouldn't leave me alone. "Come up."

Will waited while I locked the door behind us and then pulled me to him, pressing his lips over mine.

I put my arms around his neck as his hands traveled under my skirt, over the tops of my stockings and tugged at my thong. "Moving a little fast, aren't we?" I asked against his mouth.

"I had to watch that waste of oxygen touch you," Will said. "I'm not waiting."

Leading him backward to the bed, I agreed, with my hands on his fly and my lips on his neck. I wanted someone to be next to me who wasn't predatory, who I could be honest with.

Will slid down the sheets, pulling my underwear with him, until his head was between my thighs, running his hands up the skin and stocking. I gasped when I felt his mouth against me and arched my stomach, inviting his attention.

Sliding his hands under my ass and lifting me, Will worked until lights started to swim in front of my eyes, which with him usually wasn't very long.

"Ready?" he asked me, raising his eyes and dipping his hand into my nightstand for a condom. I nodded, pulling him up and wrapping my legs around his waist.

"So ready."

We moved, Will urgent and I just needing not to think about the face of a murdered girl for a few minutes. He did a good job of distracting me, and I kept my eyes open, one hand on the back of his neck, brushing the short-cropped golden hair there.

Will leaned down, his breath hot against my neck, teeth searching for purchase. He was the first guy I'd been with since the one who gave me the bite whom I trusted enough to let him close to my most vulnerable spot.

That, and Will wasn't a were. He couldn't give me the bite, turn me to his pack, and take control of me. That part helped a lot.

"Luna," Will said, short and to the point like he was with most things. His hand left my breasts and stroked against me, once, twice.

"Yes," I told him, as the deep-belly shudder gripped me.

Will shut his eyes and drove into me one last time, his thumb mimicking the rhythm. It sent me over the edge and I lost myself for a second, feeling him inside me like a miniature heartbeat. Breath short and ragged, Will lowered himself on me, kissing along one cheekbone and down my jawline.

I let myself ride out the last aftershock and then unwrapped my legs, draping one knee over the back of his. "You feel like you staked your claim?" I said with a half-smile.

Will returned it. "The real question is, do you?"

"Oh, yeah," I said. "I'm ruined for all other men now."

Will grabbed a throw pillow and bopped me lightly in the head with it. "You and that big mouth of yours."

"Hey, I don't hear you complaining about what that mouth can do for you," I said.

Rolling off the bed, Will went into my small bathroom and splashed water on his face. "I'm up for taking it slow this time around if you are."

Fatigue lay heavy on me now, like the sheen of sweat on my skin. I got up and came into the bathroom with Will, spinning the taps on my ancient, rust-ringed tub. "I need a bath and a decent night's sleep," I said. "No offense to your prowess as a lover, honey."

Will squeezed my shoulders. "None taken. I'm going to sack out. Be sure to wear that little black negligee I like." He dropped me a wink and shut the bathroom door.

"Unbelievable," I told him through the wood, but not without a smile. Will made me feel relaxed instead of jumpy with his very presence, and that was new for me, too. I stripped out of my clubbing costume and sank into the bathwater, draping a washcloth over my forehead.

Steam closed over the mirror, filled the air, and I felt my hair grow damp against my neck. I slid lower into the water, trying to float.

The faucet dripped, a Zenlike meditation in the white non-space of the water and the steam. I breathed in, out, watching my breath move wisps like skeleton fingers across the tile.

Lily Dubois stood at the edge of the tub, her skin and hair waterlogged and white, her clothes tattered, the gaping hole in her sternum red-black with clotted blood. "Help me," she said, and then reached out her hand and shoved my head under the water.

I thrashed and struggled, her tiny arm stronger than a piece of rebar, and white lights exploded in front of my eyes. This was it—I was dead and I'd open my eyes in the afterlife.

My lungs convulsed and I jumped upright, coming out of the water, thrashing and sending a minor tidal wave across the tiles to soak my wicker basket of towels and a pile of discarded laundry I hadn't had time to lug down to the laundromat.

Awake and choking, I pulled myself out of the tub and rested on all fours for a moment, shivering and coughing.

Will came bolting through the door, grabbing me by the shoulders. "Luna. Luna, what happened?"

"I don't know," I croaked. "I had a bad dream . . ."

Will's hair was mussed from the pillow and his eyes were black with worry. "Are you sure? You didn't hit your head and go under?"

I checked myself over and found I was free of bruises and scrapes. "No . . . I must have dozed off . . ." I grabbed a damp towel, suddenly freezing. "I saw Lily. She was dead."

"She is that," Will agreed. He grabbed my ratty terry-cloth robe and wrapped me in it, guiding me to the bed. "Come on. You're not the first cop to dream about the bad ones."

I let him lay me down and hold me close. I didn't tell him how real the whole thing had seemed. I have plenty of dreams, most of them perfectly normal Jungian archetypes like we all have, but this—this was different. If I breathed deeply, I swore I could still smell sea water and decomposing flesh, as if Lily were still standing there, watching me with her clouded eyes.

Dellarocco looked up when I came into the ID lab the next morning, carrying the shoebox I'd found in JB's apartment. "I was just about to call you."

"Must be psychic," I said, and then grimaced. The nightmare was still dogging me, and even two tall hazelnut lattes couldn't chase it away completely.

"I got an ID on your wallet's owner, the talented Mr.

Black," said Dellarocco, sounding ridiculously proud of himself. He brought up an AFIS file and sure enough, there was Johnny Boy. "Does the name Ivan Salazko ring any bells?"

"No," I said. "But that's who he is, really?"

"Really," said Dellarocco. "He has a bust from about five years ago, in Miami. He was running whores, and buying coke to give to said whores, and he bought from an undercover cop. It was a minor thing, and he did two years and skated out west."

"Lucky us," I said. "Maybe he wanted to see the California Disney." Or take up running whores again, judging by the snapshots under his bed.

"He got his fake ID from the same place that gave your girl Lily hers," Dellarocco said. "Any leads yet?"

"Not yet," I said. "But I'll have some today, you bet your ass. Can I get a printout of that?" I indicated the screen. Dellarocco obliged me, and I took my evidence and myself to the SCS.

"Check it out," I told Bryson, slapping the booking photo on his desk. "I found us a new suspect *numero uno* and I didn't even break a sweat."

Bryson frowned. "Who the hell is that guy?"

"This is Ivan Salazko," I said. "Pimp and maker of the fake ID that Lily got herself into clubs with."

"He Russian mob?" Bryson asked. I blinked.

"I don't know. Why would you say that?"

Bryson jerked a thumb at my closed door. "Because the FBI is in your office."

Through my blinds, I saw the shadows of two large, male figures. "Shit," I muttered. "How long have they been waiting in there?"

"Long enough to become a huge pain in the ass,"

Bryson said, turning back to his computer. "And Nor-ris told me to tell you that you have a bunch of voice-mails from the Dubois family and that they sounded, quote, 'less than thrilled.'"

"Real quick—are the End Times also upon us? Be-cause that would make the day pretty much perfect."

"Not yet, but I'll buzz you if a guy with a flaming sword shows up," Bryson said.

I took a breath and then pushed open the door. "Sorry to keep you waiting."

The agents were both men, both white, both wholly unremarkable in that dead-eyed federal way. They even had the same color tie. "Are you Lieutenant Wilder?" said the slightly taller one, with the better haircut.

"Dang, you got me," I said. "She's on vacation and I'm just using this office to impress my dates. It drives the ladies wild."

Not a flicker of humor from either of them, so I sat down at my desk. "I'm Luna Wilder. What can I do for you?"

They closed in, Fed and Fedder. One drew out a small, neat picture. Ivan's mug shot, wallet-sized. "What is your department's interest in Mr. Salazko?" the tall one asked.

"I'm sorry, Agent . . . ?"

"Senior Special Agent Hart. This is Special Agent White."

I cocked an eyebrow at White. "You're kidding me, right?"

He grimaced, as if to say it wasn't his fault. "You've been talking to Ivan Salazko. One of our surveillance teams spotted you last night at the club. Nice outfit, by the way."

"Yeah," I said. "J. Edgar would have been all kinds of jealous. What's the point of you coming in here and looming over my desk?"

"Salazko is our boy," said Hart. "He's involved in an ongoing investigation by the OCTF—that's Organized Crime Task Force."

I returned his smirk. "I've seen *Goodfellas* just like you, Agent."

"We need you to back off," Hart continued. "We don't want him spooked."

"Salazko is a homicide suspect," I said. "Whatever your little Mafia squad has going, he's being investigated in the death of a fourteen-year-old girl."

"Tragic," said Hart. "However, you understand that a federal case takes priority."

"I understand that you're telling me some scumbag mobster who is going to make a deal and disappear into Witness Protection is more important than the girl he killed," I said, standing up and glaring at them both. "I'd expect nothing less from the Feebs."

"We understand that you're upset . . ." Hart started, in his poor-little-woman tone.

"Don't even start with me," I said, holding up a hand. "Just get out. I'm going to nail Salazko for this murder and you're going to stay the fuck out of *my* way or I am going to come down to the federal building and scream my head off to your agent in charge."

Hart's mouth crimped. "That, I'd like to see." He opened the door into the bullpen. "We'll expect all of your case notes and any evidence you may have collected from Mr. Salazko's apartment by the end of business tomorrow. Have a nice day, Miss Wilder."

Miss. What a Hexed charmer this guy was.

White gave me a regretful look once Hart was out of hearing. "My advice? You want to do something about this, do it before you have to turn over your evidence. Salazko has skated before."

"Not going to happen," I said. "Thanks for your advice all the same."

"Can't say I didn't try," White said, and scurried after his partner. I heaved a sigh. Between the Duboises and the FBI, who else was going to come through my door and screw with my case?

I needed real advice, not the bullshit White was handing out. I forwarded my calls to my cell phone and went back to my car, driving up to Highland Park, to the 24th Precinct that was my old stomping ground.

Parking on the street, I pushed through the front doors and nodded to Shelley, the day sergeant. "Is he in?"

"In his office," Shelley said, turning a page in her magazine. I walked through the bullpen and knocked on the glass door labeled *Troy McAllister—Lieutenant.*

"Luna," he said in surprise when I opened the door. "What brings you from the hallowed halls of the Plaza? They slash your budget? You need to steal office supplies and stale donuts?"

I slumped into the chair opposite Mac's desk. He'd been my lieutenant in Homicide, and he was my cousin Sunny's boyfriend now. I trusted him as much as I trusted anyone. "The FBI is trying to fuck with one of my murder cases, the victim's parents are pack leaders who are going to tear me into little tiny pieces if I don't close it—and I'm not being hyperbolic there—and everything is just a mess."

Mac pulled a cigarette out of his desk drawer and lit it. I cocked my eyebrow. "Thought you gave that up for true lurve with my cousin."

"You stress me out, Luna. I can blame it on you," Mac said. "Besides, I have breath mints in the car."

"This asshole senior agent, Hart, says that I have to turn over my case notes by the end of the day tomorrow or the OCTF is going to come down on me."

"What, is this suspect mob?" Mac said. "Jesus, Luna, let the feds have him. You investigate supernatural crimes. There hasn't been a were Mafia in Nocturne City since Frank and Dino were playing at the Sands."

"No, that'd be the parents of the vic," I said. "They're champing at the bit for pack justice, and if I don't deliver, I'm sure it will end in a lot of snarling and posturing and possibly bloodshed." On the bright side, maybe they'd eat Special Agent Hart.

Mac laced his fingers behind his head. "Give it to them."

I blinked. "What?"

"You can't fight the federal government, Luna. They have a case against this guy, and they're going to slap you with an injunction if you don't give them what they want." He sighed. "You fight the good fight, kid, but you lost this one."

"And what about the Duboises?" I said. "Do I just roll over for them, too?"

"Hell, Luna, I don't know," said Mac. "Weres are your territory. That's why you're in charge of the SCS. I have faith in you. You'll figure it out."

I stood up and gave Mac a half-smile. "That makes one of us."

"You don't look good, Luna," Mac said as I opened his door. "You been sleeping?"

"I had a bad nightmare," I said. "The dead girl."

"Huh," said Mac. "She talk to you?"

I nodded. Mac stubbed his cigarette out in an old cup of coffee. "I had a kid once, a boy about sixteen. Shot to death in the street over a fifty-dollar watch. Nothing special about him, but I saw him for years, those three bullet holes staring back at me like eyes." He laced his fingers. "I'll have Sunny give you a call. Have some girl time or whatever it is you women do when you're not painting your nails or cooking delicious casseroles."

I gave Mac the finger and a friendly smile as I left the 24th. It felt good to be back. When was the last time I'd had a desk within view of a window?

My BlackBerry rang as I cleared the front steps and I ducked into the Nova to avoid the rain that had started to fall like the last tears of someone too tired to cry anymore. "Luna Wilder."

"Miss Wilder. You're a hard woman to get ahold of."

I groaned and pressed my forehead against the steering wheel. "Hello, Mr. Dubois. What can I do for you?"

"Is it true that you have a new suspect in my daughter's case?"

"Hex me, *where* are you getting this from? This is a confidential investigation, even, I'm sorry to say, to a victim's family."

"Reporters have their sources," Nate Dubois said. "I have mine. You close this case and nail this bastard or the pack is going to consider you an enemy along with this John Black."

They didn't have his real name yet. I had a little time. "I don't appreciate being threatened, Mr. Dubois. Or didn't Teddy tell you that?"

"You have our warning, Miss Wilder," he said, shortly. "Now I have to go make arrangements for my daughter's funeral, when you people finally release the body."

"And you have mine," I said, cold. "Good-bye, Mr. Dubois."

When he hung up, I started the car and drove, too fast, just to drive and try to shake off all of my problems. I ended up at the Port of Nocturne again, which in daylight was as sad and run-down a spot as you could ever end up in. I turned onto the access road before the gate and drove down to the vast columns of the Siren Bay Bridge, humming softly from the traffic above.

There's a troll under the Siren Bay Bridge. He—at least, I think it's a he—came through the temporal rift left by a Wendigo hunger god when he was reborn. Exploited by the Thelemites, he now lives safe and sound, bound by magic and the sea.

"Hey there, big guy," I said, getting out and sitting on the hood. The rain had stopped as suddenly as it had begun, and mist rolled off the bay, obscuring the roadbed of the bridge two hundred feet above us.

The troll was dozing against the cement embankment. It cracked open one eye when I pulled up and then went back to sleep.

"So," I told it, "I have a case that will never be closed

and a were pack that will kill me if it isn't. And I have a day to make it right. Got any ideas?"

The troll grunted and shifted, scratching its scaly green back against the concrete.

"You're a big help," I said. "I suppose if we caught Salazko in the act, we'd have something to hold him on and the district attorney could tie up the federal prosecutor long enough for me to find some evidence."

The bills of lading were still in a plastic baggie in my glove compartment and I felt for them, reading the tiny, faded type. All of the shipments were outgoing from the same berth in the port, a week or a week and a half apart.

"You know what they say," I told the troll. "Consistency is the hobgoblin of small minds. No offense, if you two are related."

I'd have one night, at the most, for my plan—stake out the port, get hard evidence of Salazko importing girls or exporting gods-knew-what, and get him in custody before Agents Hart and White caught on to my scheme.

For that, I'd need help, and I wasn't going to find it sitting around talking to a troll. "Appreciate the help," I told it, before I got back in the car and called Will.

CHAPTER 7

"So let me get this straight," Will said, once I'd assembled him, Bryson, Batista and Zacharias in the conference room of the SCS. "You want us to stake out the Russian mob on their turf under the nose of an ongoing FBI investigation that we've specifically been told to stay out of?"

"Yes," I said. "Which is why we need you, my darling."

Will shrugged. "I don't follow."

"If *you* are leading the operation then it's not our fault, is it? The FBI has nothing to screech about."

Batista nodded. "I like that. Who the Hex does the FBI think they are, anyway? Coming in here, stepping all over us."

"Yeah," Bryson said. "Fuck 'em."

Andy blushed, but he looked excited, like I'd suggested sneaking into an R-rated movie. "I agree, ma'am. This is our investigation."

"You do realize that if my supervisors find out about this, I'll be written up and probably lose my job?" Will said. I gave him my best innocent expression.

"Please? For me? I'm adorable."

"Sure," Will snorted. "For you."

"And you get a chance to make the FBI look like a bunch of flatfooted federal donut-munchers," I said. There was no love lost between the ATF and the feds. Will's mouth quirked.

"Well, sure. There is that. I'll requisition some equipment from my friend in technical services and we'll meet at the pier once it gets dark."

"I'll call the port authority and let them know we're coming," Andy said.

"No," I told him. "Anyone in the port could be in bed with the Russians. Why don't you try to find out who Salazko is working for, instead? And requisition a surveillance van from the motor pool. One of the new ones, not the one that smells like old hot dogs."

Andy nodded and went back to his computer. If there was one thing I could count on him for, it was obsessive fact-checking and following my instructions.

"What do you want us to do?" Bryson asked.

"Until tonight, sit there and look pretty," I said. Natalie Lane stuck her head into the conference room.

"Sorry. Am I interrupting something?"

"Always," I said. "What can I inconvenience myself for you and do this time?"

Lane rolled her eyes. "May I see you for a moment?"

I stepped into the hallway with her. "What? What is it?"

"I understand you're set on this Salazko as a suspect?" she said. "Not that you've been sharing any information with me willingly."

"He had the motive and opportunity," I said. "He looks pretty good from where I'm sitting."

"And you base this on the fact that he's involved in prostitution?" Lane said.

"Lady, what is your point? Are you only around to state the obvious?"

Lane sighed. "Look, I don't take any pleasure in this, but I think Salazko has an alibi."

Fan-freaking-tastic. "Are you really that hard up? You want to show up the freak squad that badly?"

"Believe it or not," Lane growled, "I'm doing my job, something you seem distinctly uninterested in."

"What?" I snapped. "What could you possibly have to prove by alibiing a mobster other than to show me up and get a pat on the head from all of the other sex detectives?"

Lane's eyes narrowed. "Maybe the truth? Salazko may be bad, but he's not our kind of bad."

I crossed my arms, not wanting to admit she had a point. "I assume you can show me some proof?"

"Would we be talking if I didn't?" Lane said. "I do my job well, Lieutenant. I don't have the luxury of screwing around and hoping no one notices."

"You are just aiming straight for my fist in your face," I muttered, grabbing my jacket and following Lane. "I'll be back in an hour," I called to the others.

"I've worked with these girls before," Lane said when we were in her silent-running Japanese toy of a car, "when a customer roughs them up and we're lucky enough to find out how old they really are." She drove us toward Needle Park, the section of the city where drug deals were as plentiful as ice cream trucks.

"And Salazko brings them in?" I said. "I figured that was his deal."

"His name rang a bell," Lane said as we turned

down an alley stacked on both sides with boxes and discarded appliances. "A girl had eyeballed him as one of her regular customers when we brought her in on a solicitation rap. Fifteen."

"A year older than Lily," I murmured.

"This can be a little rough if you're not used to it." Lane drew the hybrid to a stop at the end of the alley.

"I've pretty much burned out my shock and horror at the human condition," I told her. "Between the shootings, ritual murders, death threats, black magick . . ."

Lane stopped me. "Fine. Just let me do the talking, and don't act like you're here to bust anyone. These girls are in enough trouble as it is."

I followed her to a graffiti-covered door at the end of the alley. The markings were mostly wards from various witch gangs, all of them spent and faded. Whatever lived here now was much, much worse.

Lane buzzed, then pounded on the door with the flat of her hand. "*Privyet!* Open up."

"Maybe nobody's home," I said. At that moment, the door cracked and a thin-faced girl stuck her head out. Hair that had seen at least five bleach jobs too many was piled on top of her head like a bird's nest.

"*Da*? I help you?"

Lane smiled perfunctorily. "I was wondering if we might talk to Mika?"

"Mika is sleeping," said the girl, starting to shut the door. I caught it, not even having to strain. The girl, all skinny bones and huge eyes, was about as strong as a kitten.

"Please," I said. "We just want to talk. It's important."

"Look," the girl said. "We have papers, all. We not do anything wrong."

She jerked against the door until I let go, and slammed it shut. I looked to Lane. "Okay, clearly the Mother Theresa act isn't gonna work." I pounded on the door, feeling in my wallet for cash.

"Go away," the girl hissed when she opened up again. "You will scare customer."

"First of all," I said, "It's two P.M. on a weekday. You don't have customer. Second of all . . ." I flashed her a twenty. "We just want to talk to Mika. We're not here to go all *la migra* on your fine establishment, all right?"

The girl pursed her lips, looking over her shoulder. If her pimps found out she'd let two cops into their brothel, she'd catch hell, probably in the form of a fist. But money that didn't have to be shared with said pimps was a stronger temptation, and she snatched the twenty from my hand.

"Upstairs. The second door on the left."

Lane nodded her thanks, and we stepped into a dank back hall that smelled of unwashed bodies, stale cooking and staler vodka.

A few girls were sitting against the wall, smoking or nodding, and a pop station burbled from the front of the building, which I guessed at one point had been a restaurant.

The industrial kitchen was to my right and I glanced in, just to make sure Sergei the Russian Pimp wasn't waiting for us with a shotgun. Just another girl, singing to herself in Ukrainian as she stirred a pot on the range.

Dmitri, my ex, would have been able to tell me what the song was, probably even from what town in Ukraine the girl was from.

But he wasn't here, so I followed Lane up the stairs. She knocked on the second door. "Mika? Mika, it's Detective Lane."

Shuffling, and the door opened on another skinny girl with pale, bruised skin and deep half-moons under her eyes. Mika had a short, dark bob, one I was willing to bet a wig covered during work hours. She was pretty, in a wide-eyed Wednesday Addams way, but she had the slippery, slow glance of a junkie. There were bruises on the insides of her arms, handprints, and I pegged her as a pill-popper. Cheaper than heroin and doesn't leave unsightly track marks.

"Yeah? What is it this time?" she sighed. Her English was good, her accent the clipped and rounded syllables of Moscow.

Lane looked at her reprovingly. "I told you to go to a hospital, have those bruises checked out."

Mika snorted. "Nothing's wrong with me except I lose money every night I don't work because of these fucking marks and then I have to spend another day in this place working off my debt."

I was starting to like Mika, chiefly because Lane turned pink and puffed up like an angry mama blowfish at her words. "Listen," I said. "We're here about Ivan Salazko. Is he the one who roughed you up?"

"Johnny?" She spat the name. "Yes. Him. Fucking pig almost tore me apart and then he beats me and takes back his money, and the house allows this because he sells them good fake papers. I told Detective Lane all of this already."

I slid my gaze to Lane. "Then maybe she should file a report and bring Salazko in so I don't go chasing my tail in a murder case?"

"I did all of that," Lane sighed. "There's no evidence besides the word of an illegal and someone like Salazko can just buy an alibi from one of his scumbag mob buddies."

"Wow." I shook my head. "You wouldn't know it to look at you, but I think you have even less faith in humanity than I do, Natalie."

"It's not like I didn't try," Lane hissed at me. "The Russians can do whatever they want with the money they earn off the sweat of these girls' backs, and we're virtually powerless to stop them. The system in this country isn't set up to deal with . . ."

"Spare the lecture and spoil the lieutenant, will you?" I said. "Mika, when did Johnny do this to you?"

"Two nights ago," she said. "I'm tired. Can I go back to bed now?"

"How late was he here?" I said.

She shrugged. "I don't know. Sunup?"

Hex it all, anyway. "Thank you," I said. "Go back to sleep. And lay off the Oxy—that stuff will put holes in your brain."

She curled her lip at me. "I take care of myself."

"You're what?" I said. "Seventeen, eighteen?"

She stuck out her bony hip and I saw more bruises, disappearing into the waistband of her pink workout shorts. "Sixteen. So what?"

"And Salazko shipped you over when you were fourteen or fifteen?" I said. Mika sneered.

"Johnny Boy isn't part of the outfit. He likes to think he is, but he's just a geek with Photoshop and a laminator. Thinks he can act like a gangster because gangsters pay his bills."

Lane held out her hand. "Come with us. We can get you into rehab and I'll talk to INS. Maybe you can stay here."

"Promises, promises," Mika said, and slammed the door in our faces.

"If Salazko isn't bringing the girls in, who the hell is?" I said. "And who had a reason to kill Lily Dubois?"

"You got me," Lane sighed. "I don't deal with the intricacies of the mob, I just deal with the fallout they leave behind."

"Something funny about the Russians," I mused as we left the brothel and climbed back into her car. "They're not like the Italians and the cartels. They don't send messages with their killings—no two in the back of the head, no you-know-what cut off and stuffed in your mouth."

Lane crinkled her button nose. "Is there a point to your frequently inane rambling, Luna?"

"Oh, it's Luna now, is it?" I pulled out my Black-Berry and scrolled through the address book to Bryson's number. "I mean that if Lily got herself into something bad, a mob hit might look a lot like black magick."

"Okay," said Lane. "But Salazko has an alibi. Who could have done this to her?"

"Mika said that Salazko liked to play gangster," I said. "Maybe he introduced her to some real ones."

Bryson mumbled hello around a mouthful of food. "David, call Dellarocco for a lab report and get it over to Fraud. Tell them they want to pick up Ivan Salazko ASAP."

"What about the FBI?" Bryson said. "And our surveillance setup? You don't like Salazko for this homicide anymore?"

"The FBI can deal with Salazko on their own time," I said. "And don't worry about that, David—you'll still get to peep through binoculars at hapless gangsters."

"On it," he said, sounding considerably more cheerful. "Where you want I should send the Fraud boys?"

I gave him Salazko's address and turned to Lane. "Home, Jeeves. Let's show some inter-task-force co-operation."

Lane frowned. "Pardon?"

"Drive, woman!" I said. "I have something I need to say to Salazko before I cross him off my suspect list."

"Fine," Lane said. "But then you're going to let me get back to work."

"It'll be worth it," I said as we turned into Salazko's neighborhood. "Trust me."

CHAPTER 8

A plain motor-pool car was parked the other way across the street when we pulled up to Ivan's building, and I went over and knocked on the window. "Hello, there. My good friend Detective Lane and I happened to be driving by and thought you could use the assist." I showed my shield to the two detectives in the car.

"Detective Kilkenny, Detective Bolton," said the guy behind the wheel. Kilkenny was as Irish as his name sounded, with red hair and skin that looked like it would scorch under a lightbulb, while Bolton was a mountain of muscle that would have stopped me in my tracks even fully phased.

"It's your warrant, boys," I said. "I'm just here to help."

Bolton jacked himself out of the passenger seat, running a hand over his shaved head. "Freak squad here to help. Sure."

"Look," I told him. "I'm very useful. I can dazzle the suspect with my feminine wiles and kick down doors and all sorts of skills normally reserved for the cop shows on TV."

Kilkenny snorted a smile. "Salazko. This guy connected?"

"Likes to play that he is," I said. "Probably has a gun."

Kilkenny heaved a sigh. "Great." They went into the lobby and started up the stairs, and Lane and I followed them, guns drawn. Bolton pounded on the door.

"Ivan Salazko. We have a warrant."

The door opened a crack, and Salazko stuck one bleary eye to the space. "You have the wrong apartment. Go away."

"That's him," I said.

I had to give Bolton and Kilkenny credit—for guys who spent most of their time chasing identity theft and white-collar scams, they were a well-oiled machine. Bolton kicked the door in and Kilkenny made a hard entry, shoving Salazko backward onto his ass and covering the room. Bolton covered him, hauling him to his feet.

Johnny was in boxers, an Orthodox cross studded with diamonds hanging in his mat of chest hair. "What the hell is this? You can't just bust in here! This isn't Stalin's Russia."

"Funny you should mention that," I said, hauling him to his feet and pulling out my cuffs. I snapped them on his wrists. "I met one of your countrywomen earlier today."

Salazko met my eyes. "I know you. You were at the OK . . ."

I hit him in the stomach, the soft spot just below the bone that makes all of your air rush out. He doubled over, and I held him there by the back of the neck, leaning close to his ear. "That girl is sixteen, Ivan. Strung out on pills. She was totally helpless when you beat her."

I drew back my knee and drove it in again, same spot. "Let's hope your cellmate will be a little bit nicer."

"Hey," Bolton said. "What the hell?"

I stepped back from Salazko, spreading my hands. "He just fell over. Maybe he has an inner ear problem."

Bolton smirked at me. "Right."

"You can return the cuffs at the SCS office," I said. "Pleasure doing business with you Fraud gents."

"Likewise," Bolton said. "Take it easy, freak squad."

I turned to Lane. "We can go back to work now. My good deed for the day is done."

When we were in the car, Lane kept looking at me, a small smile on her face. I'd call it smug, if I were being uncharitable. Hex that—it *was* smug. "What?" I finally demanded.

"You pretend that you don't have a heart," said Lane. "That you're all grit and instinct with that were-wolf thing. But you do have a heart—a big one, and you're trying to make sure it doesn't get broken."

"Thank you, Dr. Phil," I said. "Is it time for my free car yet?"

"That's Oprah," Lane said.

"I am disturbed that we're even having this conversation," I said.

"Fine, deflect," Lane said. "But it's true. You keep this hard shell around your heart so you don't feel the pain of the people around you. That's why you may be a decent cop instead of just a burnout."

"Gee, Lane," I said as we pulled into Justice Plaza. "Any more of this and I'm gonna start to think you like me."

She chuckled under her breath. "Don't get any ideas."

Lane went to her desk, and I said, impulsively, "We could use one more for our stakeout tonight. You like bad coffee and sitting in a small van in close proximity to a few smelly cops?"

"It's what I live for," Lane said, her expression completely serious.

"Great. We're leaving as soon as it gets dark."

I thought about Ivan Salazko while I waited for the shift to end and the sun to set. I was sure someone in the crew he sold to had killed Lily. Which one of them was the question. The bills of lading were still in my pocket. Whatever had gotten Lily's heart cut out was waiting for me at Pier 33.

Surveillance can be as simple or as complicated as you make it. In this case, there were five of us parked in a van, with a microphone. A box of take-out sandwiches sat pressed against Bryson's knees, and Lane ran the recording equipment while Will manned the listening device and I peered through the windshield with binoculars at the pier. Which was completely deserted.

Excitement, Nocturne City–style.

"Nothing," Lane yawned. "It's 3:30 A.M. We should call it a night before I have to get up for work."

"Not yet," I said. "This is our one shot before the feds swoop in."

"I'm so tired I think I may legally be a zombie," Will declared. "And these headphones chafe."

"Suck it up for another few hours and if nothing happens, we can shut down," I said. I wasn't inclined to give my compatriots much sympathy—if we didn't catch Lily's killer tonight, I was as good as Hexed.

Batista let out a soft snore, and I reached back and clipped him on the shoulder. "Stay awake!"

He grunted, and glared at me. "Tonight was my date night with Marisol. Last one before the baby comes, most likely. Thanks a lot, LT."

"Your sex life is not really my concern, Javier," I said. "But thanks for sharing, all the same."

"Hey, shut it," Bryson said, peering out the back windows of the van. "Someone's coming."

A silver Jaguar pulled up to the pier, dislodging four guys in various stages of no-neck disease and one tall gent with a goatee and a bald pate that gleamed under the sodium lights.

I dropped the binoculars and grabbed the surveillance camera with the telephoto lens. It was digital, night shots nearly as clear as day. I snapped the four heavies and Goatee Guy, and looked back at Will. "They saying anything?"

"Chatting in Russian," he said. "Two of the fatties are from St. Petersburg, sounds like, and the bearded one sounds almost Chechen. Definitely from down south."

Everyone in the van turned to look at Will and I gave him the eye. The fact that he'd lived long enough to learn every major language several times over if he wanted wasn't exactly broadcast news among my squad.

"I did an exchange program during college," Will said, a little too quickly. Lane still looked at him askance. "They're complaining that the container crane is late. Their port employee is lying down on the job."

Goatee yelled something at one of his heavies.

"What do I pay him for?" Will translated. "Only without all the cussing. They have a crane operator paid off to come in here and move their containers?"

"Gotta be," I said. I snapped more pictures, watching one of the thugs grab a ring of keys and start trying them against the U.S. Customs lock on one of the two shipping containers resting on the pier. He got it open and to my great relief, it was empty. I wasn't looking forward to busting five Russian mob tough guys with only myself and Batista, Bryson, Lane and Will.

"If that thing is empty," Lane said, "what the hell are they doing here? They should be moving the girls who come in from here to their brothels around the city."

"Maybe they're loading the crate to send back? Pick up another shipment?" Batista said. "Lieutenant Wilder said all of the bills were for outgoing cargo."

"More arguing," said Will. "Apparently no one in the mob is punctual. They're waiting on a truck."

"A truck of what?" Lane said.

"A truck of unicorns and pink ice cream for all I know," Will snapped. "I'm just translating here."

"It's fine, Will," I said. "They're waiting, we can wait."

I watched the five Russians mill around, light cigarettes, check their phones for text messages. "Come on, comrades," I muttered. "I haven't got all freaking night."

An engine rumbled, and a panel truck pulled up to the pier. I snapped a picture of the logo on the side, a meatpacking warehouse. "Subtle," I said. Bryson chuckled.

"No one accused the mob of having a sense of irony," he said. "What's going on out there?"

"They're unloading the truck," Lane said. I stared through the lens of the camera.

A thug stamped out his cigarette and opened the back of the truck, illuminating the contents, and I let out a small gasp. Will muttered something under his breath and Lane exhaled sharply. "Is that what I think it is?"

I put the camera back to my eye and twisted the focus. The back of the van revealed rows of sitting figures, some of them slumped over, some clutching their knees to their chests.

Goatee clapped his hands and shouted in English with a heavy accent that would have done a cheap extra from an eighties action movie proud. "Everybody out! Don't make me move your skinny asses!"

The women stumbled up, alone or in pairs, and practically fell out of the back of the truck. I've had enough experience with people who are fucked up on one substance or another to recognize the gait of a person stoned out of her mind. Maybe fifteen of them, all in rumpled clothes, some in pajamas, all with the vacant, dopey expressions of trusting livestock walking into a slaughterhouse.

The Russians herded the girls into the container, shoving them when they didn't move quickly enough. One girl, a small redhead who looked like she taught school, nursed sick animals or something equally wholesome, fell, twisting her ankle. Goatee grabbed her up and slapped her. "You think this is a joke?" he snarled. She fought him, feebly, and he slapped her again. "Move, bitch!"

I stopped snapping frame-by-frame shots of the encounter and tossed the camera into the passenger seat. "I'm going out there."

"No, you're not," said Will.

I shot him a look, my eyes flickering to gold. "Excuse me?"

"It's my op," he said coolly. "And they haven't done anything illegal yet."

"Um . . . they're loading women into a cargo container," said Lane. "He's hurting her!"

"It's a simple assault at best," said Will. "The girls aren't restrained. None of them are protesting. What we've got here is a large case of trespassing and a whole lot of circumstantial evidence."

"He's right," Bryson said.

My face heated up and before I could exercise my cop judgment, my were spoke for me. "Are you fucking kidding me? They're doing something to these women and if we don't work fast, they'll be gone."

"There's no ship docked here," Batista said, in what sounded like infuriating logic. "We've got a couple of hours before they can move them, at least, if that's even what they're doing."

I put my hand on the door. I had to do something. Had to stop more Lilys . . . I swore she was staring back at me against my pale reflection in the glass, her milky eyes accusing me of something I couldn't undo.

"Luna." Bryson was the one to hold me back. "I can't believe I'm the one sayin' this, but don't you think we should have some hard evidence before we go rushing in there?"

I snarled at him, lips pulling back over my teeth. My gums stung and I tasted blood as my were fangs grew. "Don't touch me. They're moving girls *out*, not in, don't you get it? Something worse is going on here than sex slaves and mob money."

"They're just going to walk straight back out on our arrest once their mob lawyer comes into the mix," Will said quietly. "I know this isn't ideal but we need to take what we've gotten here and use it to build a real case, one the FBI and the U.S. attorney can't step on."

"And we still don't know which one of them killed Lily," Lane put in. They were all trying to talk me out of doing something stupid, and they were all right. I was the one putting my case in jeopardy. If I even had a case.

I shut my eyes, tried to push back the monster that lived in my hindbrain. It was a useful monster, to be sure—it shared my life and my blood, my fears and desires. It was the dark half of me, the side that ran on all of the impulses I fought in a given day of one of the worst jobs the civilized world has to offer.

I lost.

The door was open before I realized my feet were on the pavement, the salt air on my face and stinging my eyes.

"Luna!" Will bellowed. "Luna, goddammit!"

A body chugged up beside me, and I recognized Bryson. Lane was just behind him, her gun already out. Huh. Maybe I'd misjudged her Girl Scout act.

"Nocturne City police!" I bellowed, as a mobster loaded the last of the girls into the container and slammed the door. Above me, the crane whined as its magnetic arm lowered. "Stand where you are!"

I don't know what I'd expected, really, but it wasn't

for the fattest of the heavies to open his long duster and pull out a Kalashnikov.

Bryson had time to say "Oh, shi—" before we all hit the dirt.

Automatic-weapon fire is like being trapped inside a pinball machine—it's louder than the voices of the gods and a spray of bullets in your general direction feels like the air is punching you. Bryson and I took cover behind a Port Authority cart parked between us and the mobsters, and Lane rolled behind a Dumpster. Batista and Will were dug in beside the van, returning fire.

"I told you to stay inside!" Will bellowed at me.

Amid the chaos, the crane arm caught the container of girls and whisked it upward and out of my vision. I went low, between the small, fat wheels of the cart, and aimed for Kalashnikov's legs. Two shots, one for each. He went down, but impressively didn't stop firing. Tough fat bastard.

One of the mobsters had the presence of mind to back the car between us and them as both sides opened up like we were John Dillinger and Melvin Purvis. Handgun slugs tore the poor little cart to shreds, and Bryson cursed as it rocked and threatened to tip over.

"Wilder, we do not have the fuckin' advantage here!"

The mobsters grabbed the guy I'd tagged and got him into the Jaguar. The car's engine roared and I came up, planting two slugs in its bumper out of pure spite.

The Jag fishtailed, righted and then, as quickly as the shooting had started, the car was gone. The container. Everything except a stink from the spent shells and a roaring in my abused ears.

I lowered my gun. "*Shit*," I said viciously. "Everyone all right?"

"We're okay, LT," Bryson said. Will holstered his weapon, shaking his head. At least he had the grace not to say *I told you so.*

"We've got plenty of evidence," Lane said to me, almost gently. "We'll have them IDed and arrested in a couple of hours with these photos and recordings to speed warrants along."

I looked at the spot the container had occupied. "Somehow that's not making me feel any better," I murmured.

Will tried to put his arm around me, give me a squeeze, but I shrugged him away. He gave me a hurt look and I kept my face stony. Those girls with their vacant eyes were all I wanted to think about right now. Men who would do this to innocent people had a monster inside, too.

I couldn't wait until I introduced them to mine.

CHAPTER 9

"You should sleep," Will said when he saw me under the lights of the motor pool.

"No," I said. "I should find out who those men are before they ship those poor girls off to god knows where."

"Luna . . ." Will sighed and pushed his hand through his hair. "You have to take a step back and remember that this is a case, not a crusade."

I blinked at him. "Excuse me? I know you didn't just get federal and all-knowing with me, your hysterical little woman."

Will shook his head. "Don't start. You know that's not what I meant."

"Then what did you mean?" I snapped. Lane, Bryson and Batista gave us our space, offloading the cameras and the recording equipment without a word. Once IA had gotten done with their shooting report, it had nearly been morning, and I was no closer to finding one shot-up gangster and his friends.

"Do you really want to have this fight in front of your subordinates?" Will asked me softly.

"Is that what we're doing?" I said. "Fighting?

Because from where I sit it just looks like you're ordering me around."

"Listen," Will growled, grabbing me by the arm. "I know your damage, all right? I know you have a pathological fear of being pushed around, but I'm telling you this as a fellow professional—you are going to have to let this go. You have no case, even if you could get a warrant for the container that the FBI doesn't sit on. Nothing those men did was beyond a misdemeanor until you started waving your gun around."

"You know as well as I do that something rotten is going down over there," I said. "You know that the Russians got Lily Dubois killed. You know *nothing* good is going to happen to those poor women who are probably on their way to some third-world hell-hole this very second."

Will shoved his hands through his hair, leaving a ruined trail of golden strands across his face. "Knowing and proof are two very different things, Luna. I learned that the hard way, just like you. That's all I'm going to say, since I can tell I'm already in the doghouse."

I turned away from him, so furious that I knew if I stayed I'd slap him across the face. How dare he be so condescending and smug and, well, right?

Absolutely right. I had not a shred of hard proof that would allow me to make a case against anything except the shooting. Lily Dubois was a were, but her case would be solved because I was a detective, not a night creature. I had to set my emotions aside and let those women, those victims, sail away into the night.

Out of all the shitty things I'd had to let ride in my

career, this was the worst, the largest. By far. It settled in my stomach like a small ball of ice, cold and foreign, the knowledge that their welfare was on my head. If they died, were hurt, were sold . . .

"Lane?" I said, as something fell into my head, a piece that stood out as mismatched with what I knew of the gangsters who had murdered Lily.

Lane looked to me like she expected to be screamed at. "Yes, Lieutenant?" Lieutenant. Great. Now she thought I was a hysterical broad like most of the rest of the Nocturne City PD.

"Why are they taking girls out of the city?" I said. "Russia exports sex slaves, it doesn't buy them from the decadent capitalists."

"Actually, Russia is a democracy now, with a premier that functions much like the British prime minister," said Bryson. I gave him my *Are-you-kidding-me?* glare. "What?" He shrugged.

"He's right," Lane said. "And I can't think of a reason. The sex trade in Russia depends on men in this country paying to exploit the girls from the former Soviet Union."

"Then why?" I said. "Why send women out?"

"I'm sorry, Lieutenant," Lane said softly. "I have no idea."

Me, either, and it was costing me this case. I decided that punching the rear panel of the van would be an appropriate response, and did it, leaving a dent. Lane flinched. "I do have an old friend who works organized crime," she said. "I could call him for some background on the men at the port, assuming they manage to keep their friend out of a hospital."

"Fine," I sighed, realizing that everyone, including

Will, was staring at me like I'd just started speaking Klingon. "Do it in the morning. The real morning." Sun was peering over the top of the Justice Plaza in a thin gold line. "I'm going to offload these photos onto the department server. The rest of you should go home."

Batista and Bryson withdrew gratefully, but Lane stayed with me. "It's never easy to lose an offender, Luna, but it happens. To the best of us."

"In what kind of a world?" I sighed.

"In the kind of world where you wait until you can nail the motherfucker to the wall for life," Lane said calmly. "Don't worry. We'll get these sons of bitches."

"Your optimism is infectious," I assured her when she looked disappointed that there wasn't more excitement at her speech. "But now I have to write my report and find some coffee that won't give me an ulcer."

Will touched my arm. "You need company? You seem a little . . . high-strung." His nice way of saying, *Honey, when you punch a van you scare all the plain humans.*

"No," I sighed. "You might as well go home and get some rest. No sense both of us being irrationally exhausted." I made sure to kiss him in front of Lane, so he'd know I didn't hold our little confrontation against him. Those days, of blaming all of my problems on my asshole boyfriend, were behind me.

Leaving Lane at her desk, I went into my office and loaded the photos on the SCS network drive, making sure Pete would see them when he came into work in a few hours.

Then I stretched out on the battered sofa in my office and took a nap, waking up with a kink in my neck and Lane standing over me. She'd changed to an entirely new conservative pastel blouse and freshened her makeup. I felt grit in my eyes from yesterday's mascara and sort of hated her.

"My friend up in organized crime is ready for us," she said. "And I'm pretty sure they have coffee in their office."

"I'm up," I grumbled. I checked myself in the mirror hanging on my door. To say I looked like I'd been dragged through five of the seven hells was an understatement. I tried to do something about my smeared makeup and my Siouxsie hair, but there was nothing I could fix about the grumpy first-thing-in-the-morning attitude.

Lane and I rode the elevator up to the daylight climes of the Plaza proper, and she led me to the warren of Organized Crime, which shared a vast open floor with Fraud. I saw Kilkenny's swath of red hair and tipped him a salute.

"This is Detective Han," she said, gesturing to a fellow sporting a shaved tattooed head, a few earrings more than department issue and a leather jacket. "Shi, this is Luna Wilder."

"Pleasure," Han Shi said, standing and shaking my hand. "I've heard a lot about you since the department opened the SCS." He had a firm grip and an infectious grin that transformed his face from hard to open. "You'll forgive the getup—I've been out on the street for a week working on the Golden Snake gang."

I was kicking myself for not washing my face or at least finding some deodorant before we came up here. Han was cute. And still smiling at me. Dammit.

"So, Natalie here tells me that you're having troubles from our comrades in the Russian mob," he said. "Care to take a look at the pyramid of shame?"

"What's that?" I said. Han led me to the end of the row of cubicles and pointed to a large corkboard covered in mug shots, surveillance photos and crime-scene shots that varied from garden-variety dead bodies to parts that even your mother couldn't identify.

"Jesus, Mary and Joseph," Lane said. "Animals."

"The Chinese are worse, believe it or not," said Han. "They have that creative edge the Russians haven't quite mastered. The new leader of the Golden Snake cut out his predecessor's eyes and sent them to the detective in charge of watching the gang's head-quarters. Sort of a *Spy Versus Spy* thing. Only with eyeballs."

Lane started to turn green, but I was looking at the mug shots. "This is the hierarchy of the Nocturne outfit?"

"As far as we've been able to tell," Han said. "We don't have anyone on the inside with the Russians, and neither does the FBI. *Eastern Promises*, this is not."

I scanned the board, seeing a lot of hard-bitten, tattooed men glaring back at me. "Him," I said, landing on a mug shot of Goatee. "That's who I shot it out with last night."

"That's Nikolai Rostov," said Han. "He's an enforcer, a high-level one in line to be the boss. Very old school. Did time in a couple of Soviet prisons before he fled to the wicked, wicked West. That doesn't exactly turn you into a cuddly sort of guy."

"Is he involved in the human trafficking going on through the port?" Lane asked. Han nodded.

"Probably. Rostov is who you send in when you don't want to get your hands bloody. Blood doesn't bother him overmuch."

"Or selling women into slavery . . ." I said, taking his photo off the board. Han made a sound of protest.

"You better bring that back. My captain gets very upset when we disturb the pyramid."

"Don't worry," I said with a wink. "I promise I'll return him and he'll still be ugly."

I yawned as I rode back down to the SCS to pull the computer file on Nikolai Rostov. I just needed to get a fix on him, and then I was on him like a fat kid on a birthday cake until this case was closed up tight.

My nose warned me that someone was in my office seconds before the door banged shut behind me. My Sig came out as I turned around and I found myself looking at Nate Dubois over the barrel.

"Hex me," I sighed, lowering the gun. "That's a real easy way to get yourself killed, Nate."

"Maybe I don't care," he muttered, his shoulders slumping. "You arrested that man John Black. Is he the one?"

I scented him, subtly so that he wouldn't take it as a threat to his dominance, and caught a whiff of cheap bourbon on his skin and breath. On a second look, Nate didn't seem so hot. His hair was sticking up all over the place and the lines on his face were twice as deep as when I'd seen him last. "I don't know," I said, and then added, "I don't think so. He has an alibi."

Nate grabbed my citation plaque for bravery off my desk, the only one I'd managed to earn in Homicide, and flung it at the wall. "Why the hell not?" he bellowed.

"Okay," I said, tightening my grip on the Sig. "You can calm down, or you can leave."

Nate glared at me, his lips pulling back over his teeth, and then he crumpled, missing the edge of my sofa and sitting hard on the floor, legs akimbo.

"No one knows who hurt my little girl," he sobbed. "No one cares . . . She's just gone . . . I can still smell her in her bedroom, I think I hear her coming into the room, laughing . . ."

I crouched down next to Nate and gripped him by the shoulder. "I promise you that I am going to make this right. Where's your wife?"

"Home," Nate sighed. "She's taking this so well . . . she's being so strong. I went out last night just to get away from the house and I ended up here . . ."

I stood up and dialed Norris, our office assistant. He was old as the hills and twice as crotchety, and we didn't talk if I could help it, but this was an emergency. My life is full of those. "Norris, can you get Petra Dubois on the line and tell her that her husband is here and needs a ride home?"

"Very good, Lieutenant," he said prissily, and hung up on me. It was probably the most civil exchange we'd ever had.

Nate tried to pull himself up, and I helped him onto the sofa. "You wife will be here soon," I said. "You need to go home and be with her, and take care of yourself."

"I miss my Lily so much," Nate sighed. "Pack justice won't bring her back to me." He swiped his hand over his face. "You really pissed them off sending Theodore back like that. They're going to come for you now, just like Lily's killer."

"I thought you were the pack leader?" I said gently, even though his words sent an involuntary tingle of fear through my gut.

"I'm broken," Nate said, slumping. "One of the younger ones will use this as an excuse to oust me and then we're both fucked."

"I'll close this case," I said. "You just have to have a little faith in me."

"What kind of a world do we live in when this can happen to a sweet little girl?" Nate asked me.

"No kind of world," I said. "But it's the only one we've got."

Nate and I sat in silence for a time, him nodding in and out and me scrolling through the photos from the night before. Just a glutton for punishment, that's me. I paused on a clear shot of Nikolai Rostov's face. My last lead. My last hope.

My phone buzzed and I switched on the speaker. "What?"

"Mrs. Dubois is here," Norris said.

"Thank you. Send her in."

Petra came through the door a moment later and her face fell when she saw her husband. "Nate, is this really what it's come to? Stumbling around like a bum?"

"I'm not strong like you," he said matter-of-factly.

"Thank you for bringing this to my attention, Lieutenant Wilder," said Petra. "I'm so sorry that he barged in here."

"Look," I sighed as Petra pulled Nate to his feet. "This may be out of line, but you two need help. Take the grief counselor's number. He's supposedly very good."

Not that I had ever gone to the guy. I'd seen the department psychiatrist, Dr. Merriman, more than a few times, but someone to help me actually deal with my problems was a luxury not afforded to most cops, unless they beat up their girlfriends or tried to eat their guns.

"We're dealing with this in our own way," Petra said coldly. "Something you obviously know nothing about."

"You know what, Mrs. Dubois, I'm doing my job to the best of my ability," I said. "Maybe if you didn't keep harassing me I'd be able to build a case against the man who hurt your daughter."

"So you *do* have someone in mind," Petra said, rounding on me. "Who is it?"

"I'm afraid I can't reveal the details of an open investigation," I said primly. Nate Dubois I felt for. His wife was just starting to piss me off.

"Not even to the person who could call her pack off of your scent?" Petra said, her eyes darkening as the pupils expanded. My were snarled inside my head and I felt my fingernails sting as my claws started to grow.

I beat the were back. "I'm not playing this game with you," I told Petra in a deliberately quiet tone.

"If I removed you from this case, I could get some real progress," Petra snarled. "Believe that I'll be talking to your chief in the morning. We have plenty of friends, including the commissioner."

Nate put a hand on her arm. "Can we just go home, please?"

Petra put her hands over her face, and her shoulders started to shake. "I'm so sorry, Lieutenant Wilder. I know that every time we meet, I treat you horribly." She grabbed my hands. "I'm so, so sorry."

"It's fine," I said, looking to Nate with a *help me* expression. He put his arms around Petra as she started to sob in earnest.

"Come on, love," he said. "Let's go home."

I pulled up Nikolai Rostov's file on the department database once Nate and Petra had stumbled out, and checked his known addresses. None were current, no businesses listed. Aside from enforcing mob law, Nikolai was a ghost. No wonder no one could build a case against him.

The pictures were still sitting on my desktop and I looked at the meatpacker's logo again, faded and patchy. I punched the company name into the department database search and found an address sure enough, with a notation that the company was in foreclosure.

I hit my intercom. "Norris, forward my calls to my cell." He grunted at me.

"And what should I tell any further drunken, disgruntled werewolves who invade our office space?"

"That you're an enormous curmudgeon?" I suggested with a bright smile. "I'll be back in an hour."

"Don't get yourself shot," Norris said, turning back to his computer. "That would be terrible. Just terrible."

CHAPTER 10

The drive to the suburbs took me across the overpass of Ghosttown, the burned-out wreckage of the government housing project that the Hex Riots destroyed in 1969, through the tract houses that were starting to finger out from the center of Nocturne City, and finally into the industrial wasteland, old chemical factories like patient, rusted sentinels by the roadside, weeds and birds and graffiti spreading life over their carcasses.

The meatpacking warehouse was just another ghost along the strip, sandwiched between a restaurant supply warehouse and a strip club called Tit for Tat. About as classy a locale as I would expect from a mobster who trafficked in sex slaves.

I pulled into the parking area, empty except for my car and a few pallets of old refrigeration equipment that had rusted to lace in the elements.

I locked the car and headed into the warehouse through the cargo door, pushing aside bloodstained plastic strips designed to keep the cold air in. Arrows painted on the floor guided me toward the FRONT OFFICE. I followed them along a white-tiled hallway illuminated by half-dead fluorescent tubes, only to find the shades pulled and a sign crookedly shoved into the window that proclaimed CLOSED.

I tried the door anyway. It was locked, in a shocking development. I looked at the frame for alarm wires, and saw nothing but an antique security camera. I pulled out my lockpicks, which lived on my belt next to my handcuffs, a packet of rubber gloves and the waist rig for my sidearm. I'm a good lockpick even without tools, which comes more from a teenage life as a delinquent than training as a cop.

Either way, I got the lock open in about fifteen seconds. The door clicked open an inch, and I scented the room beyond. Cheap carpet, dust, stale air and perfume.

Keeping my hand on my gun, I pushed the door open and edged inside, hoping that I'd caught Nikolai with his pants down.

A secretary stared at me from behind a reception desk. "We are closed."

"Um," I said, easing my finger off the trigger guard of the Sig and brushing my hands over my jacket to smooth it. "Your door was open."

"No, it wasn't," she said plainly.

"Okay," I said with a sigh. "Just tell me where Nikolai is."

"I do not know who you speak of," she said, her accent managing to make her sound prissy even though she was wearing a garish floral-print blouse, had red hair that could have been put out with a fire extinguisher and bright blue eye makeup. "You leave before I call the police."

"That's good," I said. "You calling the police on your front—I mean, your 'meatpacking warehouse.'" I made sure to use air quotes.

She glared at me. "You are a very rude woman. You will leave now."

"Tell you what," I said, leaning on the desk. "I'm fresh out of patience, so you toddle on back and tell Nikolai I'm here, or I'll give you a reason to wear that much cheap makeup on your face."

Her lip curled back and I started when I saw fangs. She didn't smell like a were, but then again, she was sporting about a gallon of cheap perfume. "I wouldn't do a thing for you, except throw you out on your fat ass."

"Word of advice, Fuzzy," I said. "You don't want to go there with me. I'm what you might call a sensitive type."

She pursed her lips. "What do you want I should do, pull him out of thin air?"

"Look, I know he's here or you know where he is," I said. "I'll speak to him now, or I'll get very, very unpleasant until he shows his face. Your choice."

After a long second of snarling at each other like wolves on a nature program, she sighed. "I buzz him." Her hand dipped below the level of the desk.

My gun came out fast, the safety off, aimed less than an inch from her eyes. "Don't move."

She didn't gasp or cry, like someone who *wasn't* reaching for a gun would. She just glared at me, like a small child who's been denied a reach into the cookie jar.

"Slowly," I said. "Show me the piece."

Sniffing in fury, she brought out the long-barrel

revolver and slammed it onto the desk. It was a .38, plenty large enough to ventilate me at close range.

"Now I call Nikolai?" she asked hopefully.

"You wish," I said, taking the gun and tossing it into the trash can on my side of the desk. I unhooked my cuffs from my belt and gestured to her. "Up."

"Nikolai will kill you," she snarled. "He will make you into pieces so small you will not fill paper cup for a funeral."

"Scary threats, scary gangster, blah blah blah," I told her, handcuffing her to the office door and re-locking the deadbolt.

She cursed at me some more, in Russian, but I turned my back on her and walked around the desk and through the door behind it, finding myself in a chill metal-lined hallway, freezer lockers on either side filled with nothing but permafrost and empty hooks for meat. I gave a small sigh of relief. Another dead body would really ruin an already crappy day.

I walked on, pushing through another plastic curtain into the main freezer, from which a chorus of male voices emanated.

I didn't hesitate before I banged the door wide open. "What, no strippers? No pool table? No humidor? Nikolai, this is one sucky secret clubhouse."

The group I'd surprised slowly stopped what they were doing, which was counting stacks of worn bills and banding them. Four pairs of eyes turned and bored into me. Rostov stood up slowly, deliberately setting down his fistful of bills.

"I'm sorry, miss, but this is a private business establisment. Can we help you find your way back to wherever it was you got lost?"

"Is this where you took Lily Dubois?" I said, gesturing at the featureless warehouse and plastic pallets, the cold air drifting down from the vents in fingers and cloaks of white vapor. "Not exactly a romantic hot spot, I have to say."

One of Rostov's companions reached for his gun, or whatever the bulge inside his windbreaker was supposed to be. Could have been a hero sandwich, but I doubted it.

"No," Nikolai said. "I'm sure the young lady is here in an official capacity."

"Smart boy," I said. Rostov gestured to a an empty plastic chair at the table covered in money.

"Please. Sit."

"You're pretty polite, for a gangster," I said. Rostov chuckled. It was a deep, fatherly sound, like a jolly Eurotrash Santa Claus.

"My dear, whatever rumors to the contrary—I'm a legitimate businessman who happens to run a concern built largely on cash transactions. What you see here is merely an . . . accounting meeting."

"Lucky for you, I'm not interested in your money laundering," I said. "I'm interested in the girls that you're selling overseas."

Rostov shrugged broadly. "Girls? I'm lucky if I find myself a date on match.com, Officer."

"Okay," I said, sitting in the offered chair and propping my feet on the table, sending cash to the floor in a minor snowdrift. The heavies traded glances but Rostov waved them off. I said, "I have a proposition for you."

Rostov seated his bulk in another chair. He wasn't fat, just solid—twenty years ago he might have been a heavyweight boxer or just one hell of a big guy, but he had run to softness around the eyes and jaw, and he looked like a mopey cartoon character. "I am listening, Officer."

"It's Lieutenant," I said. "Lieutenant Wilder."

"Whatever flips your skirt up," Rostov said, and suddenly he was no longer a friendly Santa but one of those innately creepy ones you see on *Dateline* exposés.

"Here it is," I pressed on. "You admit to killing Lily Dubois . . ." I took out the picture and shoved it across the table at him, "and I'll let you tie up the case the feds are making against you with local prosecutors for a couple of years. You plead guilty and you'll serve your time at Los Altos instead of some federal hellhole."

"I do not know this girl," Rostov said dismissively. "She is not my type." He shoved the photograph back at me. "Too skinny. Too pale. I require something to grab on to when I fuck them."

I had planned to stay cool and calm and to whittle Rostov down with common sense instead of threats. All of that flew out the window when I got a look at the gleam in his eyes.

"Although in a pinch, I would have taken her on trial basis," Rostov continued in a clinical manner. "Some men's proclivities are not the same as mine. Her youth could have served her—" He let out a yelp when I came across the table and grabbed him by the neck, squeezing down on either side of his windpipe, burying my fingers in the space between the thick cords of his tendons.

"Word of advice," I snarled, feeling the sting as my

eyes changed color from gray to gold. "I'm real, *real* low on patience these days." Hex me, this was not how things were supposed to go. I didn't lose it and jump the gun anymore. I was in control of the were, not the other way around. The crippling rage stayed locked in a box in the dark part of my mind, not always prowling the surface.

I heard noise behind me as the heavies fumbled for their weapons, their eyes wide with shock. Rostov fumbled for something in his waistband and I beat him to it with my free hand, grabbing a Browning pistol and tossing it over my shoulder. "Here's how it's going to go," I growled. "You're going to tell me who killed Lily Dubois and why. Then I'm going to arrest you and drag you out of here, and everyone is going to be happy. Except you, because you'll be rotting in jail for twenty-five to life."

Rostov laughed wetly under my hand, his face turning purple-red under my ministrations. "Even if you live to walk out of this place . . . you think the FBI will let me serve a day in prison? I will turn on my bosses and I will go into Witness Protection. I will retire to someplace like Tucson, where the sun is warm and the women wear halter tops, and street cops like you will never be able to touch me again."

I used my were strength to leverage Rostov out of his chair and slammed him into the wall of the freezer, hard enough to shake the calendar of topless women circa 1991 loose. "That day? It's not today. Now *tell me about Lily*."

"Nikolai . . ." said the largest of his buddies. I turned on him with a snarl.

"You shoot at me, you hit your boss," I said. "We're

having a private conversation. Shoo." They were scared enough by my eyes and fangs to be hesitant, but for how much longer?

"Go," Rostov croaked. "Let us speak." When his goons retreated, he turned his eyes back to me. "I will tell you nothing. You're just a whore like all the rest of them," he grunted. "A whore who doesn't know her business."

Black closed in on my vision, my animal side taking over with a vicious snarl that ripped out of my throat. I shook Rostov like a rag doll, impressing myself with my own strength. "Call me a whore one more time."

Dimly, I realized that I was losing control, lack of sleep and stress and rage creating a perfect storm in my hindbrain that had allowed the were to rip free of the tight harness I'd maintained on it since I'd phased and ripped a murderer to shreds, nearly two years ago.

But I can't say, in that moment, that I really cared. I just wanted Rostov to pay for all of my frustration and anger and for the visions of Lily that danced in front of my eyes.

It made me sloppy. Rostov wriggled an arm free and drove a fist into my gut. He was, as I'd predicted, disproportionately strong and I felt all of my air sing out of me.

I sagged, my grip on his throat loosening, and Rostov grabbed me by the scruff and tossed me like one would a bag of garbage. I went backward over a pile of pallets, landing in a heap.

Shit, Wilder. Get yourself together. Rostov came over to me, his feet in my field of vision, cheap shiny patent loafers that I could see my startled face in. He picked me up again. I struggled, but after the rush of the were it was a pitiful fight. I was disoriented and the animal in me was panicking while the cop in me was watching the whole thing with a resigned sigh.

This was why there are procedures. If you go off half-cocked, you just end up on the floor, getting beat to shit by a mob enforcer with terrible taste in footwear.

Rostov gave a grunt, and breathed in my ear: "Whore." Then he heaved me away from him, and I went through the freezer door, plastic sheeting shredding around me. I landed in a cutting room, with long metal tables, rusty hydraulic scissors hanging from hoses, knives and meat hooks piled in the sinks along one wall.

The three heavies came after me, their steps deliberate. They gathered in a half-circle, looking down, waiting for Nikolai's order as patiently as Rottweilers trained to attack. I gave them a weak smile. "How's it going, fellas? You get good dental in this line of work?"

Rostov brushed off his hands. "She's a filthy, disrespectful cop. Anton, deal with her. You two, get back to the count and don't let me find it fucking short tonight, eh?"

Anton, the one who'd been staring at me with such intensity, came over and got me up, even though my legs wobbled. The other two retreated, opaque plastic whispering shut after them like a shroud. Anton put me in a police hold with remarkable efficiency and shoved me down onto the cutting table, grabbing my legs and laying me out flat like I weighed nothing.

"Oh, good, torture," I said. "You in the secret police or something before you came to the bright lights of America to seek your fortune?"

Anton grunted. "Shut your mouth."

He went to a row of metal equipment lockers and pulled on a plastic apron stained dark purple with animal blood, and heavy gloves, never taking his eyes from me or giving me a chance to be sneaky. This whole situation couldn't have telegraphed *body disposal* any louder if there were bright flashing lights.

So this was it. This was where they'd find me, days later, when someone finally retraced my last steps. If they found me at all.

"You women are all the same," Anton said, reaching into his waistband. "Putting your business where it should never be." I heard the click of a pistol's safety coming off. "Turn your head," Anton ordered. "Away from me."

I twisted my neck around so he'd have to look me in the eye. "No."

Anton snarled, and I saw with shock that he had twin fangs growing from his top row of teeth. Another were who didn't smell like a were. What was this, my lucky fucking day?

"Don't look at me, bitch," he ordered again, and cuffed me in the jaw, drawing blood from my lip. It was either be executed like a good little girl or end up too beaten for an open casket.

"I hate this," I sighed. Another reason why I'd stopped kicking down doors that I had no business kicking down. More often than not, I found situations like this on the other side. *You never really learn, do you, Wilder?* "Shut up, will you?" I told myself crossly. Anton raised an eyebrow.

"Are you a crazy woman on top of it?"

"Quite possibly," I agreed. "But not as crazy as you are to shoot a cop in the head." The metal was freezing under my back, and the small .32 pistol Anton held looked disproportionately large so close to my face.

"One cop," Anton said, raising his pistol. It was shiny and nickel-plated, one of those penis replacements gangsters like to wave around. "Lots more where you came from."

So much for scaring him straight. He was the one who was armed, so I would have to be the one who was faster.

"Do me a favor," I said. "Shoot me so that they can have an open casket? My mother will kill herself otherwise." I cut a glance at him, putting as much sincerity in my voice as I could muster in my current state of *Oh crap oh crap I'm going to die.*

Anton muttered something in his native language. "Please," I said again. "Right through the heart. Kill me just as fast as in the head. I'm not wearing body armor. You can check."

"You have *no* leverage to make demands of me," he snapped.

"Anton," I said, putting as much sincerity as I could into my voice, considering that I was panicking on the inside. "All I want is to have my cousin and my aunt and my mother be able to say good-bye to me. I know what's coming. I'm not going to fight you. Just shoot me in the heart. Please."

Anton's nostrils flared. He was tall and thin compared to the pudgy thugs in the other room, and his face was drawn with blue varicose veins snaking across his cheeks, burst vessels in his nose. An ex-junkie, maybe, certainly not current, but his eyes had that blankness that comes with witnessing too much that people aren't meant to see.

He dropped the pistol, reaching out his free hand, patting me down. "Roll onto your stomach."

I did as he asked and he felt down the length of my back. He touched my Sig and threw it away from us. "You think you're smart, huh? You think you're going to grab your police gun and shoot me instead?" He grabbed my hair and slammed my face into the metal table. "Deceitful whore. Now I'm going to do it right between the eyes. For your mother."

"No," I said, "No, you're not." I grabbed his wrist, twisted the hand holding my hair, and bit him. Hard.

Anton screamed as my fangs sank into the fleshy part of his thumb, the blood coursing over my tongue driving me straight back into that black pit that lurked in me, where the monster waited, pacing and chained.

I shoved him away from me and he windmilled, bleeding, the gun moving away from my head. I snatched my holdout weapon from my ankle and went after him, instead of shooting him on the spot like I should have. I was lost in the lust for the hunt, and I hit Anton in the midsection, tackling him to the tile with a grunt from both of us.

Straddling his torso, I pressed the snub .38 against the soft part of his jaw with a growl. "Shoot *me*?" I demanded, pulling the hammer back. It was a double-action revolver, so I didn't need to cock it to fire, but the effect of the chambers rotating scares the piss out of anyone with sense.

"I . . . I'm sorry," Anton muttered thickly. Blood

dribbled from his mouth. He had bitten his tongue when he went down. I bared my own bloody teeth at him and he gave a shiver. For such a big bad werewolf, it sure didn't take much to break his dominance.

Then again, having a gun pressed against your chin has that effect on most people. "You're damn right you're gods-damned sorry," I told him. "Who killed Lily Dubois?"

"I got no idea what you're even talking about," Anton hissed.

"Right, because I totally and completely believe you," I said. I pressed harder, curling my finger around the trigger. "You have three seconds. One."

"I don't know!" Anton panted. "There are a lot of girls. Nikolai ships them by the week. I don't know her!"

"Two," I snarled.

"I don't know her!" Anton howled. He latched his hands to my shoulders and tossed me off of his torso. I went tumbling to the floor, the .38 skittering out of my grasp. He was strong, too strong for his size, and I hit the floor hard enough to crack tile.

Anton scrambled for his pistol and I grabbed for the .38, and we both brought the guns to bear at the same moment. He was back to smirking. "You like to be in charge, eh? Think you're getting what you want and you go soft."

"You're a very good actor," I said. "You might have a career if you quit your day job."

Anton spat on the ground. "You put that gun down."

"I don't think so," I said, backing up slowly. If I could just get some cover between us, I could make a run for the Nova. That was a hell of a big *if*, though.

"I'm going to keep holding it, and we're going to work out our differences like adults, and not little kids playing cops and robbers."

"I'll shoot you in the fucking head!" he yelled, obviously fed up with my mouthy ways.

I risked a quick look over my shoulder. There was a dark hallway and a set of stairs beyond, dark and slick with mildew and moisture as the cold air ended and the dank smell of below ground began. I snapped my head back to Anton. "If you're going to shoot me in the head, then do it," I growled.

His finger tightened on the trigger, and in the second between my taunt and his gun firing, I ducked and ran. One bullet dug into the wall next to my head, another into a pile of sawdust pushed into the corner with a puff of air and wood fibers. One thing was to my advantage—angry weres don't make the best shots.

I lost my balance on the second stair and pitched forward into the dark, tumbling, limbs cracking against the cement stairway and metal railings until I landed in a heap at the bottom of the stairs. "Graceful," I grunted, pulling myself up.

I fumbled for my penlight and flicked it on, flashing it around the basement. Rusted piles of metal, old hooks and saws, pallets and cages for chickens, stacked like steel cairns to a dead civilization. The witch's alphabet cascaded across the walls, the standard language of spells for caster and blood witches, and most disciplines in between. I pointed the light at the floor and breathed a sigh of relief when I wasn't standing on another binding ward or in a circle.

Then I'd really be Hexed.

Anton shouted from above, in Russian, and I heard him and at least two other bodies start down the stairs.

There were showers and lockers at the far end of the basement, ribbons of rust staining the wall beneath the taps, and I doused my light and dove behind the half-walk, crouched in the damp, smelling the mildew from the drains. I tried not to breathe too loudly in the small pit of decay where I'd landed, and to still myself. If they lost me here, I could double back and get to my car.

Way to go, Wilder. You play the sheriff and now you're screwed.

This was why cops didn't go Lone Ranger, unless they wanted to end up dead. This was why my monster was rarely a real asset to my job. It might make me stronger or faster, but there were plenty of days when it just got me stuck in a creepy basement chased by a bunch of Russian gangsters.

Anton's footsteps and his panting breath were fast behind me, and another flashlight beam glanced off the wall above me.

"Nothing here," one of the heavies wheezed. "You prick, Anton, you let her get away."

"She has to be down here," the other said. "There's nowhere else to go."

"Shut up," Anton said. "Just go back upstairs."

"But Nikolai . . ." the first heavy whined.

"Nikolai ordered me to deal with her," he snarled. "And I will. *Leave.*"

They retreated, cursing, and Anton snapped off his light. I heard him draw in a ragged breath, his wiry frame cutting off the light from the stairwell like a living scarecrow. "I know you're here, wolf girl," he singsonged. "I can smell you. I can *taste* you."

I held on to my Sig like a drowning man would clutch a piece of flotsam.

"I can hear your heart beating," Anton hissed, and then with a whisper of air he was standing over me. "And I see you."

Trapped, I goggled up at him, at the gun. Not my most proactive response by a long shot. *How* had he seen me in the pitch dark that even my eyes were having trouble penetrating? How was he so goddamn fast?

"Nothing to say this time?" Anton said. "Perhaps you have something you would like me to tell your family when Nikolai kills them as well?"

It didn't really matter how Anton had managed to find my hiding place—he was about to kill me and something needed to be done about that.

So I resorted to that old staple of fighting dirty, and lashed my foot out as he prattled on, kicking him squarely in the balls.

Anton doubled over, but he didn't lose his grip on the gun, and I cursed silently, raising my own. I aimed for his shoulder, just something to put him down long enough for me to get the hell out of the warehouse.

I squeezed the trigger, in the half-dark, and Anton *flowed* to the left, out of the way of the bullet, and came upright as if he'd never had a steel-toed boot to the testicles in his life.

Well, shit.

Anton let out a low laugh. "You won't get me that way, bitch."

The only thing I'd seen even close to Anton was a Wendigo, and he wasn't *that*, thank all the gods. If he were, I might as well give it up. You couldn't kill Wendigo except with fire, and I was fresh out of flamethrowers.

I stood up, slowly, holding my gun out to my side. "All right, Anton. Here's the thing—I'm leaving here one way or the other. You can let me go quietly, or we can fight, and you can lose, and I can hurt you. Your choice, since you started this."

That was a lie, of course. Anton had about six inches and fifty pounds on me, and while that would normally just make things more fun, he had also proven himself to be faster, freakishly strong and nigh-on impervious to pain. I really hate it when the bad guys have all the aces in their hand.

Anton drew himself up, baring his teeth. "I'll enjoy tearing pieces off of you, bitch."

Bitch, bitch, bitch. Didn't he know any other gender-specific insults? "Do it, then," I said, trying to circle him so that my back was to the stairs, to the exit.

Anton lashed out at me with a hand that sprouted claws under my eyes, faster than any were I'd run into before. *Crap.* I was already losing and he was just getting started. The claws caught my shirt, tearing ribbons across my midsection.

I danced away, keeping myself in profile, presenting a small target. Anton snarled and then gathered his legs under himself and leaped, a spring straight up and out. It was terrifying, like watching a zombie jump at the camera in a scary movie, and my split second of hesitation cost me.

Anton's weight slammed into me and he took me to

the floor, tangling his hands in my hair, slamming my head into the concrete. Lights flamed and dulled in front of my eyes and my vision went blurry.

How had he made that jump? What the hell was he?

Questions for another time, all. Anton bared his teeth, fangs fully extended now, and angled for my throat. I struck out with my free hand, feeling for anything, and finally closed my fist around the end of a rusty iron meat hook.

It would have to do. As Anton closed his teeth around my throat for the finishing blow, I swung the hook up and buried it between his shoulder blades.

A crunch, like a cleaver cutting into a bunch of fresh celery. Anton quivered on top of me and then went still except for a convulsive twitching through his limbs. I felt a warm trickle of blood over my collarbone and shoved him away from me, rolling out from under his weight.

The hook didn't look to have hit anywhere vital, not even a deep wound and very little blood, but from the way he was gasping and twitching, I wagered Anton was not long for this world.

I found my Sig, and backed away from the body, the irrational fear that it would get up again and start chasing me bubbling up from the animal part of my brain.

It's happened before, and I wasn't taking any chances. I slipped up the stairs, hearing the heavies muttering to each other in the freezer and Nikolai snapping at them. *Get back to work* sounds the same in any language.

I headed for the emergency exit, shoving open the

heavy fire door. I was tired, bleeding, sore every-where from the tussle with Anton, and I was shaking with delayed shock. So I nearly jumped out of my skin when the fire alarm started screeching.

It just figured—a condemned warehouse and they still worry about fire safety. I took off at a run and made for my car. I threw myself into the Nova and fumbled for my keys, jamming them into the ignition and gunning the engine.

Nikolai came barreling out of the warehouse with a gun, stepping into my path. I pressed my foot down on the gas. He could be pavement pizza or he could get out of my way. I didn't care particularly which he chose right at the moment.

He leaped out of the way, and I sped out of the of-fice park, laying rubber on the main road and speed-ing all the way back into the city.

My rage dissipated as the road hummed under the Nova's tires, and all that was left was fatigue and shock. I've encountered a lot of weird people in my time, but Anton was something new. He'd come close to winning our little dance and that didn't sit well. If I met another like him, I'd be Hexed.

Hands shaking, I took the exit off of the Appleby Expressway into downtown and tried to hold it to-gether. I felt like I wanted to vomit, but I sat in the car instead after I parked at the Plaza, sweating and shaking.

I gripped the steering wheel and looked at myself in the rearview mirror. I'd done something unforgiv-ably stupid and probably just Hexed any chance I'd had to start with of closing Lily's case. "Nice going," I told myself with a sneer. Nothing to do now except go back to my office, call the body in to Bryson and Batista, and deal with the fallout of letting my monster have its head.

Just when I thought I had a handle on the were, it tricked me again, laughed at me from dark corners. I wished, not for the first time, that I could just rip it out of me, be a plain human again. Mundane had to be better than this.

CHAPTER 11

Lane followed me into my office when I arrived back at the SCS. "You don't look so good," she said.

I slumped in my chair and ran my hands down my face. "I'm lucky to be alive, never mind looking fresh and fabulous, Natalie."

"So I take it bursting into a Russian mobster's office and confronting him didn't yield the fruit that it always does in the movies?" Lane said, sitting on the edge of my desk.

I glared at her. "I'm really not in the mood right now, okay?" I rolled my neck, trying to work out a few of the kinks, and then buzzed Bryson's desk. "David, can you and Javier come in here for a second?"

"Sure thing, LT," he said. He gave me the same look as Lane when he clapped eyes on me. "Shit, Wilder, did you run yourself through a cement mixer?"

"There's a body at Rostov's meatpacking plant," I said. "It's a were, so it's an SCS beef. Can you and Javier take CSU and go down there?"

Batista paced. "And how do you know about this body?"

"I created it," I said shortly. "I'll be in tomorrow and you can take my statement."

"Internal Affairs is gonna shit a brick," Bryson said.

"Were body," I repeated. "SCS case. It's not a hard one to figure out, David."

Batista touched him on the arm. "Come on. We'll grab Anderson and get right on it, Lieutenant."

"Thank you," I said. "Less questioning, more following orders. Go on, shoo."

Once they'd left, Lane gave me her motherly, disapproving look. "It sounds like things got way, way out of hand with Rostov, Lieutenant."

"I know what I'm doing," I said, stubbornly.

"I'm going to give my opinion here," she said. "And then you can get angry, because that's what you do."

I rolled my eyes at her. "Please. Enlighten me."

"I think you'd do anything to get this guy," she said. "Obsession can be a very narrow edge to walk, Luna."

"Are you my shrink now?" I asked, probably more snappish than she strictly deserved.

"Just someone who's been where you are," Lane said. "Mine was the father of a ten-year-old girl who'd been systematically abusing her for five years. My captain put me on unpaid leave when I started following him from place to place, and he reported me to Internal Affairs when I hit the guy in the face with my baton."

I looked up at her. Lane didn't seem like she had the stones for anything except procedure. "What happened?"

"I got ordered to go to anger management classes and the prick sued the department for a fat settlement." She gave me a sad smile. "At least the little girl isn't in his custody anymore. Even if he never did see a day of prison."

"Prison is too good for some people," I said softly.

"Agreed," said Lane. "But it's not up to us to decide that, is it?"

"Not judge and not jury," I agreed. "Just the long, often ineffectual arm of the law. It sucks."

Lane patted me on the shoulder. "Go home. Hug your loved ones. And take a shower. You smell like old meat." She went back to her desk, shutting my office door gently behind her.

I leaned back in my chair and pressed my hands over my eyes. I knew I looked tired and wrung out, and that I'd been acting less like a lieutenant and more like a detective who'd gone over the edge. I hadn't let a case sink its teeth into me like this one in a long time.

This used to be me, always. This shell, with circles under her eyes and too much coffee in her system. I used to snap at the drop of a hat because I would get so tired my were would take over.

Lane was right, much as I hated to ascribe that quality to someone as sanctimonious as she. I picked up my phone and called my cousin Sunny.

"Luna," she greeted me. "Troy said you'd come to see him and you were in a bad way."

"I need to talk," I said. I couldn't think of anything else that conveyed what sort of a time I'd been having.

"Of course," Sunny said. She'd known me my whole life. She knew when it was serious.

"You know that wine bar on Grove Street, the snooty one that you dragged me to a few months ago?"

"Vines? Yes, of course," Sunny said.

"Meet me there," I told her. I needed someplace far

away from my usual haunts of Devere Street and Waterfront. A tony Cedar Hill wine bar was just the ticket.

"I'll leave now," Sunny said. "I was going to stay in and cook dinner for Troy, but he can fend for himself for a night."

"He's been doing it for twenty-five years," I agreed. Mac was once divorced, long ago, and had been a content bachelor until he met my cousin. I was still trying to figure that one out. "But don't hurry," I said. "There's one thing I need to do first."

"You're insane," Will said when I'd laid out the whole humiliating story of my day. "Absolutely around the bend. In what universe did this seem like a good idea?" We were standing in the light drizzle outside of the federal building, underneath the overhang where the smokers from his office congregated.

"Thank you for your support and sympathy, dear," I told him. Will rubbed his forehead with his index finger.

"That came out wrong. I meant, I don't really know what to say. I'm glad you're all right, certainly, but you can't think there won't be a reprisal . . ." That was my Will, practical to the point of insensitivity.

"I've dealt with the mob before," I said, thinking of my dealings with the O'Halloran family, a gang of caster witches who had done their damnedest to erase me from the planet. "It's gone bad before, too." Car bombs, beatings, and when that didn't work, a plunge off of the Siren Bay Bridge. They were persistent, I gave them that.

"If Rostov finds you again anytime soon, it won't

be just 'bad,' " Will said. "It will be you, in tiny pieces, as a message to anyone else who tries to screw with their business. And not just you, Luna. The Russians don't believe in loose ends. They'll go after your whole family. Sunny, your grandmother, me . . . anyone who cares enough to get revenge for your murder. If you won't stop this for your own sake, back off for theirs."

"I don't exactly have a choice here, Will," I snapped. "I'm dead if I don't do this because then I will *never* get hard evidence on who killed Lily Dubois and her pack will rip me to shreds. With Rostov, at least, I know what I'm dealing with." Mostly. Anton's snarling face flew back to my mind.

Will reached out and ran a thumb down my cheek. "You're awfully sure of yourself, Luna, and I respect that and I respect you and all of the crap that a supportive boyfriend is supposed to say, but you don't *know*. You just don't know what's going to happen."

"Neither do you," I said, leaning over and kissing him lightly. "And you worry too much. You must be getting old."

"Very funny," Will told me and then he faced me, taking my hands in his. He pressed them against his chest, so I could feel the steady flutter of his heart under the crisp cotton of his dress shirt. "Luna, I didn't want to have this talk in the smoker's area of my work, but I have to say it—I care about you, a lot. More than I've cared about a woman in a while. Like fifty, sixty years."

I met his eyes, their inky depths usually so inscrutable that I could spend hours looking. Will's eyes were one of the things I liked about him, along with the smile, and the body, and the evil sense of humor. "Thanks. You know how to make a girl feel special."

Will gripped my hands tighter. "Marry me."

"What?" I said, oh so coherently. Will's mouth quirked.

"You heard me."

"*Marry* you?" I sputtered. "Will . . . I . . . you . . . How long have you been planning this?"

"Well, originally there was a night of great sex, a few bottles of wine, a box under your pillow when you woke up next to me, but then you came and told me about this, and . . ." He sighed. "You mean something to me, Luna. I love you, and I want you to be my wife, and I may not get the chance to ask again so will you please put me out of my misery and say yes or no?"

A litany of excuses flew through my head. *It's only been six months. You're cursed, I'm a were—it would never work. I fear commitment like a vampire fears a spicy marinara sauce . . .* "Will . . ." I sighed. He was still holding my hands, and I gently extricated myself. "I just don't know."

His face fell, and he stepped back, running his hands through his hair and dislodging a blond chunk to hang in front of his eyes. "Not the answer I was wanting to hear."

"I know, and I'm sorry, but this was just so sudden and no one has ever proposed to me before, so I don't know the etiquette . . ." I babbled, trying to salvage something from this.

"The etiquette is, you say *yes,*" Will said testily. "And I don't embarrass myself."

"I'm sorry, but I don't think this is supposed to be

about you being embarrassed," I said gently. He grimaced, and paced a few steps away from me. I stayed where I was, suddenly feeling very cold and small in the scheme of things.

"This isn't about trying to control you or trying to make you settle down or my own happiness," Will said. "This is about *us*, being together. If you don't love me in the same way, tell me now and I'll walk away and we can end this before it causes some real pain."

I looked at my feet. Six months was, in the larger timeline, no time at all, but to me it was huge. Six months was the longest I'd managed to be with *anyone*, except Dmitri, and we'd had enough fights and problems to make maybe a handspan of weeks in those six months actually good.

Will was not Dmitri. He was solid, dependable, loving. And more than any of that, he accepted me exactly as I was. He'd never tried to make me change or conform to his ideas of what a woman should be.

I didn't want Will out of my life. I just wasn't sure I wanted to be his wife. "Please don't go," I said. I came to him and wrapped my arms around his waist. Will had a few inches on me, enough so that I could lay my head on his shoulder.

He sighed and stroked my hair. "I cocked this up royally, didn't I?"

"It's not you," I said. "It's me."

"That'd be funny if we weren't standing right here," he said. "What do you need, Luna? A guarantee that I won't make you wear a frilly apron? Me to proclaim adoration from the rooftops? A complete list of every other woman in my life? What?"

"Well, since that last one would take literally years," I said, "I'm not gonna go there." I pulled back and pushed the gold strands of hair out of his face. "I just need time, Will. Time to process. Time to decide." Part of me whispered that if I were really sure one way or the other I'd know already, but I told it to shut the Hex up.

He shut his eyes, and I knew gut-level that this was the end. He was going to throw up his hands, like all of the men in my life eventually did. I was just too much trouble for my own good.

Will opened his eyes and gave me a crooked smile, one that did a fairly good job of masking the hurt in his expression. "Time, I've got."

I blinked. "Really?"

"Really. For you, doll, I'm prepared to wait."

I started to shake with relief for the second time that day. "Thank you," I said, covering Will's mouth with kisses. "Thank you."

"You'd better get going," Will said, checking his watch. "You're going to be late meeting your cousin."

"We'll talk about this more when this case is closed," I said. "I *promise*." Whatever I decided when I had time to actually think, I'd never meant anything more.

Will kissed me chastely on the cheek and squeezed my hand. "Be careful, Luna. I mean it. I know you're a tough broad but the Russians are tougher."

I gave him a reassuring smile. "Honey, they've never met anyone like me. Trust me on that one."

* * *

Vines, the wine bar I'd told Sunny to meet me at, was a discreet stone building on a discreet corner in Cedar Hill. The waiters all wore black, as did most of the customers, and the music was the kind of self-conscious world tracks that no one *actually* likes to listen to.

But it was quiet, it was dim and no one looked at you to do anything except size up your hair and clothes. Once the clientel realized that I was in a wrinkled pair of suit pants and an off-the-rack blouse, they ignored me.

Sunny was in the corner with a glass of water, twisting it between her fingers. "You're late," she said when I slid in across from her. "I was starting to think you'd ditched me."

"Will proposed," I blurted. Sunny's mouth opened a fraction, and she froze, her perfectly curved eyebrows in a perfect arch. Sunny is the petite, polished, pretty one in the family. I'm the one with surprise proposals.

"Come again?"

"He proposed marriage. Legal union between two consenting adults."

Sunny grabbed a passing waiter. "House Merlot. Make it quick."

"I hate Merlot," I protested.

"You stroll in here looking like you just punched a semitruck in the face and tell me that your immortal boyfriend proposed. It's not for you." She folded her arms. "Now, why don't you explain why you look like you just rolled out of a gutter in Times Square, circa 1979?"

"I . . ." I sighed. "That's the other part of what I need to talk to you about. There was this enforcer, with this Russian gangster I paid a visit to today and it was like . . . he was a were, but he wasn't phased. Wasn't even close."

"Not a Redback?" Sunny asked. I shot her a black look.

"Not like Dmitri, no. No phasing at will. He was just strong, and fast, and . . ." Frightening. "A little crazy," I finished.

Sunny spread her hands. "A pack you haven't encountered before. A pack that's extra strong."

"No, it's more than that," I insisted. "It was like . . ." I sighed. The waiter set a glass of Merlot in front of Sunny, bloody and a little thick like a Merlot should be. The smell of the grapes overtook my nose and I coughed into my hand.

I couldn't articulate what about Anton had scared me so, but it was more than a pack that was stronger than the average were. It was something primal that my were understood but I didn't.

To understand it would be to allow the were to roam free again, and my life now was predicated on that not being the case. My job, Will, sitting here with my cousin instead of alone at home, because my rage wouldn't let me be safe with other people.

"Luna, tell me about Will," Sunny said, taking a long drink of her wine. "Tell me what happened."

I laid my hands on the table and looked at them. My knuckles were scraped on the left, my nails scrimmed with dirt, and they shook a little, from being hungry and tired. "I need to go," I sighed. "I need to get some sleep."

"Luna . . ." Sunny started, reaching for me as I stood. I shook her off.

"I'll talk to you tomorrow, Sunny. Enjoy your Merlot."

"Luna!" she snapped as I walked away. "Luna, you can't turn your back on this! This is *important*. This is your *life*."

I looked at her over my shoulder. "Sure doesn't feel that way sometimes, Sun."

Leaving Vines, I drove home through a light mist, my headlights beams of dancing droplets, like gems. I rubbed my eyes before I shut off the Nova and locked it, making sure I had my bag of dirty clothes from work to take to the laundry, my laptop bag, my badge and gun, a few extra clips I'd left in the car.

My apartment doorway was a cocoon of light in the mist, and I walked toward it, feeling the weight of my bags and of the day lean heavy on me.

Footsteps sounded behind me, and I heard the drunken giggle of a college girl and the lower rumbling of her boyfriend's voice as they turned into one of the bars on the next block.

What would I say to Will? How could he expect me to spend the rest of my life with him, when I couldn't even spend one day without succumbing to the were?

Footsteps came again, and I felt air against my neck. I spun, my dirty laundry slipping out of my hands.

Victims who say things like *It all happened so fast* always sound like they weren't aware, that they were caught flatfooted, but it did happen fast, too fast for me to see.

There was a touch against my throat, a hand sliding across my chest, two more figures out of the fog in front of me, a sting against my neck.

I didn't smell or hear them. All I felt was the terrible cold in my blood, the one I knew all too well. Silver.

The entire right side of my body went numb from the kiss of it, and I felt my knees buckle. I fell to the sidewalk, twitching. What had they done to me? I'd never felt this way, not when I'd been drugged once before, not when I'd been hit with a silver round. It hurt, yes, but nothing like this.

This felt like dying.

As I lay there helpless, with no control over my body and only the haziest sense of what was happening to me, I heard a voice.

"Get her up. Nosy fucking cop has got a long trip ahead of her."

CHAPTER 12

I fell through layers of cotton, the sting in my neck disappearing. It was strangely soothing . . . everything smoothed at the edges and sounds came to me from a distance, calming like waves on a black sand shore.

My gun, badge and holdout weapon were gone, their familiar weight light. Hands pulled at my clothes, palms a kiss of cold on my skin. Once they'd determined I wasn't wearing a wire, they left me alone. I couldn't care less. I floated down, landing gently on a rough automobile carpet, feeling lighter than air.

"Gods, Nikolai," said a voice. "How much did you give her?"

"Enough for a were," Nikolai said. "And she's a bitch, believe me. She smacked me good when she came to my office."

"Just get her into the van," the second voice snapped. A woman. The quality-assurance portion of the prostitution ring, no doubt. Trust a woman to judge a woman. "You're less than worthless, you know that? What if she dies on me?"

"She's a cop who came into my business asking all kinds of fucking questions," Nikolai growled. "Ques-

tions that are troublesome. You'd be starring in a re-
make of *Caged Heat* right now if it wasn't for me."

I drifted out then, coming back to myself with the
rumbling of an engine running through my body.
Dimly, I wondered how long it would take Will and
the SCS to find me. Tomorrow morning, later? How
long before someone like me was missed, and not just
a relief not to have around?

The engine stopped and the door opened. I was
hauled out, stumbling like a prom date on spiked
punch, and dropped next to other warm bodies that I
felt but didn't see, my vision blurring in gentle waves.
There were other women around me, halos of light
softening their features as my drugged eyes struggled
to focus.

Will would find me. Will would miss me. I just
wanted to sleep, to dip into the dream sea and swim
forever.

No. My were snarled, howled and scraped its teeth
over the inside of my head, but I couldn't rouse myself. They'd dosed me too strong; I couldn't think,
couldn't move . . .

None of it mattered in the next second as a new
parade of images took over from my hope that someone would find me before the truck reached the port.

Will, Sunny, my grandmother. Faces and images
I hadn't seen for years, as if my mind was flipping
through a mental catalog and not liking what it saw.

Hands levered me up again, faces slid past, and I
felt my gut rebel. Weres heal fast and my body was
doing its level best to expel whatever I'd been dosed
with before I was irrevocably fucked.

I managed to vomit onto the shoes of the girl next to me, as we were shoved into an echoing metal space. The cargo container, of course. The girl groaned and tried to slide away from me, and ended up falling over.

The metal walls of the crate brought a cold certainty with them—no one was coming for me. No one was going to rescue me. No one knew where I was, and by the time Will missed me or Bryson and Lane thought to track the GPS in my cell phone and found it in the hands of the bum who had undoubtedly stolen it to pawn, I would be halfway around the world.

I still had no power over my own body, so I did the only thing I could do, that hadn't happened since I was a small child—I curled into a ball and started to cry.

When I woke up, I thought I was dead. I'd had the notion before, but this time I was absolutely sure. I smelled bile and piss, I ached everywhere, I was cold and my surroundings were rocking in steady time, like the beating of a heart.

I could hear crying, too, sobbing, hysterical and ongoing. Wasn't the Christian hell supposed to be full of the wailing of sinners or something equally melodramatic?

"Shut up!" someone shouted, banging on metal and making my head echo. "Jesus fuckin' Christ, what's her problem?"

The sobbing continued, and I ordered my eyes to open. If I was in hell, I at least wanted to see which of the seven I'd landed in. I hoped it wasn't the fire hell. I don't do well with heat, even if it is a dry heat.

I recognized my racing thoughts for what they

were—panic. Maybe there was hope after all. Could there be much purpose to panic in the afterlife?

The first thing my eyes caught was a steel wall, swinging shadows slicing back and forth like some kind of macabre puppet show. The same witch's alphabet I'd seen in the meatpacking warehouse cascaded along in ripples of shadow, like a moving river of magick. It hurt, so I dropped my eyes from it to the floor.

There was a shoe lying on its side—a nice shoe, a Louboutin—level with my face, and I reached out for it, as something tangible and real.

Where the Hex was I? I tried to sit up and felt as if I'd hit my head against a Dumpster. Dizziness and pain raced through me and I threw up again, all over the front of my shirt.

"Fuck, bitch, what's wrong with you?" the same voice shouted.

Wait, *again*? I'd thrown up before. Recently. Something poked through the black cloud that had taken the place of my brain, flashes of stumbling, vertigo, my stomach welling up into my throat . . .

"Oh, shit," I breathed, clapping a hand over my mouth. "I got dosed."

"Welcome the bright penny to the club," snarled the woman. "Yes, sweetie, you're not supposed to drink the roofie cocktails. Lesson learned?"

Underneath the stench of the filth sloshing back and forth on the floor of the container, I placed the musky smell that had been tickling my nose as female weres—a lot of them, scared and pissed off. I reached out for the side of the container and levered myself up.

"I wasn't roofied."

Rostov. He'd shut me up in here, just like the group of women I'd been trying to save.

"Hell you weren't." The voice laughed, bitter as a pill on your tongue. "Look at you. You're a hot mess."

Silver, burning from the inside out . . .

My stomach lurched, but fortunately there was nothing left. I put eyes on the bigmouth. She was short and busty, clipped bright red hair still half-spiked from a night out in the mosh pit. Her outfit was the sort of carelessness that punks cultivate when they're trying too hard—tight bondage pants, ripped men's tank, full sleeves of tattoos bright with cherry blossoms and dragons and other pilfered symbolism. "Mind keeping your voice down?" I rasped. "My head is killing me."

"Yeah? Aren't you special." She folded her arms, making the dragons flex. "On the bright side, I'm about to kill little Miss Sobs-a-lot over there if she doesn't *shut the fuck up!*"

Red beat her fist against the container wall again. That was where we were. A cargo container, painted with workings on the inside, airless and dark. "Let me out, fuckers! I'm an American! You can't do this to me."

"If they were inclined to let us out, they would have done it," I said, suddenly weary. "We're in here until we get to our port of call." There was no mistaking the lurch and roll underneath us for open sea, now that I was conscious.

"Oh, yeah, and what are you, some kind of expert on freak kidnappings?" Red snarled. Her claws were out, flexing in fear.

"No," I said wearily. "I'm a cop."

Her mouth opened at that, but I turned away from her and crawled over to the girl who was sobbing. Her noises had taken on a hypnotic rhythm, droning, like an animal caught in a trap.

"Hey," I said, trying to get a look at her. "Hey, what's your name?" I didn't bother asking if she was all right. It was a stupid question.

She hiccupped, staring at me with wide, terrified eyes. "What do you want?"

"Just to know your name," I said. "I'm Luna." I reached out to put a hand on her shoulder and she flinched back, squealing in fear. "I'm not going to hurt you," I said. "I promise."

"My name's Dolores," she managed. "Dolores Stern."

The name was vaguely familiar, and I tried to sift through the leftover fragments of my brain from my silver roofie coma for the memory. Bold print, a picture of the willowy blonde before me staring out at me from a page . . .

"Dolores Stern, the reporter?" I said. "You're with the Nocturne *Inquirer*, aren't you?"

"Y-yes." She shuddered. "And you're Luna Wilder, that werewolf cop who runs the freak investigations for the NCPD."

"That's one way of putting it," I allowed. Focusing on Dolores and her trauma was allowing me to shove mine into a box and lock it. As long as I didn't let myself think about what had led me to be here, I'd be fine. Functional. Able to get out of this alive.

I was good at compartmentalizing way before I became a cop, but it certainly comes in handy for the job.

Dolores let out another choked sound, which may have been bitter laughter. It was hard to tell. "We sure make a pair, don't we?"

"I suppose we do," I said. "How did they scoop you up?"

"I was talking to this asshole in a bar," Dolores sniffed. "Lots of club girls turning up missing lately. Thought I might get a story. I only turned my back for a second to take a call because my editor was checking in . . . there was no way he had enough time . . ."

"This asshole," I said. "Did he happen to be about six foot, slick-looking, black hair, accent?"

Dolores blinked. "You know him?"

"Ivan Salazko," I said. So they were all in a little club together. It'd be cute if it wasn't so nauseating. I didn't know what I was most furious about—that I'd slipped up or that it had been that slimy little rat's asshole Nikolai Rostov who had dosed me. I was supposed to be smarter than that, harder to get to, and he had waltzed up to me on my own front steps and snatched me. I felt my neck where the silver had touched me. There was nothing there except a dime-sized burn, which would heal in a matter of hours.

"Sounds about right," Dolores said. "About six months ago a sister in my circle went missing. 'S what put me on to the whole thing. The police couldn't give a crap—no offense—so I started digging and more and more women with the blood and the bite turned up gone as I went along, all of them from Russian-run clubs. I'm not stupid, so I followed the story."

"You're a witch?" I said, thinking that if she could pull it together it might be useful in getting us out of here. Magick can do a lot of things brute strength and a set of claws can't.

"Shaman," she said. "It was one of those stupid teenage things—you might have guessed 'Stern' isn't a family with a long proud line of circle-scribblers in it. Anyway, your standard vision quest gone bad and then . . . certain powers."

I'd only met one shaman before, and Dolores was an improvement even in her hysterical state. She hadn't tried to kill me yet, and no one had needed to shoot her. Definitely a step up.

"Can you do something to get us out of here, if you have a chance to calm down?" I asked.

Dolores shook her head. "Steel. It Hexes up my ability to pull down power, plus they've put bindings on it. None of us are getting out of here, witch or were."

So much for my brilliant escape plan. Red snorted from the corner. "Well, princess, with or without you, I'm getting the fuck out of here at the first gods-damned opportunity. The rest of you bitches are on your own."

"Let's not be hasty," I said. "We don't need anyone getting killed."

"Bitch, are you blind?" she snapped. "We're locked in a fucking *crate*. On a *boat*. Headed to Thailand or some gods-forsaken place where they chain you up and fuck you in the ass until you're too old to make them a buck."

"Oh, gods . . ." Dolores whimpered. I put a hand on her shoulder and squeezed.

"Not Thailand. Ukraine," I said. Red cocked her head.

"What?"

"The shipping manifests I saw were all going to the Ukraine. That's probably where we're headed. Since the collapse of the Soviet Union it's hard to keep track of what comes in and what goes out."

"You're just a regular little *Encyclopedia Could I Give Less of a Shit?*, aren't you?" she said with a saccharine smile.

"I told you," I said evenly. "I'm a cop. A lieutenant with the Nocturne City PD."

She bared her teeth, testing my dominance. I didn't bite. No pun. "Why should I believe you?" Red sighed, finally, when she saw neither of us was going to get to hump the other's leg.

I pointed to her forearm, to a small portion of the tattoo sleeve that described a dead tree with a gravestone beneath it. "You spent three years in the McClintock Women's Correctional Facility in Chino. The branches on the tree are the years, the gravestone means you were there for murder and the Roman numeral on it is the number of days you spent in solitary. Seventy-four. Impressive."

She grimaced. "It was involuntary manslaughter."

"How did you put it? 'Could I give less of a shit'?"

Red's defensive posture relaxed an iota. "So you're either a cop or a fellow con."

"Look at my outfit," I said, gesturing at my vomit-soaked ensemble. "Could a con afford this?"

"What's your pack?" she said. I held her gaze.

"I'm an Insoli. You?" As such, I was subject to the dominate of any pack I ran afoul of, unless my lone will was stronger. So far, so good, but I had a feeling Red might give me a run for my money.

"Lobo del Diablo," she said finally. "I guess that makes me dominant."

"Until we're out of this crate, all of us are working together," I said. "And since I don't hear anyone except your convict ass speaking up as troop leader, I'll be figuring out our next move."

"Yeah," said Red. "Because you've done such a great Hexed job getting yourself stuck here in the first place."

"Listen . . ." I gestured at her for her name.

"Esperanza," she said.

"Huh. Mouthful. I think I'll stick with *Red*. Listen, Red. You're obviously strong and capable and all that shit but I've actually dealt with kidnappings and hostage situations before. I was a SWAT officer for six months and homicide detective for five years before that, so if you've got relevant experience, now is the time to speak up."

Esperanza dipped her head to her chest and muttered something that I didn't catch. I turned back to Dolores. "Are you going to be all right now, Miss Stern?"

"You can call me Deedee," she murmured. "Everyone does."

"Deedee, are you going to be all right?"

"I don't think so," she said. "I feel like I can't breathe. My heart is racing. I have to get out of here."

"You're having a panic attack," I said. "I need you to shut your eyes and focus on something that calms you down, and take deep breaths. Calm breaths. Nothing worse is going to happen to you than what's happened already. I'll make sure of it."

Red grunted a guttural laugh. "Big Hexed heroine, huh? Saving the day?"

I ignored her and raised my voice. "Who else is in here? Speak up." The container only had the single bulb, and my eyes were so dry that my vision probably wasn't any better than a plain human's. That was a depressing thought. "Tell me you're all right," I said softly. "Please."

"Me," someone whispered from the darkest corner of the container. "I'm here."

"What's your name?" I said, squinting into the dimness. A petite girl with a long fall of brown hair pulled her knees up to her chest, hugging herself.

"Anna."

"Anna, I'm Luna. Are you a witch or a were?"

"A caster witch," she whispered. "He invited me to happy hour after my nursing class let out and I woke up here." Her numb recitation spoke to shock, and I scooted over to her, trying to keep myself out of the filth on the floor of the container. It was mostly vomit—I wasn't the only one who'd lost their cookies upon waking up in this small square of hell, apparently.

"It's not your fault," I said. "We're going to find a way out of here."

"Yeah," Red snorted. "When they sell us into sexual slavery."

"Will you shut the Hex up?" I snarled. "You're really not helping morale here."

"It's okay," Anna whispered. "I know I'm not getting out of here. They took my caster. I can't pull down energy, either."

"Don't worry about it," I said. "Anyone else?"

"My head hurts," said a fourth voice. "Do you mind keeping it down?"

I looked further into the shadows, seeing the hunched figure only in profile. "Sorry. I think we're all a little out of sorts."

"Yes, well." She sighed. "I couldn't care less about making friends, so could we please just wait to find out what they want from us and how much it will cost to get me out of this metal box of idiots?"

"What's your name?" I said, ignoring the lumping in with the other idiots. "We all know each other now, so it's only fair."

"Charlie," she said. "Now please leave me alone."

"You don't seem real upset," Red said. "Maybe this is everyday for you, but for the rest of us, well . . . *We're locked in a fucking box!*" She beat her fists against the side again.

Charlie sighed. "Go right ahead, if it makes you feel better. Like the reporter said, we're bound in here. That door could be wide open and we couldn't walk out. The working would put us on our backs."

"Are we going to die?" Anna asked.

"No," I said, at the same time that Red said "Maybe." I shot her a look. "We don't know," I said. "I have a feeling we're worth more alive."

"I am," Charlie said. "But the rest of you . . ."

"You're kind of a bitch, aren't you?" Red growled. Charlie flashed some fang in return. I didn't protest— Red hadn't said anything I wasn't thinking.

People deal with trauma in different ways, I reminded myself. Most lose their heads, some get angry, and some, like Charlie, go cold. "Listen," I said loudly. "Is anyone hurt? Anyone who can't walk or needs meds right away?"

"I cut myself when I woke up," Charlie said. "I was

trying to get out and I sliced my hand on the binding. It might already be infected."

"All right," I said, ignoring the whine in her tone that was clearly hunting for our undivided attention. "Anna, can you take a look at her? You're a nurse, right?"

"Student nurse," she murmured. "I'm not certified yet."

"Well, it beats my two weeks of EMS training," I said with a smile. "Just make sure that she's not going to bleed to death or go septic, all right? Can you do that for me?"

"Okay." She nodded, crawling over to Charlie. I looked at Deedee.

"You okay?"

"I'm doing better," she said tightly. "Still can't breathe. I don't like small spaces."

I started to tell her that everything would be fine, even though I had nothing to back it up. I figured the least I could do was to try and stay calm, but before I could say anything there was a rumbling outside and the doors of the crate started to swing open.

Red rocketed out of her crouch. "Holy shit. They're here."

Deedee let out a small cry and Anna flinched against Charlie, who rolled her eyes. "It's not the Gestapo out there. Jesus."

"You don't know that," I said shortly. "Everyone stay still and do what they say. You live longer by co-operating with kidnappers."

"You're bossy," said Charlie. "I bet you were a hall monitor, weren't you? Before you went to community college and got a job that lets you push people smarter than you around?"

"Hey, *puta,* shut your mouth," said Red. "I don't see you trying to help us out of this."

I shot Red a grateful look. Charlie was getting on my last nerve with remarkable speed.

"You little . . ." Charlie started, but I raised my hands.

"Enough. Both of you be quiet." The doors swung back with a groan and a bright beam of spotlight sliced into my eyes. Red and Charlie let out a groan.

"Nobody move," said a heavily accented voice. "We are in charge." I made out two shadows behind the light, one of whom was holding a rifle, trained on us.

"He's got a gun," I said. "Take it easy."

"Shut up!" the same voice shouted at me. "Get up, all of you!"

We all managed to get to our feet, Charlie tottering on a single shoe. Anna tried to shrink into herself even more while Red snarled.

"These are the rules that will enable you to live to see the light of day again," the voice said. "One: You will not try to escape. You will not make noise and you will not cry. You will be fed once a day. You will be clean. If you are sick or filthy, no one is going to help you."

There was a creak, and the light fell a bit, giving me a look at the men's faces. They were white, tattooed, ugly to a man. They had that nothing-behind-the-eyes chill of career criminals, and I knew that if one of us stepped out of line she'd be dead as quickly as the gun-toter could depress the trigger of his Kalashnikov.

"You will hold still and be cleaned. If you scream, we will punish you." The raspy-voiced leader of the pack sure had a thing for punishment.

"Come over here and say that, you pasty-faced waste of sperm!" Red snarled.

There was no response, except a humming rush and then a blast of frigid water slammed into us from the ship's fire hose. Anna and Charlie screamed, Deedee threw up her hands to cover her face and I grabbed one of the struts in the container to stay on my feet. Magick crawled over my hand from the binding, and I yanked it away.

The water was so cold that my skin lost feeling almost immediately, and the hose coursed over each of us in turn, washing the filth out of the container and beating us down until all I could hear was the roar of the water.

"You're warned," said the leader. "Any back talk, any resistance, and you'll get worse." A plastic five-gallon bucket landed at my feet. "Use that from now on, you filthy whores."

"Hey!" Red shouted as they started to shut the door. "Hey, what about our clothes? We're freezing!"

The clang echoed, rattling my teeth. I started to shiver uncontrollably, my pants and blouse doing nothing to keep the cold from me. I might as well have been soaking wet and naked.

Focus, Luna. Think. There were two minders, for three weres and two witches. They knew we had nowhere to go, even if we broke the binding and overpowered them. We were in the middle of the ocean on a cargo liner, with no way to call for help. They counted on us to be passive, terrified, womanly. And we had no choice but to be exactly that, or take a bullet in the head.

I slid back down the wall, water pooling around my feet. My shaking became less from the cold and more from panic. I turned my face toward the wall, trying to hide my meltdown from the other women. I might need them later, and they needed to see me as unflappable, a leader, if we were going to live.

Anna was still crying softly, and Charlie heaved a sigh, moving away from her. "Look, someone is bound to be looking for me. I'm a very important person back in Nocturne City, a lawyer. Not like the rest of you. They'll find me."

"Bitch, are you out of your head?" Esperanza snapped. "*She's* a cop and they're sure as shit not breaking down the door to rescue her."

"They're not going to be able to find any of us," said Deedee. "My editor wouldn't even know I was gone until I didn't come to work on Monday."

"No one's looking for me," Red said softly. "No one in the pack cares about one bitch."

They kept talking, and all I thought was that I had to stay focused, had to not panic, had to keep myself until control.

Because no one was coming for me, and no one would help. I couldn't count on a rescue or a brilliant plan.

I was alone.

CHAPTER 13

A week went by, if I counted by how many times the men came and fed us expired MREs with Cyrillic lettering on the labels. The bucket got emptied, but only if we were lucky. Esperanza cursed and screamed at the men every time they came—their names were Mikel and Peter. Mikel was the one who held his gun like a girlfriend. Esperanza got hosed down each time, but it didn't seem to do much for her temper.

I was starting to like Red. The rest of the girls drifted in and out, Charlie periodically monologuing about her fabulous life as an attorney, Deedee telling me about her grandmother, Anna crying more often than not. She was always quiet about it, but her eyes had started to get that hunted, all-whites animal look. Much longer and she was going to lose it.

Drifting gave me plenty of time to think, but not much that went through my head made sense. This wasn't just sex trafficking—if it was, there wouldn't be only witches and weres in the container with me. They wouldn't be kidnapping us from the United States and sending us overseas. Quite the opposite.

Mostly, I thought about everyone that I'd left back in Nocturne. Will, Sunny, the SCS. Will would think that I'd freaked out and ditched him, at least for the first few days. Sunny would lose her mind with worry. My detectives would know exactly how stupid and hardheaded I'd been, and how wrong it had gone, and I'd lose whatever respect I'd managed to build.

I was starting to get weak, a low-grade fever raging through my system. No one except Esperanza was still fighting. We existed in the box, in the small metal world that was our prison. Charlie's hand was infected, Anna had stopped talking and Deedee was so dehydrated she couldn't do much more than lie on her side.

"We're not making it out of here, are we?" Red said, sitting down next to me.

"It's not *if,* it's what condition we're in when we do," I muttered. "What percentage of us dead is an acceptable profit/loss margin?"

"There's a happy thought," she said. "You must've been a regular cheerleader back home, huh, Luna?"

"How the hell are you still so peppy?" I demanded, wiping sweat off my face. I felt like someone was banging a drumstick slowly against my brain, in time with my heart. I knew that the repeated soakings, the lousy food and the appalling sanitary conditions had given me the flu, if not something worse. The were couldn't heal me if it kept getting exposed to more trauma.

"Benefit of the Diablos," said Red. "Fast healing. And I do mean fast."

"We're all so happy for you," Charlie muttered.

"You should rest," said Red. "Rest is the best thing for a cold, my mother always said."

"Before or after she kicked your slutty ass out of the house?" Charlie said.

"You know what?" Deedee said. "There's no call for you to be so mean. We're all here, and we should be sticking together."

"Pollyanna, you and I are nothing alike," said Charlie. "Excuse me if I don't want to be lumped with you sad sacks while all hope of a rescue slips away from me. I am not being the sex slave of some sweaty Soviet farmer, all right? That's for you saps to hold hands and cry over."

"Ignore her," Red said, stroking the sweaty hair back from my forehead. "Try to sleep."

My survival instinct said that I shouldn't, that I needed to be awake and alert, lean and hungry in case of attack. *Hypervigilance*, the books I'd read during training called it, the symptom of posttraumatic stress that put the grinning imp of fear on your back, made you keep that back to the door at all times, never sleep, see enemies everywhere . . .

I was so tired, though, that I felt my eyelids flutter even as I remembered sitting in the dusty classroom at the Las Rojas Police Academy, listening to Dr. Corchran drone on about trauma and abuse and lingering symptoms of both.

Sleep came fleet and dark, but it didn't last long. I woke up to see Lily Dubois looking down at me, her hair clinging to her blue-white skin, spots of lividity on the side of her neck.

"You better not forget about me," she snarled, her hand reaching for me. The pads of her fingers were white and wrinkled, shriveled around her small bird-like bones.

The hand closed around my throat, and it was the

cold of deep water. "You better not let me be forgotten."

I gasped myself awake, sitting up and banging my head on the side of the container. Deedee touched me on the shoulder and I flinched. "What's wrong, Luna?"

"Bad dreams," I said, though if I hadn't known with my own eyes Lily was dead I never would have called it a dream.

"This whole place is a bad dream," Deedee sighed. "I thought I was getting the story of a lifetime, and look where I am."

"I thought I closing my case," I said. "I thought I was doing the right thing . . ."

"I can tell you from experience that the right thing isn't always the obvious thing," said Deedee. "Or even the thing that seems right, on the face."

"Fucking profound," said Charlie. I vowed that if we ever got out of this, she was due for a slap.

"Listen," Anna whispered. "*Listen*."

Charlie and I cocked our heads, as did Red, three pairs of were ears tuned to noises outside the crate. There was shouting in Ukrainian above us, and footsteps.

"Notice anything?" Esperanza said. I put my hands on the side of the container, trying to ignore the crawl of magick. I can Path it, absorb it and use it, but this working wasn't anything I wanted in me.

"The engines," I said after a moment. "The engines stopped."

"We're saved," Deedee said. "Someone must have stopped them."

For a while, the hope that spread among the other

women was almost infectious, and I allowed that some kind-faced Interpol agent might open the door and put a blanket around my shoulders and help me get in touch with Will and file charges against Rostov and Salazko and all the rest.

As the time stretched out, I knew that we weren't rescued. "What's taking them so fucking long?" Red snapped.

"We're not saved," I sighed. "They've gotten to where we're going."

A cargo crane carried us, swaying and bouncing, to rest on a dock somewhere. Light flickered from the seams of the crate, and then male voices approached, along with the rumble of an engine.

The door swung open and the spotlight hit us again. Mikel shouted, "Stand up, whores!" He tossed in a bundle of plastic handcuffs. "Put them on each other and step out! Keep your eyes down. No talking!"

Charlie grabbed up the bundle. "Come here, Nurse Anna." She whipped the cuffs around Anna's skeletal wrists with surprising efficiency.

Anna flinched, dipping her head so her hair fell in front of her face. Charlie rolled her eyes. "I don't want to get sprayed again. Cowgirl up."

"You are so fucking compassionate I may cry," I said.

"No talking!" Mikel barked again.

"You know something?" I said, my fever and my general state making me reckless. "You're a nasty little man and you're going to get exactly what you deserve when I get out of here."

"I'll look forward to getting you alone, then, beautiful," he said, licking his lips. He grabbed me and shoved me into Esperanza, who in turn stumbled out of the crate, hissing as the light hit her eyes for the first time in a week.

A tumbledown truck was waiting for us, and once we'd been shoved in the back and the door rolled shut, we moved again, bouncing over rough ground.

"Just like home," I muttered. "It feels so good to be back."

We drove for hours, or even days—my sense of time was so Hexed that I could have been in there for a year. When we stopped for the last time, it was in a bleak warehouse. Peter hauled us out of the truck while Mikel held his trusty Kalashnikov on us. We frog-marched across the warehouse and into a warren of cinder-block corridors that exuded the same dampness as an old tomb.

There were cells, metal doors half-rusted, mesh with no glass attached, faint spray letters the only hint to what the warehouse had been before the gangsters took it over. There were girls in the cells, dozens of them, dirty, matted hair and skinny to a woman.

Mikel prodded us into the farthest cell, and slammed the door, locking a padlock that was the newest thing in the warehouse. The three men retreated, the lights went out, and we were alone in the dark again.

The next morning—I could tell it was morning because of the convenient hole in the ceiling that let in a fall of rain during the night and weak sunlight now— Mikel and Peter reappeared. There was a third figure behind them, and Peter stood aside deferentially.

I nudged Deedee. "That's got to be a boss."

"Fantastic," she muttered. "Can't wait to meet him."

Charlie stood up. "Excuse me. I don't belong here with them. You want money? I've got money. I could probably buy this whole godforsaken country with what I make in a year. Just tell me how much and let me out of here so I can call in a wire transfer. As much as you want. American dollars. Simple, right?"

The slim figure was silent in the shadow thrown by the door to our makeshift cell, and Charlie swallowed. It was the first time I'd seen her actually display some emotion. "Speak English?" she asked loudly. "Lots of money. All for you. Me, go home."

Stepping forward, the figure smiled at Charlie. "I speak English," she said in a cultured accent, Russian with a touch of Brit from whomever had taught her the Queen's language. "I speak, I would wager, better English than you do."

Charlie blinked. "You're a woman," she said flatly, as if that was the most shocking thing about this entire situation.

"You're so very observant," said the figure. She was barely a woman—tiny and willowy with flowing dark hair and hard green eyes, she looked more like a teenager. The only thing that made her seem like something other than a figment of my fevered imagination was the twin scars bisecting her right cheek from her mouth to her ear and to the corner of her eye, as if someone had stroked two fingers of hot iron against her perfect Snow White skin.

"My name is Ekaterina. As of this moment, I am your mother, your priest, your warden and, if you displease me, your disciplinarian. Do exactly as you are told and we'll get on famously. Disobey me and you

will find out very quickly how bad my temper can be."
She snapped her fingers at Mikel. "Get those four.
Leave the one with the tattoos. She's good for the
sport only with all of that ugly ink."

Mikel jerked his rifle at us. "Up, you four. Blonde,
brunette, skinny, loudmouth. The ugly one stays."

Esperanza's eyes filled with panic. "Don't leave me
here. Don't you fucking leave me alone."

"It's going to be fine," I tried to reassure her. "I'm
not going to forget about you. Just stay calm."

Red lunged for me and grabbed my wrist. "Don't
you fucking leave me!"

I had an unwelcome memory of Lily Dubois, her
waterlogged dead hand clamped around my skin.
"Esperanza," I said quietly. "You have to try not to
panic. I'm getting us out of here. I *promise*."

Peter grabbed our wrists and tried to jerk us apart.
I snarled at him, baring my fangs. He backhanded me,
the sting putting the taste of blood on my tongue, and
then grunted something at Mikel in Ukrainian. Mikel
stepped in and jabbed the butt of his Kalashnikov
into Esperanza's forehead. She let out a yelp and fell
backward, clutching her head and going still.

Peter grabbed me by the back of the neck and
threw me out of the cell and into the opposite wall of
the hallway. I rebounded and came for him, determined to break his nose, his ribs, tear out his throat
and hurt him for everything he'd put me through. I
didn't care if I ended up shot. The were clamped down
on my vision and I could see in shades of silver,
monster-vision at its finest.

"Enough!" Ekaterina stuck her arm in between us,
shoving me back with surprising strength. "Do that

again," she murmured in my ear, "and it's the sport for you as well. Don't think you'll be spared because you're pretty. I can make short work of that angelic face."

Aside from the fact that she was the first person in history to refer to me as *angelic* in any capacity, Mikel was now pointing the rifle directly at me, and my human sense of self-preservation kicked in.

My vision cleared, and I was back to being freezing, filthy and starving, with more invested in staying upright than in clawing the smirk off of Mikel's face.

"Better," Ekaterina said with a curt nod. "I can see that I'm going to have to watch you. What's your name?" She took my chin between her fingers, and even though I had a good four inches on her, I felt the undeniable spark of magick between us. I can always tell when a witch is in my personal space by that crawling sensation up and down my spine.

Ekaterina felt cold, like I'd rubbed up against a frozen statue. I jerked my chin away from her grasp. "Luna. Luna Wilder." I wish I'd said something like *Remember my name* or *It'll be the last one you ever hear* or something equally Bronson-esque, but I was so exhausted that I just plodded after Anna, Deedee and Charlie.

We got into a car this time, a Cadillac, shiny and new as if it had just rolled off a lot. "The fall of communism's been good to you, I see," I said.

Mikel gave me a shove and I fell into the back seat, landing on Charlie. She shoved at me, managing to fold my five-foot-ten-inch frame into the space between her bony knees and the front seat. "Get off. I don't want your sweat on me."

"You don't smell like a rose, either," I said as the car started to roll. I could see the tops of buildings out the window, telephone wires, chimneys. Everything was washed out, browns and grays of forgotten industry and ever-present poverty. A few fat sparrows clung to the wires as the Cadillac rolled past. Mikel and Peter fought over the radio, and Ekaterina sat between them, facing back, regarding us all with her cool emerald-chip eyes.

"You will be washed and dressed," she said. "You will be fed, and tonight you will be put to work. This is the easiest job you can be given, and it can be lost very easily if you fight, cause trouble or don't bring in enough money for my liking. Understood?"

Anna nodded, her knees pulled up to her chest as usual. Deedee was watching out the tinted windows, though what we could see was just a parade of urban decay punctuated by the occasional sign in Cyrillic. I wished that I'd made Dmitri teach me Ukrainian. My chance of getting away would be so much better . . .

The car rolled to a stop at the rear of a building that proclaimed APARTMENT in both English and Cyrillic. Same drill—pull, push, brandish Kalashnikov and march forward. Up a dank set of fire stairs, down a hallway that smelled overwhelmingly of perfume, under bulbs dressed up with small red shades.

The building had been, at one point, luxurious. The wallpaper was a rich rose brocade that was tearing off in strips, and what was left of the carpet was expensive Persian wool. The doors still bore their script numbers, along with penthouse suite names in Ukrainian.

Ekaterina pointed at rooms as we passed, snapping

orders. First Charlie, then Anna, then finally Deedee
was shoved through a door, which was promptly
locked again from a ring on Peter's belt. I filed it in
my memory for when I escaped. *When,* not *if.* Even
in the hell of the shipping container, that had never
changed. I just needed an opening, the smallest slip,
and I was going to run, find a phone or the U.S. embassy, bring all the weight of the law down on these
people.

The last door was a double set, the presidential
suite, probably. The thought made me giggle, and I
clapped a hand over my mouth. Ekaterina shook her
head. "In. No more of your sass."

She must have learned English from a kindly old
schoolteacher in some small British village. She
talked like she was about eighty years old and was
about to offer me a crumpet. That just made me giggle
more, and Mikel rolled his eyes and put his foot into
the back of my knee, sending me stumbling through
the doors.

The lock clicked behind me and I stopped laughing
when I saw the room. I've seen my share of brothels,
but this one was beyond what I'd ever imagined.

The bed was round, hot-pink bedding in a leopard
pattern, and there was a large mirror bolted into the
crumbling plaster ceiling above. The rest of the furniture was cheap, in a style I'd classify as Vintage Las
Vegas Pimp, plenty of satin and animal prints. There
was a small platform for dancing and an armoire full
of skimpy outfits that a stripper at Tit for Tat would
be embarrassed to prance around in.

"Crazy?"

I started as a voice spoke up from the corner, in the

chair by the window. The window looked out over the courtyard, but it was heavily barred and padlocked from the inside. There went my bright idea to tie the tacky bedsheets together and rappel down the face of the hotel, Bond-style. I stilled as I took in the vista. It wasn't just one apartment building. There were five, arrayed on a wagon wheel, all of them with barred windows, all with armed guards patrolling the rooftops.

Women, like small bright tropical birds, looked back at me from their cages, down into the empty courtyard, the dry, crumbling fountain and the heavy black iron gates with electrical wires attached to the top. A guard with a German shepherd on a leash walked along the quad. This wasn't just a brothel, this was a compound.

"You," the woman sitting in the chair said, taking a drag on a black cigarette that smelled like the morning breath of Satan. "I said, are you insane?" She enunciated each word like I might be stupid as well as mental.

"No," I said. "But I was locked in a shipping container for a week. It'll do wonders for your stress level." I slumped down on the bed. Never mind getting out the window . . . I'd be lucky to get two steps once I was on the ground. I can't heal from bullet holes.

"I wouldn't," the woman said. "I had a customer about half an hour ago and they haven't changed the sheets."

I bolted up like I had springs in my legs. "Hex me."

She snorted and took another drag. "Fuck, these things are disgusting. All that they smoke here. Real cigarettes are worth their weight in gold. I have to beg the high rollers for a drag." She got up and appraised me. "You look rode hard and put up wet, lady."

"Shipping container," I reminded her. "And there was the whole thing of me getting kidnapped, before my little cruise."

"Yeah, well. Welcome to the club." She stuck out a hand armed with cheap acrylic tips in a purple that made me think of gangrene. "I'm Lola."

"Like the Kinks?" I just couldn't stop myself. My mental filter, what little I'd had in the first place, was completely gone.

She frowned at me, smoke coming out her nose. "What?"

"You know—*Well, I'm not dumb/but I can't understand/how she looked like a woman/but talked like a man/oh, my Lola.*"

Her eyes, done in the same shade of shadow as her tips, narrowed. "You trying to say something, Princess Vanilla? Because I'll tell you—you could win first place in a drag show with the shape you're in."

"I'm just exhausted," I said. "I apologize. I'm Luna Wilder."

"Don't tell me your real name," Lola said. "I don't want to know, and you don't want the johns to know, so come up with something fake. Fast." Lola's accent was pure New York, all flat vowels and clipped syllables, and she puffed on her cigarette like she was attempting to create her own little smog cloud.

"Johns?" I said. Of course I knew what was waiting for me here, in the Ukraine, but it still seemed unreal. Maybe if I just willed myself hard enough I'd wake up somewhere that wasn't an annex of hell . . .

"Customers? Clients? Daddies?" Lola said. "You're

a whore now, sweetie pie, and you better cozy up to the idea before you end up like my last roommate."

"I'm not a whore," I said, raising my chin. "I'm a cop. I was kidnapped. And you're not a whore, either. What were you back in the States?"

Lola shook her head. "Oh, no. None of that matters here. You keep your head down and you live. You fight, and you die. They drag you out of here and take you to sport, like they did Charity."

"Okay, what's 'the sport'?" I said. "Ekaterina talked about it, and one of the girls I was in the container with got left for it. Please, just give me the rundown on what's going on around here and I swear I won't make trouble for you."

Lola sighed, stubbing her cigarette out into a cup of tea that already had several dead soldiers floating in it. "You're gonna make trouble one way or the other, lady. I see it in your eyes. Were?"

"Insoli," I said. "What are you?"

"I'm a seer," said Lola. "A piss-poor one, too, or I would have figured out that guy in the Village who wanted to buy me a coffee was a rat-bastard Russian gangster kidnapper. You think I'd be smarter, right? I watched the *Dateline* specials, both of 'em, and that Lifetime Television movie. Jesus."

I took a seat on the least offensive of the chairs, a zebra stripe, and sighed. Something soft, that didn't grind my bones and muscles, felt close to heaven.

"Up," Lola said. "That chair is for customers. They see you in it and it's an ass-beating. Besides, it'll be dark soon and business will pick up. We need you dressed and changed by then or Madame Scarface will send both of our asses down to the ring."

She strode over to the armoire and started jerking things off of hangers. "What are you, a six? Maybe an eight with your legs?"

"Six," I said. "I'm not wearing any of that."

"Unless you want to be in a bloody heap on the basement floor, you're going to put it on and you're going to shake what your mother gave you," said Lola.

"Okay," I said, taking a red stretch vinyl dress out of her hands. "I'll clean up and put this on if you explain to me what you mean by that statement."

"Bathroom is in there," said Lola, pointing through a beaded curtain. The plumbing must have been state of the art when Khrushchev was in power, but now it was rusted and filthy beyond belief. Still, spinning the tap produced a trickle of orange water from the showerhead and I stripped off my filthy clothes, shoving them into the overflowing trash can.

"How long have you been here?" I asked Lola, who leaned against the doorjamb, lighting another cigarette. I didn't even care that she was looking—the temptation of hot water was too much to take.

"A year," she said. "Maybe more. No family, you know. No one misses me. My boss probably figures I quit, my so-called friends got one less person to pass the roach to, and no one else gives a flying fuck."

"And what goes on in the basement?" The water left me feeling only marginally clean, but I dried myself off with an itchy towel and slid into the dress, which was too tight and smelled like stale tobacco.

"The basement? That's where you go if you're no good at this," Lola said, exhaling.

"What, does Mrs. Bates live down there?" I combed back the tangles in my hair and twisted it up in a knot.

"Makeup under the sink," Lola said helpfully. "The basement is where the ring is, and it's where they take the girls who fight the johns or make trouble, or are just too used up." She rolled her cigarette between her fingers. "Fucking, fighting and gambling under one roof. It's a regular one-stop vice shop in here."

The mirror over the sink was cloudy and cracked, like someone had put their fist into it. It was easy to see why they might have. I turned to Lola instead. "What happens to the girls who go into the arena?"

"They fight or they die," said Lola. "It's all the same to the customers, and Ekaterina and her brother make more money if the fight is to the death."

"Brother?" I said, going to the window. The street I could see beyond the front gate was quiet, a few cars puttering by, no people who could help me, even if they were inclined. Even if they could ever hear me scream.

"Yeah, he's a real piece of work," said Lola. "You think Ekaterina is bad, you ain't seen nothing yet. He's gotten rid of girls before for wearing the wrong shade of lipstick."

I went over to the door and rattled the handle. Locked, of course. "He sounds charming," I said, scanning the corners of the room. Sure enough, a pinhole camera resided in the crown molding opposite the bed. I'd run into an operation in Nocturne City selling footage of their girls on the Web. It looked like scumbags thought the same no matter what country you were in.

"He's dangerous," Lola said seriously, taking her old seat by the window. "You steer clear of him, if you know what's good for you. Don't rock the boat."

"That's sort of why I'm here," I said. "Who's the boss of this operation? The brother?"

Lola snorted. "What are you, a cop?"

"Yeah," I said. "And look where it got me."

"You want to live long enough to tell *Dateline* your story," Lola said, "you don't go asking about who runs this charming little compound of sin. Hell, you keep it up and *I'll* shank you."

I started to say that I usually had a hard time in that area, but the lock turned and the door banged open. Ekaterina and Mikel stood there. Ekaterina gave me a cursory examination. "You managed to look human. Congratulations. You have one hour to eat your supper and then you'll be expected in the parlor." She crossed her arms. "Has Lola explained to you how we do things here?"

"I look pretty and wait for sleazebags to come screw me?" I said. "Then you take the money and I get locked back up in this tacky nightmare?"

Ekaterina jerked her head at Mikel and he walked over and slapped me. I can't say it was entirely unexpected. My cheek started to bleed again and my headache intensified by an order of ten. I just smiled at Mikel. "Bad idea, buddy. You're going to get exactly what you deserve, and I'm going to be the one to give it to you."

"You got a big mouth, yeah?" he said, grabbing his crotch with his free hand. "Why don't you put it to some real use?"

Ekaterina snapped something at him and he backed off, going out of the room, returning with a tray. Ekaterina was definitely the boss, at least of the thugs.

You never know what information will come in handy when you're a hostage.

Mikel slammed the tray down on our table. Two plates of smelly instant macaroni, two sets of plastic utensils so flimsy that I doubted I could even stab myself in the jugular with the broken end, if I were so inclined. "Eat," Ekaterina said. "You'll get used to the way things work here. You're a commodity, and you'll be healthy or you'll be sent to the sport. It's not complicated."

The door shut, and I looked at Lola, my eyebrow cocked. "She really gets into that whole Mrs. Goldfinger thing, doesn't she?"

"It's bullshit," said Lola. "They get you hooked on something if they can. It makes you easier to control."

I sniffed the food suspiciously, detecting a tang underneath the general stink of preservatives and fake cheese. "There's something in this."

"A little ground-up Valium," said Lola, grabbing a fork and a plate. "Keeps you docile."

"Don't *eat* it," I said, making a grab for her. She danced out of the way with surprising dexterity.

"Fuck off, lady. This is everything we get today. You're either drugged or you starve. Me, I think a full stomach and a head doped enough not to remember is the way to go."

I paced, trying to keep my mouth from watering. Foul as it was, the macaroni was the first real food I'd seen in over a week. "So this place—it's all weres and witches?" I said.

"Yeah," Lola said. She'd already polished off her plate. "Yeah, it's all bloods and bites around here.

That's why we come here, you know? No laws, no regulations. People pay a lot to fuck the monsters."

Her voice had gone slow and dreamlike. Someone starved and weakened would be a puppy with a full dose of Valium in them.

"One last thing," I said. "What happens to the women who lose the fights? If they don't die?"

"Fuck if I know," Lola sighed. "Now be quiet and let me doze until we have to go downstairs. This isn't exactly fun for me, you know. We're not roommates."

"Sorry," I murmured, looking out the window again. The guard with the dog was still pacing the quad. "Just making conversation."

CHAPTER 14

By the time a sour-faced girl with artificial hair woven into her own with a comical mismatch effect banged on the door and told us with gestures to get downstairs, I had had plenty of time to come up with and discard fifty escape plans in my head.

A straight run for my life was out—between the bars, the cameras and that son of a bitch Mikel and his ilk, I'd be dead before I'd gotten ten steps out of the room. I had to get the layout of the place, find a phone, find the weak spots.

All before I got jumped by some kink fan who wanted to get his jollies off with a woman of the hirsute persuasion. *No pressure, Luna.*

Lola nudged my shoulder. "Come on, fish. They dock you if you're late, and you have to service the employees to work it off."

The thought of Mikel or Peter anywhere near me turned my stomach. I hustled after Lola, tottering on the platform sandals I'd put on. Girls descended the stairs in pairs and threes, never any alone. Their eyes, to a woman, were the doped, haunted eyes of long-term sex slaves, all hope long ago drained out like so much dirty water.

The parlor was the same sort of elegance I'd come to expect from Ekaterina's operation, red satin and black carpet with a deep shag pocked with cigarette burns. Heavy curtains blocked out the windows and low lighting gave the whole room the aura of a cheap porn set.

The girls milled, a few of them lighting cigarettes, a few more discreetly popping pills from pillboxes or their bras and washing them down with vodka or cloudy water from a tap behind the wet bar in the corner.

Lola positioned herself against the bar, hip cocked, face carefully arranged to look bored. I sat myself on the edge of an armchair, grateful to be off the too-small shoes, which had already raised blisters.

While I sat, I went over the facts I'd garnered about the sex trafficking operation, like they were beads on a rosary that would somehow deliver me back to the light. Ekaterina was a boss, that much was clear, and I knew from briefings on the Russian mob that a female boss was unheard of. Then again, so was a brothel full to the brim with non-human prostitutes with a blood-sport arena in the basement.

Rostov and his men were enforcers who scouted women in Nocturne, and plenty of other cities had the same setup, if Lola was any indication. They transported the women to countries with few laws, where no one would question a bunch of Americans and Canadians and Brits locked up in a defunct hotel and sold as sex slaves. When I thought about it, it was really a perfect operation. I wondered how long it had been going on.

Laughter and shouting filtered from the lobby, and two men in cheap suits stumbled into the parlor, big sloppy grins on their faces. Ekaterina was behind them, wearing the obsequious posture of a helpful employee. She gestured at me, at Anna, who was trying to fade into the wallpaper, and at Charlie and Deedee. Deedee was holding it together, and Charlie was staring into space. She must have eaten the macaroni.

The johns clapped and grinned approvingly at the new meat, examining each of us in turn. When they got to me I tried to resist snarling or flinching, even though I've never done well being touched by anyone, never mind two sweaty office workers who reeked of cheap vodka. I just had to hold on a little longer, had to keep it together. No one was getting me out of here but me.

"You are very pretty," one of the johns said to me in labored English. I tried to smile obediently. Ekaterina stepped in.

"This one is a bite, brand new, from the West Coast of the United States. A true California girl. She will be insatiable, or your money back."

The john caressed my knee. "Care for a drink and a talk in private?"

Private, I could do. More and more johns were filtering in, none of them any better than the one currently pawing at me, some considerably worse. A blue pall of cigarette smoke hung over the parlor and the drinks and false cheer were flowing. I thought I caught a familiar scent amid the carnival assaulting my nose, clove cigarettes and the distinctive scent of a male were, but it vanished just as quickly as it drifted to me. I shook my head to clear it.

"Go," Ekaterina said, as the john pulled me up. "And behave yourself."

"Ekaterina." Someone else had come in the door and stood behind the john, his face in shadow in the dim reddish light. Ekaterina turned in surprise.

"What are *you* doing here?"

"I was passing by, and I saw we had new visitors." The man stepped forward, and the john fell over himself to get out of the way. The man looked him over, lip curling with faint disgust. "What is your name?"

"Illya," the man quavered.

"Illya. Find yourself another woman to reek all over."

"I don't think . . ." Ekaterina started, but the man cut her off.

"Be quiet. Go attend the front of the house so the whores don't rob us blind."

Ekaterina nodded and did as he said, instead of castrating the patronizing bastard like I would have. Illya, too, stumbled away, and pressed up against Lola, who seemed all too happy to have him.

The man looked at me, stretching out a finger and putting it under my chin. "You are very beautiful. I would even call you rare."

I sized him up while he was staring at me. Pale skin, dark hair slicked back, green eyes that could have cut glass with their sharpness. The guy would have been drop-dead handsome, except for the utter lifelessness of his expression. He looked like a creature who had decided to try on a human skin and found it lacking.

This had to be Ekaterina's brother, the one Lola had warned me about. Fucking fantastic. I swallowed the lump that had grown in my gullet. "Thank you."

The brother extended his hand to me. "Shall we retire?"

"Is that allowed? I mean, I'm supposed to be earning money . . ." Anything to stall him. Anything for time to think.

The brother reached behind the bar and felt around for a bottle, unmarked. The good stuff.

He took my hand in his. "This way. Don't worry yourself over such things. I'll take care of you." We started up the stairs, back to the apartments. I was going to have to knock him out. Then I'd be the girl who assaulted the boss and got sent to the basement. If I was lucky. Crap.

"What is your name?" the brother asked.

"Joanne," I said without missing a beat. I decided to be brave. "What's yours?"

"My name is Grigorii," he said. "Grigorii Nikolaivich Belikov." He had the same precise, Oxford-accented manner of speaking as his sister. "It is very nice to meet you, Joanne."

My middle name was better than nothing. I wasn't going to lose myself in this place, hide behind a construct like Lola. "Yeah, whatever," I told Grigorii, opening the door to the suite. "You'll understand if I'm not thrilled to be here."

He grinned at that and dropped himself gracefully into the zebra chair. He was my height and moved like liquid. Again, it would have been sexy if he didn't remind me of a hungry snake.

"Sit with me here, Joanne. Let me get to know you." He uncapped the bottle and took a long pull, patting his finely tailored, genuine-Armani lap.

"I've got a better idea," I said, as he took a second swing, each pull at least a full shot of vodka. He didn't seem the worse for it. I backed up to the bed and sat down, patting the spot next to me. "You come here."

The first thing you learn about unarmed combat is to control the situation. Put your opponent where you want them and then execute a takedown move as soon as possible to end things. Don't get fancy and don't get cocky.

Not that I thought it was going to take much to put Grigorii out. He wasn't a big guy, by any stretch. I was more worried about what happened after. The camera would see whatever I did.

"I like this," Grigorii said as I tilted my head coquettishly. "Come and have a drink with me. It would make me happy." His English was getting better with each drink, not worse.

Struck with an idea, I got up on my knees and ran my hands over my body. Grigorii perked up, but he didn't move.

"I dance," I said. "You drink. I like that idea the best."

He grinned, lips thin and bloodless, and downed more of the booze. We were at half a bottle. This guy must have a liver made out of titanium. "Very well, Joanne. Dance for me."

I got off the bed and started a slow hip shimmy, fighting to stay calm and look sexy. What I really wanted to do was bolt. "If you finish that bottle by the time I'm done, big man, I'll give you a little present."

"You can be sure of it," he slurred, missing his mouth and dumping a few droplets down his front. Finally.

"Oh," I said, dancing closer, hands running up and down my body. "Careful there, sweetie pie."

"I'm very careful," Grigorii muttered. Utilizing more focus than most people would to launch a bullseye at a dart board, he upended the bottle and dumped the remainder down his gullet. "There. Now, then, my present," he commanded.

"Soon," I assured him. "Stand up. Dance with me."

Grigorii came to his feet when I beckoned, and came to me, grabbing my waist and yanking me against him. His body was hard under his suit, and I felt a gun in a holster in his left armpit. I met his eyes, and saw amusement, not intoxication, flickering in their depths.

"Not working out the way you planned?" he inquired, one hand skating down to my ass while the other drifted up and caught my cheek.

"You're not drunk," I blurted.

Grigorii let out a laugh. "Of course not." He ran his thumb over my cheekbone and I felt the pop of magick. "I'm drunk, or I am not drunk, as I see fit. Very freeing. My body is my magick, and I look after it."

His gentle caress became a hard squeeze, and he held me by the back of the neck, his expression furious. "Is that your plan? To make every man who chooses you a drunken fool and escape their attention? Do you think *I* am a fool?"

"No," I said honestly, softly. "I don't think you're a fool."

Grigorii's jaw twitched and he gave me a shake. "The right answer, much too late."

He shoved me away from him, onto the bed, and got on top of me, flipping me on my stomach. He knotted a hand in my hair and pushed my dress up, his cold touch raising goose flesh on my skin. "My sister told me you were going to be a problem, and as usual, she was not wrong." He wound his hand tighter in my hair and I groaned, pain lancing my scalp. "Fortunately, I specialize in problems. I'm the—what's the English?"

Grigorii leaned close to my ear, his lips touching the outer edge. "I'm the troubleshooter."

One good thing about macho assholes is that they don't expect you to fight back, so awed will you be by their manly speech and manly beatings. Grigorii's free hand reached for the elastic of my panties and my own hand lashed out and grabbed the cheap clock radio from the bedstand. I whipped my arm back and slammed the thing into his head, plastic case breaking into pieces.

Grigorii groaned, falling off of me and off of the bed entirely. A second later, he started to snore. He may be a witch, but he wasn't invulnerable. For the first time in weeks, things were going my way.

I climbed off the bed, pulling the dress right, and went into the hall. Ekaterina obviously didn't expect anyone to misbehave once they'd come this far. She was in for a serious fucking surprise from me, that was for sure. I just had to be fast enough to get out of here before the underlings came to shoot me.

The hallway with the girls' suites was devoid of anything helpful, so I went the other way, past the stairs to the parlor and back toward the hidden part of the building; more apartments, these in disrepair like the suite bathroom had been. Voices spilled out from behind closed doors, a tinny laugh track and a familiar theme song. *The Facts of Life* dubbed into Ukrainian. Funny stuff.

I stuck my head around an open doorway, just enough to give me a sightline, and saw Mikel and Peter sitting on a battered sleeper sofa, sharing French fries out of a fast food bag and laughing at the TV like a couple of normal guys.

The urge to storm in, grab Mikel's best friend the Kalashnikov, and open fire on them both was almost overwhelming. Those two men had been responsible for my suffering, for the suffering of the other four girls, and they deserved to die for us and who knew how many others before.

And once Ekaterina and the rest of the thugs hear the shots, you're Hexed. I couldn't very well shoot my way out of the hotel on my own. Besides, I had to at least take the four from the container, plus Lola, with me. My dreams would never be silent if I left them.

I slipped past the door and continued on. No one shouted at me. My stealthy reputation was intact. The next opening was a makeshift office set up in an efficiency unit, and I almost sobbed when I saw a telephone sitting plain as you please on the desk, along with a sleek new laptop and a set of instruction manuals for a bookkeeping program and Excel.

Slipping in and shutting the door, I picked up the phone and depressed the disconnect. A dial tone buzzed and I punched in 0.

"*Da?*"

That was most definitely not an operator, unless the operator was a three-hundred-pound man with a smoker's rasp and a cacophony of pop music in the background.

"Hello?" I said.

"*Da?*"

"Crap," I muttered. "Operator," I said loudly into the phone, "I need an outside line."

"Who are you? You whores can't use the telephones."

This wasn't getting me anywhere, clearly, and I was about to hang up and start trying random numbers when the door banged open. Ekaterina and Peter stood there. Peter had an old-model stun gun in his hand.

"What do you think you're doing?" Ekaterina demanded.

"Calling for a pizza?" I said. "That Valium macaroni really left something to be desired, let me tell you. I'm a growing girl."

"The phones are wired for internal calls only," said Ekaterina. "You think we'd leave a means to call for help so close to the hands of your kind? You Western women all think you're entitled to a white knight, someone to save you from the harsh realities of this world." She jabbed her finger at me. "Where is my brother?"

"Dreaming a little dream back in my suite," I said.

Ekaterina snarled. "If you've hurt him . . ."

I held up my hands. "Relax. He's fine. Concussed, but fine. Far better than he deserves to be. Listen, do me a favor and spare the lecture on my un-whore-like behavior? My head hurts enough as it is."

Ekaterina gave me a cold smile, all perfect, gleaming teeth. "Very well."

Peter depressed the trigger of the stun gun and the

darts arced out and landed in my side. Just a small sting, and then I was on the floor, every muscle seizing, pain dropping a black curtain over my vision.

As I felt hands grab me under the shoulders and start to drag, I thought that I hadn't really expected Ekaterina to shoot me. I was going to have to do something about those assumptions of mine.

CHAPTER 15

I woke up on a cold cement floor, curled in the fetal position. Everything hurt, but at least I appeared to be reasonably intact. I rolled onto my back, seeing nothing but a plaster ceiling with a stain that looked like Fidel Castro's head. A look to the left gave me a windowless brick wall scratched with graffiti and a look to the right gave me a door of heavy-duty mesh with a lock.

Another cage. This was getting old real fast.

"You're awake." I saw shoes, male, Gucci. Very posh, and not a speck of dirt on them. I raised my head with difficulty. Getting Tasered is a lot like having six shots of tequila in a row and then beating your head against a wall. Unpleasant at the time, one hell of a hangover after the fact.

"More or less," I said. "For certain values of awake."

"That was a nice move with the clock radio. You honestly did take me by surprise. Trouble, just like Ekaterina said."

The face that belonged to the Gucci came clear. Grigorii had a row of Steri-Strips on his temple, but otherwise appeared unscathed. The bastard.

"That would be an accurate assessment," I said.

"My sister is usually accurate in matters of business," Grigorii said. He crouched down to my level as I managed to sit up, feeling all of my muscles scream. "But she defers to me on matters of discipline. Tell me, do you feel you deserve it?"

"Dude, your people kidnapped me out of my fucking shoes and shoved me in a shipping container straight to one of the seven hells. What do *you* think?"

He chuckled. He really was eerily beautiful, like some sort of Tolkien creature that lived for thousands of years and lost all human feeling because of it. "We weren't properly introduced before. I am Grigorii Belikov. I run this compound, and I am your only hope of staying alive long enough to regret fighting me off. How do you do?"

"I noticed you left out *rat bastard* and *witch* from that resume. And a lot better if you'd let me out of here," I said.

"Ah. But you already knew I was a witch, for you're a were." He *tsk*ed at me. "I'm afraid I cannot allow you freedom . . . Joanne, is it?"

"That'll do for now."

Grigorii sighed. "You see, I run a very large and profitable operation here, one that turns on the good behavior of my girls. If they disobey, they become . . . less useful. But not useless."

"I guess it's the octagon for me, eh?" I said, trying to be cheerful even though I was aching and freezing. The dress and shoes were gone, and I was wearing a ragged, oversized gray T-shirt and what the good Lord gave me. My feet were bare and my hair was still damp enough to cause shivers all through me.

"You're far too pretty to be torn apart," said Grigorii.

"No, you've merely been moved to a . . . specialized section of our enterprise. Sometimes there is a customer who has special needs, and you are here to accommodate him."

I really didn't like the sound of that. It was sinister even without the clipped British delivery and Grigorii's creepy smile.

"Special needs . . . we're not talking, like, wheelchair accessibility here, are we?"

"Astute as well as pretty," Grigorii said. "No, we're not. There are men who have a need for blood, for pain and humiliation." His face darkened and he folded his arms. "You will service them, until you are either dead or useless to a man, and *then* you will be used as bait in our combat ring." A smile twitched across his lips. "My only regret is that my chance to break you in was so rudely canceled. You are premium stock, Joanne."

It wasn't the proposition that did it—spend enough time in my line of work and you hear every lame sexual innuendo in the book, and a few that haven't made it yet. It was the way he said *stock*, and the look in his eyes that said that to him, I really was nothing more than a thing that had arrived for his use.

How many girls who didn't have my fortitude had he used up and spit out like *things*?

I launched myself at the mesh. It wasn't that thick, and I was pissed the Hex off. Grigorii would find out firsthand what the seven hells had no fury like.

There was a snap, I smelled burning hair, and I was on my ass across the cell, back up against the brick, electricity dancing across my nerve endings for the second time that day.

Grigorii stood up, laughing outright now. "Oh, Joanne . . . breaking you is going to be a fine thing to watch. You take care now. I'll be seeing you soon enough."

I was trying to restart my heart and command my shocked lungs to *breathe, breathe, dammit,* but I still managed a snarl. "I'll be . . . counting . . . the seconds. Asshole."

Grigorii walked away without another word, leaving me with my thoughts. When you're me, and trapped half-naked in a cage, it's not a great place to be.

I listened, mostly, since there was Hex-all for me to look at. I couldn't even see any other cells, which I'm sure was the idea. People break faster when they're isolated.

Someone else was breathing a few dozen feet away, and whoever it was smelled like BO and dirt, which I probably did, too, if not worse. Further still, I could hear the low bubble of voices and music, which had to be the party room for the fights. Beyond that, faint enough to tickle my ears but little more, I could hear screaming.

"Bright lady," I muttered, wrapping my arms around myself. It was the closest I ever came to praying. Even with direct evidence of places and people who were not human, I had a hard time believing any gods who might possibly be listening gave a damn about me. Especially now.

Time went by like a slow river current, carrying my thoughts and panic along with it. You don't expect to be the victim when you're someone like me. I relied on myself, on my strength and my skills and my inner monster to deliver me from bad situations. I never conceived that I could switch places with the people whose deaths and disappearances I investigated.

But I had. And my monster had failed me. I was still here.

So what are you going to do about it, Wilder?

"Good question," I whispered, leaning my head back against the wall. A door banged, letting in a snatch of god-awful Russian pop music as well as shouts of approval. I smelled fresh blood on the air and I buried my nose in the T-shirt, which also stank. But at least it didn't make me want to chew someone's throat out.

Two men in the uniform I'd come to recognize as that worn by cogs in the Belikov machine—windbreakers, longish hair, tattoos—dragged a girl past me. She was alive, but barely. A sucking echoed along the corridor every time she breathed from a collapsed lung.

Her face, as she passed, was a mess—I wouldn't even have pegged her as human if I couldn't see her body. One leg was twisted, broken, and she moaned softly as she bumped over the concrete.

"What are you looking at?" one of the men snapped.

I averted my eyes, but as soon as they passed, I slid over to the front of my cell and peered out, careful not to touch the mesh again.

A door banged open again, and with it came the sound of traffic, and more importantly, the scent of outside air.

Suddenly, nothing about my current situation mattered. Not the cold, not the hopelessness of what my shenanigans with Grigorii and the telephone had caused.

Because I knew where they took the weres who lost the fights.

And I was going to use it to get myself free.

I tried to sleep, tried to rest, although my empty stomach kept sending pangs letting me know that it would like some food now, thank you. I ignored it as best I could. I'd need everything I had to make this work.

Perversely, my mind cast back to *Enter the Dragon*, the scene where Bruce Lee is sneaking around the compound at night and happens upon all of the slave girls. I always thought Lee, from the movie, was a total asshole for not letting those girls go. I also wondered why they didn't just escape, really—it wasn't like anyone was paying attention.

At least I had an answer to that now.

I'd watched the film with Will, curled up on the sofa in his expensive loft, bathed in the glow of his expansive plasma screen, everything right and normal with the world. Just me, my boyfriend and Bruce Lee. As close to perfection as I'd likely come.

I laced my hands behind my head and stared at Ceiling Castro some more. I didn't let myself think about what would happen if this didn't work. It had to work. Nothing else had gone right for me since I'd gotten that 187 call to Lily's body.

This would work. I was still me, and my crazy plans didn't fail. At least, not often. Even after Alistair Duncan, the witch who'd summoned a daemon with seven dead girls as his offering, and more recently the Thelemite cult that had exploited a rift in the fabric of the ether to draw their leader back from her exile, I was still working with a fifty-percent success rate.

That had to count for something.

I drifted in and out, trying not to listen to the faraway screaming, until footsteps and two voices sounded in the corridor, once of which I recognized as Grigorii's.

"She's still very spirited, which I believe meets your requirements. She'll fight you."

The other voice mumbled something in what sounded like Russian—I only knew enough Ukrainian to be sure it wasn't that. Grigorii gave that silken chuckle that I had already grown to hate.

"Yes, but not so much that she'll do you any harm. You're a were of breeding—you understand how these things work better than I."

Fuck. Fuckity fuck and double that right on down. Another were was something I hadn't counted on.

The Russian grinned at me as he and Grigorii came to a stop outside of my cage. I tried to pull the baggy shirt down over my thighs. The Russian was tall and pale, with an Adam's apple that stuck out and big knobby hands that were perfect for hurting things softer than he was.

He opened his nostrils and scented me, the were equivalent of putting your hand on someone's ass without an invitation. I gave him the finger and a snarl. Couldn't hurt to sell myself as the perfect fantasy for his particular brand of Sick Twisted Fucker.

Grigorii tapped his finger against his teeth. "We can clean her up if you like. She's a bit rough around the edges, I know. Just in from America." He winked at me and I fought the urge to go straight through the mesh and sink my claws into his smarmy throat.

"Not necessary," the were rumbled. "Bring her to

the room. I will pay for the night." He stalked off, heels of his knockoff shoes tapping on the concrete. Grigorii flashed me the OK sign.

"You've already put us in the black for the night, Joanne my dear. Too bad you'll be out of commission for a few weeks. I could get used to this." He went to an antique circuit box on the wall and flipped a switch, then came over and unlocked my cage.

I looked up at him as he came into the cell and grabbed my arm. "Don't do this."

"Why?" he said. "Because I should feel pity, deep down past the black burnt crust over my heart?"

I leaned close to his ear, and smiled. "Because if you put me in that room, there will be no place you can hide from me and the hurt I am going to inflict on you when I get out of here."

Grigorii jerked me into the hallway, hard enough to make me stumble. "You speak very crassly for someone who has such lovely features. Then again, you do have the body of a porn star, so perhaps that explains it."

"You think of these all by yourself, or does your lovely sister write them out for you?" I said as we half-marched, half-stumbled down the corridor, toward the sounds. Toward the screams.

Grigorii surprised me by grabbing me and slamming me into the wall, holding his long, thin fingers against my clavicle with a pressure that made my bones creak. "You don't get to talk about my sister, you whore. Is that understood?"

I swallowed, my heart fluttering against his grip. "I'm sorry."

"She's a finer woman than you could ever hope to

be. Don't go opening your mouth on the subject again if you're as smart as you seem."

"I said I was sorry," I told him quietly. Grigorii showed a spark of human in his eyes for the first time, but then the ice sculpture that lived in his skin came back in control and he swallowed, straightening his tie.

He stepped back, letting me go, and gestured me toward a metal door, in a row of similar metal doors that looked to be storage units for the apartments above. I heard soft sobbing from behind the closest door.

I was at the source of the screams.

"Inside," Grigorii said.

The Russian was already half-undressed, his shirt off to showcase a powerful barrel chest.

So much for me getting a puny human to deal with. I gritted my teeth and stepped inside. "Behave," Grigorii said before he shut the door. He dropped me a wink, and then I was alone with the were.

He stood up, undoing his belt. "You want me, yes?"

I raised my eyebrows. "Not particularly. You smell like onion soup. I hate onion soup."

He growled, showing black fangs. In fact, all of his teeth were black. As far as were strains went, that was an unfortunate scrap of DNA. I backed up, fanning exaggeratedly in front of my face. "By all means, take this as constructive criticism, but—breath mints. They're a wonderful invention, even in Soviet Russia or wherever the fuck we are."

Once I got started, I didn't stop. Usually my big mouth is a detriment, but now it just might save my ass.

The Russian grabbed a pair of handcuffs from the

iron headboard of the sagging single bed and advanced on me. "I teach you respect, whore."

"Why is that the one word all of you dumb lumps of Chernobyl-addled werewolf flesh know how to say in English?" I said. "Seriously, are you really that dumb, or is it just all of the cheap vodka rotting your brains out and making your tiny little dick so limp you can't get it up unless you're beating on a defenseless half-starved girl?"

I pushed myself into his personal space, staring into his eyes and baring my teeth in a show of dominance. "Is that why you still have your pants on? You're just totally embarrassed? I don't blame you."

The were roared and backhanded me in the jaw. He was strong—it was like taking a hit from a compact car, and I crumpled in the corner, no acting required. A loose tooth scraped against my tongue. I prayed he hadn't broken anything too important.

The Russian leaned down, unclipping the handcuffs, grinning and breathing into my face. "You scared?"

I met his watery eyes. "You wish." I snapped my foot out, putting all of my strength into the kick. I was aiming for the solar plexus, which will put someone down no matter how big and mean they are. You can't fight if you can't breathe.

My kick went low, but that worked out, too. The Russian howled as my foot connected with his balls, and stumbled back from me. I was up and going for the door. I wasn't going to run for it, seeing as how splendidly that had worked out the first time. I just needed Grigorii to see exactly what I would cost him if he kept putting me in a room with johns.

A hand closed around the back of my neck and the

Russian grabbed me and tossed me onto the mattress, all of his panting weight landing on top of me. He was babbling in his own language—enraged or horny, I couldn't tell. He pinned my wrists down, grinned as I thrashed wildly under him. Why shouldn't he—this was what he'd paid good money for.

I'd like to say that I remembered all of my close-grappling techniques, that I stayed calm and focused and didn't let panic overtake me, but that would be a lie, mostly. I didn't panic.

But I did let my were overtake me.

A snarl ripped out of my throat and I shoved up with my knees, levering the Russian's weight off me by sheer force of rage. My claws sprouted, my eyes changed and my fangs grew.

The Russian stumbled back, uncertainty flaring in his eyes. Not many weres can phase at will, without a moon to bathe them and trigger the monster that lives hidden deep within their genes.

I wrapped my legs around his neck as he came for me again, and I squeezed. Just because I was down didn't mean he had all the power. I'd learned that lesson a long time ago, with the guy who gave me the bite in the first place. Never be submissive. Never give up your dominance. Dominance keeps you alive.

The Russian gurgled, scraping at my thighs, his own claws sprouting and carving bloody furrows.

The pain didn't move me, it just made me squeeze harder. The Russian started to turn blue around the edges, lips darkening, but his hand shot out and wrapped around my throat in turn.

"Bitch . . ." he wheezed. "I'll kill you and then I'll take you. You're *mine*."

"I'm no one's," I rasped. "Especially not yours."

My air was cutting off, and he wasn't passing out. My were roared, and the silver slid across my vision again, the monster in me eating up everything that made me Luna.

I gave one last desperate squeeze with my spent muscles and jerked my legs to the left.

There was a *snap*, no more than someone stepping on a stick, and then weight on top of me, suffocating, immobile.

Dead.

I blinked, coming down with a vertiginous jerk in my stomach. The Russian lay on top of me, head at odds with his body, his neck loose and pulpy. Boneless.

"Gods," I breathed, because what else could you say in a moment like that? I pushed at him, rolling him off of me and onto the floor with a thud. Eyes wide and glassy as any cadaver I'd encountered, his lips and tongue swollen from our struggle. The guy was deader than a coffin nail.

I'd killed him. And I didn't feel one iota of regret, not when the were had taken over and not now, as my heartbeat slowed and my vision came back and my claws and fangs retreated with my adrenaline. It was him or me, survival of the meanest, nastiest wolf on the block, and I was it.

I'd killed him. I stood up, stepping over the body, feeling drying blood on my legs in the cool draft. I pounded on the door. "Hey!" I screamed. "Hey, Grigorii! You want to see what a good time I gave your friend?"

My heart was jackhammering against my ribs, slow

and heavy, but my mind was calm and blank as a black pool of water. Dimly, I thought that I *should* be freaking right the Hex out, shaking and crying and vomiting. But I wasn't. I was acting like a were for the first time in years. Death wasn't personal and it wasn't always tragic. Survival was a perfectly good reason for a death, and this was survival at the rawest, most low-down level.

Screw what I *should* be doing, I'd done the world a favor. I snarled at the body once more, one final *fuck you* to a waste of oxygen that had dared to challenge me for dominance.

The door rattled and Peter yanked it open, his eyes widening when he saw what was on the other side. He turned and yelled, and Grigorii came, annoyance painted on his face.

"Oh," he said, looking at the Russian. He moved me aside and knelt, feeling for a pulse. "Oh, my dear," he sighed. "That was one of our most expensive clients. You're in a world of trouble now."

I put up my hands and gave him a toothy smile. "Take me in, Officer. I'm guilty."

CHAPTER 16

Grigorii was surprisingly gentle as he led me down the hallway toward the one part of the establishment I hadn't seen yet—the arena. Maybe it was because I didn't fight, keeping my head down and my hands at my sides.

"You know, you display so much savagery," said Grigorii. "If I were a nosier man, I might ask what you'd repressed to make your monster fly forth so."

"My mother didn't love me enough. My daddy loved me too much. I never got to be homecoming queen. Take your pick."

Grigorii chuckled. "In a different world, Joanne, you and I might have gotten along very well. It's a shame, really."

In a different world, I would have been looking at Grigorii from the good side of a police lineup, not in his cool grasp, being led toward what he thought was my death.

But he's wrong, the were whispered. *We fight. We survive.*

Grigorii pushed a set of swinging doors open, which were marked with a water insignia. I flinched as the smell hit me. It was like the Nocturne City morgue, if the air conditioning went on the fritz and somebody had left all of the stiffs lying around for about three days. Flesh and blood, sweat and fear all mingled to create a miasma that made my monster scream.

The old swimming pool was the arena, the deep end cordoned off with more heavy mesh. There were two weres inside at the moment, scrabbling for purchase on the blood-smeared tiles.

"Instead, sadly, this is your fate," said Grigorii. He passed me off to Mikel, who looked inordinately pleased to see me again. Grigorii leaned close to my ear as Mikel prodded me toward the shallow end of the pool. "Make me proud," he whispered, and brushed his lips over my sweaty cheek. His touch was like ice.

Mikel shoved me down onto my knees. "Get in."

There was a crowd at the deep end, cheering, and I heard a yelp and a snap. One of the weres fell, a gout of arterial blood pulsing from her neck. She twitched, fingers and feet racing in the few spare seconds it took her to bleed out.

I'd have to be careful that wasn't me. Looking back at Mikel, I asked, "Who am I fighting?"

"The champ," Mikel said. "For today, anyway. You watch yourself, pretty. She's a bigger bitch than you."

We'd see about that. I still had plenty of my own personal bitch coursing through me from killing the Russian, and the were was panting for another chance to run through me.

Mikel and another man jumped down into the ring and carried away the dead girl, while Peter pulled the winner through the crowd. Money changed hands, and

Mikel raised his voice. He shouted in Ukrainian, introducing me. I took that as my cue to step obediently into the ring. The blood was still warm under my feet and I fought to keep myself under control as the were rippled over my skin, bending me into a crouch.

Not yet. Not yet. Just a little longer . . . I couldn't phase without the moon, fully, but I could change enough to do plenty of damage. Enough to make this look real.

Mikel shouted something else, something that got a roar of approval from the crowd. The champ had arrived. She lowered herself into the ring and raised her arms, and the crowd just went crazier. Money floated from fist to fist like a flock of paper birds.

She turned, and I saw the red hair, matted with blood, and the tattoos. "Esperanza?" I blinked, feeling very small, human, and exhausted in a second. The wounds in my legs weren't healing and I was so tired I was starting to see double.

"You," she said, with a curl of her lip. "You said you'd come back for me."

Mikel stepped away from us, and I heard the mesh roll back into place. That was Red's cue—she sprang for me, going fully airborne. I ducked, half-slipping in the blood, and she went over my head, banging off the mesh. The crowd let out a gasp.

"Esperanza," I said. "I need to say something to you."

"Too late," she responded, swiping at me with a fistful of claws sharp as switchblades. I moved and she caught my shirt, shredding it at the bottom.

"*Listen,*" I hissed as she came in again, close, her

hands low and sloppy. I caught her in a submission hold, bending her wrist back. I'm quick when I'm desperate. "You have to beat me."

"No shit," she said, snapping at me, wriggling against the hold. "I'll beat you like I beat the three before you. That's how you stay alive when you're *left behind*."

"You can't kill me," I hissed desperately. "The maimed ones get out of here. They get taken somewhere outside the compound. If I can get away and get to a telephone . . ."

Esperanza let out a battle cry, a shriek that vibrated my head from chin to brow. She jerked, twisting, and I watched in horror as her wrist snapped and she wriggled free.

"Just for that," she said, "I'll kill you. Never mind any of the rest."

"Esperanza," I said, "I'm your best hope for getting out of here. Don't be stupid."

"I can take care of myself," she said, before she lunged at me again.

This time, I wasn't quick.

Esperanza's full weight landed on me, and I slammed into the bloody wet tiles, stars going nova in front of my vision from the blow to the head. "They like it when I do the big finish," she said. "I think I might even live long enough to become a favorite."

"Esperanza," I choked, because her claws were digging into my neck. A millimeter more and she'd have an artery open . . . "None of us is getting out of here. I tried. The only way you leave is dead or so fucked up you can't fight or screw."

"Why should I believe you?" she hissed, dipping

her face close. The crowd, thinking they were getting a good old-fashioned throat-ripping, cheered.

"Because we've both survived this long," I whispered. "And it would be a real waste for you to kill me before I have a chance to pay back the sons of bitches who did this to us."

Esperanza hesitated, doubt flickering over her face. The animal retreated and the woman came out. I wished I could say the same, but trapped and with the stench of blood filling its nose, my were was on the scent, and it was taking everything I had to lay still under Esperanza instead of reaching up and clawing out her eyes.

"Hurry," I gritted. "Much longer and I'm going to change." My spine rippled, trying to ensure that when I got up, I'd be on all fours. Hot pain reached out, all through me, and I snarled at Esperanza. "Do it now or we're both getting dragged out of here on a slab."

Esperanza balled her fist and drove it into my face. She had a hell of a right cross. My head snapped sideways against the tile and I felt her palms on me, coating me with cold, sticky blood. I flopped around, trying to make it look much worse than it was.

Esperanza shifted off of me, to hoots and cheers. "You better not fuck up this time," she hissed at me, and then her weight was gone and I felt hands on my wrists. I moaned and lolled, trying to sell recent brain damage as a possibility.

"Grigorii," a voice said. Mikel. "Take her out and dump her, yes?"

We stopped moving, and a cold hand wiped away some of the blood. *Hex me*. If he figured out I wasn't hurt . . .

"What a bloody waste," Grigorii sighed. "And no, she stays here. A fight fan has requested her for his companion."

"She can barely move . . ." Mikel said. "That red-headed bitch dented her skull." Was it my punch-drunk imagination or was there a tinge of disgust in his voice?

"The customer is always right, Mikel," Grigorii said. "Ours is not to question why. Take her upstairs."

Mikel switched to a fireman's carry, muttering something that I'm sure was about getting blood all over himself dragging my heavy ass around. I cracked one eye and saw we were going upstairs, through the parlor, back to the rooms of the girls who didn't have to fight.

After my days in the basement, it was almost welcoming. Mikel knocked. A voice rumbled at him, and I was deposited on a bed. Mikel withdrew, and I steeled myself for yet another battle. Whatever man wanted to fuck a half-dead, defenseless victim, I was more than happy to usher him into the next life. And the one after him, and as many as they sent to me.

Fight. Kill. Survive. That was what my mind was now, prey to my monster.

A hand brushed hair off of my forehead. It was large and callused, and the body that went with it sat on the bed beside me. "Are you all right?"

I made my move, and grabbed the hand touching me, shoving hard to throw the man off the bed. He fell with a thud and a curse and I was over him and against the door, scrabbling for the handle with my sticky blood-soaked fingers.

"Luna."

The voice stopped me in my tracks. It was rusty, accented, stained with tobacco smoke but so familiar. I still heard it sometimes, in bad dreams. I turned, shaking.

"Dmitri." I didn't have to question. I knew it would be him.

He stood, coming toward me, arms wrapping around my shoulders and pulling me against his chest. "Luna," he said against my hair. "Luna, what the fuck are you doing here?"

Shaking, I pulled back from him. *"Me?* What the Hex are *you* doing here, Dmitri?"

He shook his head. His hair was longer, and it fell in his eyes. "Never mind. There's time for questions later. Right now I have to get you out of here."

"Good luck," I said. "What do you think I was trying to do when you decided to get noble, genius? They take the girls who are beaten out of here!"

He blinked at me. "I didn't realize . . ."

"No," I said, jabbing a shaking finger into his chest. "You didn't. So thanks a lot, Dmitri. Once again, your pathological need to play white knight has fucked up my perfectly good plan."

His face drew into the frown I remembered so well. Dmitri and I had never been able to just sit still with one another—it was always fighting, sex, or sometimes both, one right after the other. "Oh, I'm the one that screwed up? I'm not the one who got herself tossed into a blood-sport cage match in the middle of a Ukrainian whorehouse!"

"Oh, so we're going right back to the blame, are we?"

I shot back. "Fine by me. By all means, go ahead and explain your virtuous and noble reason for being here in the first place!"

Dmitri's nostrils flared. "We need to get out of here, Luna. Now. Do you want to fight, or do you want to run?"

I curled my fists, uncurled them. "Lead the way, Galahad."

"Always with that mouth," Dmitri growled. "You can never just let anything be."

"Not this damsel," I agreed as he eased the door open. "I hate to break it to you, but you can't stroll out with me. I'm a commodity. And I don't have any clothes on."

"I'm trying to ignore that last part," Dmitri muttered. "As to the first, just be quiet and stick close."

Now I remembered why I hated alpha males so much. They always had that damn know-it-all attitude, too smug for words. "I'm not budging unless you share this plan with me," I said as we slipped into the hall. Dmitri cocked his eyebrow at me.

"You'd rather stay here?"

"Talk fast," I said as he started to walk.

"Cased the place before I came in," he said. "There's a service entrance off the catering kitchen in this building that backs up to a loading dock on the street. Kirov is waiting with a car."

"Kirov would be your sidekick in short pants?" I said, acid on my tongue.

"He's a member of the pack," Dmitri said, opening a nondescript door that I'd passed in my search for a phone. Stairs, an empty hallway, a ghostly kitchen full of rusted equipment and dripping refrigerators, and I was out the door, as simple as that.

Dmitri smirked at me as I wrapped my arms around myself. It was freezing cold, but I didn't care. I was free. "Your car is this way, milady."

I *really* hated alpha males.

Kirov, Dmitri's friend, was a stocky man with a long ponytail that would have looked better on someone taller and thinner. He raised his eyebrows at me. "Not as pretty as you described, Dmitri."

"Up yours, Fabio," I said. Dmitri guided me into the back seat and shut the door.

"Drive. Those witch gangsters aren't going to be thrilled when they find out I walked off with one of their girls."

I couldn't believe it was so easy for him. But that was the problem with Dmitri—everything was easy for him. He had never acted like anything was his fault when we were together, so why should he start now that he was here? Here, saving my ass. Dammit.

The car wound through narrow streets, gray stone buildings and small storefronts giving a deceptively quaint look to the place. I squinted out the windows. "Where the hell are we?"

"Kiev," said Dmitri. "My home."

"It's lovely," I said, deadpan, and leaned back against the seat. I didn't intend to fall asleep, but my eyes fluttered closed, and when I woke up, Dmitri was putting me to bed.

I came awake alone, in a small room that was furnished with shabby furniture, but was clean and dry.

Clothes were sitting on the chair by the bed, jeans, a tank top and a plaid overshirt. Even underwear. Everything was my size.

The bed felt like heaven, but I pushed back the covers and got dressed, shoving the stained, bloody T-shirt into the trash can with deep satisfaction.

"I have to say, I'm sad to see that skimpy thing go," Dmitri said from the doorway. "But you look better without all of that blood on you."

I spun around, putting my hands up reflexively. "How long have you been standing there?"

"Relax," he said. "Not long."

"Dmitri Sandovsky, I was kidnapped and sold to a brothel. The next time you tell me to *relax*, I'm going to knock your fucking teeth in. Are we clear?"

He raised his hands, palms up. "I'm sorry. I apologize. I'm just still in shock that you're even here."

I sat back on the bed, wincing. Dmitri's face instantly darkened. "What's wrong?"

"I got cut," I said shortly. The Russian's face flashed in my mind, broken neck and all. I felt a surge of nausea. "Where's your bathroom?"

Dmitri pointed. "Down the hall . . . Are you all right?"

I bolted up and ran into the small white-tiled space, dropping my head over the toilet. There was nothing in my stomach, but I retched anyway, miserable, until Dmitri crouched next to me and pulled my sweaty hair out of my face.

"It's fine. It's fine, Luna. I'm here now."

I looked up at Dmitri, into the eyes that I'd spent almost a year trying to forget, and I felt the dam on my emotion break with a snap against my chest. I leaned my head on his shoulder and started to sob.

"I screwed up, Dmitri. I screwed up and I'm here, and I was in that horrible place . . ." I couldn't breathe, so I just sobbed some more.

Dmitri put his arms around me. "Luna, the girl I knew would never screw up that badly. Everything is going to be all right."

I sniffed hard, and scrubbed at my eyes. "You don't know the whole story."

Dmitri stood up and opened the medicine chest over the sink. He pulled out antiseptic and bandages, and handed them to me. "You need help?"

I unzipped my jeans and pushed them down to my knees, not caring that he was still around. "No." I soaked a bandage in peroxide and dabbed at the cuts, wincing. "I don't understand why these fucking things haven't healed up yet. He didn't even cut me that deeply."

"Looks like you ran into a Poison Talon," said Dmitri.

"Let me guess," I said, biting down hard on the inside of my cheek so I wouldn't yell from the sting. Whimpering in front of my ex-boyfriend was not on the agenda, for this day or any other. "Their claws secrete something that keeps me from healing up?"

"Bingo," said Dmitri. "Nasty bastards, the whole bunch of them."

I taped down bandages over my cuts and pulled my jeans back on. Dmitri's eyes darkened, but he didn't say anything and neither did I. "You didn't answer my question," I said.

"Which one?" he said, handing me a washcloth. I ran cold water into the sink and started to wash off all the blood that I could.

"Why you were in that brothel," I said.

Dmitri sighed. "It's complicated."

"Complicated like, you-pay-for-sex complicated, or you're-in-the-mob complicated?" I wrung out the cloth and looked him in the eye.

"Luna, do you honestly think I need to pay for sex? Or would join the mob? Especially the *Belikov* mob?"

I looked at myself in the mirror. I was sporting a nasty bruise along my cheekbone from where Esperanza had clocked me and scratches on my clavicle from Grigorii. I buttoned the shirt to cover them. I didn't want to remember Grigorii. "I don't know, Dmitri," I said. "I don't know much right now."

He sighed. "I was there to help a pack member. It was something that needed to be handled delicately, because the Belikovs are the biggest witches in this city and fucking nasty types on top of that. And then . . . there you were. Imagine my surprise."

"Likewise," I said. Dmitri moved closer to me, and I backed up until I was against the sink.

"I missed you, Luna. Every day since I left. There wasn't an hour that you weren't in my thoughts."

I looked away from him, fixing my eyes on a crack in the tile wall rather than even try to answer.

"Luna?" he said again.

"We ended, Dmitri," I said finally. I stepped forward so he'd either have to back up or do a Super Bowl–style chest bump with me. "I'm eternally grateful to you for getting me out of that place, but there's no *us* anymore, and frankly it would be miles less stressful if we could just agree on that and move on."

He sighed, running a hand through his hair. "Do you ever think that no more *us* was a mistake?" he asked softly.

"Never," I said, too quickly to be anything but a lie. Of course I wondered if I'd backed out too soon. Of course I wondered if things ever could have been lasting between us.

But when I thought about it, the answer was always *no*. Dmitri and I didn't work long-term. It was a flash, a melting point of lust, and that was all we'd ever really had.

"You're a bad liar," Dmitri said, moving again, rubbing his hands up and down my arms. After days in the Belikov brothel, close contact with another were was about on par with kissing one of Dr. Kronen's rotted corpses.

"How's the daemon?" I said, knowing that the question would snap him back. He grunted and dropped his hands.

"Do you really want to know?"

"Since we're all hot for the personal questions, yes. I do." I crossed my arms.

Dmitri pulled back the arm of his shirt and I hissed. Whatever I'd expected to see, it wasn't that.

Bitten by a were possessed by a daemon, Dmitri had been infected with daemon blood, and the corruption had slowly overtaken his own monster, turning him into a man who had violent blackouts, fits of anger that terrified me more than I'd ever let on. It weakened him, too, made him a prisoner of the daemon as his own pack magick was leached away.

Now the curved black scar, which had looked like a crescent brand, was red and swollen at the edges; the veins that trailed out through Dmitri's pale skin blackened as they crossed it.

"Hex me," I whispered, reaching out for his arm in spite of myself. I took a second look at Dmitri. He had deep rings under his eyes and he'd lost weight—a lot of weight. Where there had been a solid hunk of were was skinny, bones showing at the shoulders and low in his ribs. His hair was greasy and his scent was coppery with sickness.

"Dmitri," I said. "What's happening to you?"

"Don't I wish I knew." He laughed humorlessly, pulling his arm out of my grasp and rolling his shirtsleeve down. "Now, come on downstairs and meet the rest of my pack. I need to tell them what happened."

"A member of your pack sent you into the compound in the first place?" I said as I followed him down a narrow flight of stairs. It was a house, faded and rotted at the edges, but still homey. A parade of severe black-and-white pictures of someone's ancestors glared reprovingly at me as we descended.

"Sure did," Dmitri grunted. He was uncomfortable now, reverting to that Me-Tarzan monosyllabic thing he did when something grazed too close to one of his trigger points. The daemon bite was changing him, more than I'd thought possible.

I was definitely revisiting that. But not now. "Your pack member must be pretty damn persuasive if he talked you into going in there."

Dmitri dropped his eyes. "She. Yes. It was an emergency."

The plot thickens. "She have a name?"

He grunted. "You'll meet her." And that was all I got out of him as we walked through the warrenlike rooms to the kitchen. It was huge, from a time when you needed space for ten servants to be milling around, a wood-fired cooking stove hulking in one corner and a wide farm sink in the other.

Weres were thick there, standing at the ancient refrigerator or sitting at a battered harvest table playing cards. All conversation died away as soon as they caught my scent.

"Everyone," Dmitri said in English, "this is Luna."

I tensed, anticipating the wrath that was going to come my way any second. Dmitri's pack, the Redbacks, and I aren't exactly on great terms. He gave up his pack leader status to be with me, and I'd had a few run-ins with the pack elders who oversaw all Redbacks, all over the world. They hadn't been inviting me out for drinks when it was all over.

Kirov, the driver, stood up from the table and came over to me. "A pleasure, miss. Always happy to rescue a lady in distress." His accent was much heavier than Dmitri's, and his smile seemed genuine. When I shook his massive rough-palmed hand, he nearly pulped my fingers.

"Thanks for your help, again," I said. "I'm so happy to be out of there you don't even know." Maybe this particular pack house didn't know me from Eve. Maybe I had gotten lucky.

"So you are the one who Dmitri gave up everything for," a female voice said. "You're the one who made him leave Nocturne City."

Should have known. I was never that lucky.

"Margarita, don't do this," Dmitri said. "I don't hold it against Luna. You know that."

I sized up Margarita as she wound toward us through the other weres. She was shorter than me, but not by much, with stunning auburn hair that was too bright not to be natural. Blue eyes and flawless skin. She looked more like an Irish princess than a Ukrainian were, but what did I know?

She also had a fantastic body, slender and curved, and she came over and took Dmitri by her fantastic, delicate hand. "Care to explain to me why you are here, Miss Wilder?"

"Well, let's see," I said, mimicking her conciliatory bullshit tone. "There was the kidnapping from my hometown, and it all goes sort of vague, but I'm pretty sure it ends with me being grievously injured in a fight to the death and Dmitri saving me, like the white knight he aspires to be. That work for you, sugar tits?"

Kirov muffled a snort. Dmitri just sighed. "Luna, this is who I was telling you about. Margarita, I found her in that horrible place. You can't expect me to not help her."

Margarita rolled her eyes. "Did you have to bring her *here?*"

"The Belikovs will have their weevils scouring Kiev for her. It was the safest place I could think of."

Margarita grunted, as if this were an inadequate answer at best, but I ignored her. Dmitri turned to his buddy. "Kirov, do you think you could fix a girl up with something to eat? It's been a while."

He nodded, leading me over to the grumbling Soviet-era icebox. "Take your pick. We have sandwiches, sausage rolls, whatever you want. Any friend of Dmitri's, you know."

"You seem to be taking this awfully well," I said, grabbing three sausage rolls and a diet soda out of the bowels of the fridge. "Me being that packless bitch who made Dmitri into a walking daemon contagion and all."

Kirov swiveled his head toward where Dmitri and Margarita were talking with their heads bent together like lovers. For all I knew, they were. That would explain the attitude she was copping. "Dmitri is my very good friend," Kirov said quietly.

I tore the package on the first sausage roll and consumed it in two bites. "Oh, yeah? Good enough that you're treating me nice?"

"Dmitri was my pack mate before he took his sister to the United States," said Kirov. "He has saved my life more than once and I trust him. Besides . . . you don't seem like the brazen hussy the pack elders made you out to be." His eyes flicked over me. "I figure Dmitri knew what he was doing getting involved."

"Gee," I said around the second roll, "thanks for that."

"Anytime," Kirov said. I popped the tab on the soda and washed my food down. I had no idea how it really tasted—I was so hungry, it could have been wallpaper paste on a cracker and I would have munched it with good cheer.

Dmitri and Margarita broke apart, he looking angry and she glaring at him and then pointing at me, saying something sharp. This would be the *Either that hussy goes or I do* speech. I'd gotten it from a few girlfriends of men I was seeing, over the years. I wasn't always the perfect angel you see before you. Shocking, I know.

Ducking his head, Dmitri came over to me. "Luna, Margarita has something she'd like to speak to you about."

"Fine," I said, crumpling the can in my fist and launching it at the trash. As the calories and caffeine hit my system, I was beginning to feel a little bit more like myself. "Hit me with your best shot, Ivana."

Margarita heaved a sigh. "Not here. In private. Come to our room."

Our room. This just got better and better. Not that I cared who Dmitri was sleeping with, but I sure as hell cared about having my face rubbed in it. After that little speech in the bathroom, he had a lot of gods-damned nerve.

"Lead the way," I said. I grabbed a pack of chips from the counter and another soda, and followed Margarita. The kitchen had back stairs that led into the servants' quarters, and the small, neat room at the top was furnished with a large iron bed and photos of Margarita and a girl of about ten, with a serious expression and hair that hung in front of her face.

Dmitri sat in the armchair in the corner by the window and lit a cigarette. "Tell her, Margarita."

She knotted her hands together and looked at him for help. I spread my arms. "Tell me what? That you're getting married? That she's really a man? That you're both leaving the pack to become circus performers? If so, mazel tov and all of my blessings to you. Now, if you don't mind, I need to use your phone and call my embassy."

Margarita dipped her head, avoiding my eyes, and

I realized that she was trying to be submissive, to show respect to me.

Well. That was new. "Spit it out," I said.

"I know that you want to go home, and I'm sure Dmitri will help you get to the embassy and get on a plane, but first I need to tell you why he was at that horrible place."

"Please," I said. "It's not like I'm on a schedule or anything. Not like I want to get out of your craphole country and go home. No offense. I'm sure the springtime is lovely."

"He was looking for someone," she said. She went to the bedside table and snatched up the photograph, holding it out to me. "He went looking for Masha, because I asked him to."

I took the photo and looked closer at the little girl. "She's young, even for these people," I said.

"The picture is old," said Margarita. "She's fourteen now. We don't know why the Belikovs took her, or where she is . . . That place . . ." She let out a small sob. "That place was the last."

Dmitri got up and put his hands on her shoulders. "Just because she's not there doesn't mean we won't find her," he murmured.

I met Dmitri's eyes. "Why are you looking for this particular little girl? Lots of others I saw in there could have used a helping hand."

Margarita bit her lip. "Masha is . . ." She sniffed and tried again. "Masha is our daughter."

CHAPTER 17

There are three kinds of silences—comfortable, uncomfortable, and incredulous. This was the third kind.

"*Our* daughter?" I said. "Yours and *Dmitri's*?"

"Luna," he said. "I know I should have told you . . ."

I held up a hand and cut him off. "You know what—save it, because at this point I don't even care."

All that time, the entire year we were together as lovers, as partners, and he had a kid I didn't know about. And a Margarita, too . . .

"Are you married?" I asked. She shook her head.

"No. I was very young, and Dmitri was about to be sent away to prison, so I raised Masha by myself for the first few years. And when he got out, he wanted to take us with him, but I said no, I needed to stay here, near the Kiev pack where we'd be safe . . ." She degenerated into sobs again.

"Masha has been missing for two weeks," Dmitri said. "Margarita asked me to come here and help her." He rubbed a hand over his forehead. "I'm hitting wall after wall, Luna. I know how good you are at investigation. I know how stubborn you can be. I need your help."

"We." Margarita sniffled. "We need your help."

"Isn't that just touching?" I spat. "I might shed a single tear." Spinning on my heel, I stormed back down the stairs, through the kitchen, and out the door, sitting myself on the crumbling back stoop of the crumbling old house.

I ripped open the bag of chips and consumed them, feeling rotten to my core as I did so. Masha Sandovsky hadn't done a thing to me.

But Dmitri had. He'd lied, and not about something small and forgivable like the number of ex-girlfriends he had or if my ass looked fat in those pants. He'd lied about having a *child*, an entire life that was just a big blacked-out spot on the version of his past that he'd fed me.

And that I had swallowed, hook and line. I sighed and ground the heels of my hands against my eyes. When was I going to stop being a total idiot for the guy?

The back door creaked and Dmitri came out. I could tell it was him by his scent—that clove and *him* smell that I thought I'd hallucinated back in the hotel.

"I guess you're pretty pissed at me, huh, darlin'?" he said, sitting down next to me.

"Don't even go there with the *darlin'* crap right now, okay?" I said.

"Okay," he agreed. I let out a growl.

"Thank you."

"You know," he sighed. "Margarita and I have been over for a long time. It wasn't even supposed to be all that serious to begin with. Masha, though . . . she's my kid. I gotta take care of her."

I finally looked at him. "Like you took care of her when you bolted to America and left her here in the ass-end of Eastern Europe with only her mom? Like that?"

Dmitri flinched, his newly hollow eyes wounded. "No. I screwed up there. Money doesn't make up for me not being around, so now I have to make it right." He reached out to put his hand on my shoulder, thought better of it, put his hand back at his side. "I never said I was perfect, but I am trying."

I looked out into the alley, at the blowing garbage and the taillights of cars passing on the street. Night was starting to fall and the air was cold, kissing my exposed skin. "Where did Masha go missing from?" I said.

"School," Dmitri said. He shrugged when I cocked my eyebrow. "What? Just because she's born were doesn't mean she has to miss school."

"And the small chance of her phasing and tearing the other kid to shreds when she loses at tetherball doesn't worry you?"

"Masha's not like that," he said. "She's a good girl. She takes after her mother."

I tried not to flinch at the implication that Margarita was the good woman and I was the . . . what? The necessary evil? "I need to call Will and let him know I'm all right," I said. "And my department, and the FBI. Get them working on this case from the U.S. end. After that, I'll see what I can do."

Dmitri exhaled. "Thank you, Luna. You don't know what this means."

"Don't thank me yet," I said, standing up and brushing off my butt. "You want my help, then I help you my way. You don't get to second-guess me or argue with me or do that pouty thing that you do when you don't get your way. And the less I have to see of your baby mama, the happier I'll be. Got it?"

He sighed. "Margarita isn't the bad one here, Luna. That would be the bastards who kidnapped my daughter."

I shook my head. "Just show me where I can call Will, please. And accept that I don't want to talk about yours and Margarita's endless love, all right?"

Dmitri sighed and leaned inside. "Kirov, get the car." To me, he said, "We have to drive to the night-club on the corner. They have a pay phone that can make international calls."

When we were in the car, Kirov looked at me from the driver's seat. "Who are we calling?"

"My fiancé." I said it without thinking. Dmitri let out a small choked sound.

"Your what?"

"You heard me," I said. The nightclub was still closed, neon just flickering to life in the twilight. Kirov brought us to the back door and I got out.

Dmitri followed me in. "Fiancé. Six months. You work fast, Luna."

"Why don't you phase and bite me?" I suggested. "And when you're through, show me the phone."

Dmitri set me up with the pay phone and a stack of money while he sat at the bar, glaring alternately at the taciturn bartender and at me. I turned my back on him. It wasn't my fault he got pissy when I'd mentioned I'd moved on. *He* had a *kid*. Bright lady. I was still trying to wrap my head around that one.

I punched in the country code and Will's cell

number, praying that he'd pick up. Who knew what time it was in California?

"Hello?" he muttered. Early. Or late. "Who is this?"

"Will? It's me."

"Luna?" It was a yell, something that made me hold the greasy beer-scented receiver away from my ear. Totally out of character for Will, who had never raised his voice in my hearing except when the Celtics were on TV. "Luna, where the fuck are you? Are you all right?"

"I'm fine," I said, feeling a small smile bloom. "I'm just fine, Will."

"What the hell happened?" he shouted. "You don't come home, me and Agent Hart pay a visit to that sack of slime Nikolai Rostov, he has no answers, and you're just gone!"

"Aw, honey," I said. "You spent time with the Feebs for me?"

"Wasn't easy, doll, believe me," he said. "That guy wears this terrible aftershave. Could choke a horse."

"Will," I said, not able to hide the tremble in my voice. "I missed you. A lot."

"Tell me where you are and I'll come get you," he said. "I don't care what happened, I don't care whose fault it is, I just want you home."

"I'm in Kiev," I said. "I'm all right." I looked at Dmitri. He spread his hands, obviously wondering what was taking so long. He could go Hex himself.

"Kiev?" Will sounded gobsmacked. "Gods, Luna, I knew those Russian bastards must have done something to you, but Kiev? Gods," he said again.

"I'm fine," I repeated. For certain values of *fine*.

"I'll be on the next federal flight out," Will said. "Just give me your address and sit tight."

I shut my eyes and drew in a breath. "Not yet," I said.

There was a thud on the other end of the phone. "Ow! Dammit," Will said. "I stubbed my toe on your freaking armoire. What do you mean *not yet*?"

"You're at my apartment?" I said.

"Yeah," Will said. "Couldn't sleep at mine. Stupid and girly, I know. I should go lift weights or shoot some game to make up for it."

"Will," I said. "There's something here I have to do."

"I don't buy that, Luna. You need to come home and we need to nail these guys."

"I'm sorry," I said softly. "I'm all right, and I'll be home soon."

"Luna . . ." Will started.

"I love you," I whispered, and hit the disconnect. The dial tone pulsed in my ear, in time with my heartbeat.

I stalked back to the bar and sat on the stool next to Dmitri. "Whiskey," I said to the bartender. "No ice, no water, no umbrella."

He shrugged at me. I glared at Dmitri. "Translation, *por favor?*"

Dmitri and the bartender exchanged a few snapped syllables and the bartender slid a cloudy glass of rotgut in front of me. I took a sip and winced.

"Good gods. What do they put in the whiskey in this country, nuclear waste?"

Dmitri lifted his shoulders. "You didn't say what kind you preferred."

I rolled my eyes at him and changed the subject. "Tell me about Masha," I said. "Lay it all out. The more information I have, the faster I can find her and get the Hex home."

"The fiancé," Dmitri said. "Will. How'd he take it? Is he jealous?"

I swiveled to face him, throwing down the rest of my glass. "We're not talking about Will. Not now, not ever. Understood?"

Dmitri chuckled. "Touchy. You must really like the guy."

"The precious spawn of your prolific loins," I reminded him. The whiskey against my still virtually empty stomach brought out the vocabulary words. "Tell me the details."

"Masha isn't what you'd call a model kid," he said. "She got into a lot of trouble—fights, boyfriends, probably a little pot."

Could have been me at fourteen. "Yeah, funny how that happens when there's not a father in the picture."

Dmitri snarled. "Don't do that. You said you'd help."

"I said that. I said nothing about not making snarky remarks to keep myself from punching you in the teeth for lying. Go on."

"She was cutting school a lot, and hanging out with some wannabe gangsters. Margarita eyeballed one of them after she went missing and I followed him for a while, to the Belikovs' compound. You know the rest."

"Which gangster?" I said. "Why Masha?"

"Some ponytailed asshole who likes to wave a gun around. And I'm thinking for the same reason you were there. Were girls turn a profit."

"Mikel," I said. "I've had the pleasure. But Masha wasn't in the compound."

"No," Dmitri growled, tapping one index finger on the bar like a restless secondary heartbeat. "She was gone, and I didn't have time to look around once I saw you."

"Okay," I said. "So we go back there and we ask some politely phrased questions."

Dmitri smirked. "Same old Luna. Always willing to go running in like the sheriff."

"Speaking of," I said. "Why haven't you gone to the real police? Or is that a dumb question?"

"The pack has a lot of friends in the Kiev police," said Dmitri, "but the Belikovs have more. Legends in Kiev, old witch blood, with ties back to the Romanovs themselves. Pull with regular criminal circles, and magickal ones. It's too risky. If they find out Masha is my daughter, that she's connected to the Redbacks, they'll kill her to save themselves the trouble."

"Okay," I said. "In the morning, we go back."

Dmitri frowned. "The morning? Masha is in trouble right now."

"I'm exhausted," I said. "I'm running on fumes. I've gotten maybe eight hours of sleep in the last seven days. If I don't get some sleep soon I'm going to nod off and pull a Tyler Durden, and no one wants that." I reached out, mostly out of pity, and laid my hand over his. "If they haven't killed her yet, they aren't going to do it anytime soon. Their girls are worth more alive."

I wasn't entirely sure the profits stopped rolling in when the girls were dead, having seen the way Grigorii operated, but I didn't say it out loud.

"I guess you got a point," Dmitri muttered. "Come on. We'll head back to the pack house and you can get some rest." We walked out to the curb, where Kirov was patiently dozing at the wheel of the car, and I got into the front this time. I was through with being shoved to the back, shuttled from one place to another.

"Margarita will be relieved," said Dmitri. "We were at wit's end. Masha is a good girl, even if she went off the path a bit."

His voice and face went soft when he talked about the girl, a softness that I'd only seen a few times when we'd been together. Never at the end. Even as wasted as Dmitri looked now, he managed to appear a father.

The stab of jealous heat that went through my gut was purely an animal reaction, or so I told myself. Not like I could compete with flesh-and-blood relations, even if I wanted to. And I didn't want to.

I kept telling myself that until I was in a lumpy bed on the top floor of the pack house, so tired that sleep wouldn't come. I wasn't jealous of Masha, I wasn't jealous of the family that Dmitri had hidden from me. He and I were over, and just because I hadn't rated the truth when we were going out didn't mean I had the right to get all uppity now.

I kept telling myself that, but it didn't do much good.

Someone pounded on my door the next morning and then proceeded to come in without waiting for an answer. "I have brought you breakfast," Margarita said, slamming a plate with a hard-boiled egg and some toast down on my nightstand.

"Wow," I said, running a hand over my face. "Service with a smile."

"I also need to talk," she said. "Alone. Without Dmitri hearing."

"Is this the part where you tell me to stay clear of your man?" I got out of bed, finding the jeans I'd been wearing the day before and rooting in the chest of drawers for a fresh shirt. They were all men's sizes, but I was past caring. I found a ratty Slayer band shirt from sometime in the eighties and slipped it on. Margarita studied my body with narrowed eyes, not even trying to hide it.

"Kickboxing," I said. "But don't worry—from what I've seen of his choice of women, you're way more Dmitri's usual type." He'd come back from Kiev with a mate last time, forced on him by the pack, or so he said. Now I wondered. "Irina—I dunno if you two hang out or anything—but she was like you. Bright hair, big stripper tits, that sweet farm-girl face that he likes so very much."

Margarita inhaled sharply, her nostrils flaring out. "I have given you no reason to speak to me like this. *I* have every reason to be angry with *you*."

"Oh?" I said, rolling the egg between my palms to get the shell off.

"You endangered the father of my child. Your actions could take him from us," she said. "You are reckless and dangerous by every account. I need to know that Dmitri will be safe with you, when you go to find Masha."

"Dmitri is a big boy," I said. The toast looked a little musty, but I dug into it, anyway. I was still hungry enough to clean out my favorite restaurant in Nocturne City, the Devere Diner, and go back for seconds.

"He is also blinded by what he feels is his fault, his wrongdoing," said Margarita. "He will charge in and he will not care if it costs him his life. You must be the one to have balance and to have a care for him."

I raised an eyebrow. Maybe Margarita wasn't as simple as those big eyes and big breasts let on. Most were women in packs I'd encountered were some nightmare version of Stepford—submissive, with no thoughts in their heads aside from what they could do to please their man. Since the alternative was a beating or a humiliation bite often enough, I didn't exactly blame them.

"Well?" Margarita said, standing. "Will you bring Masha *and* her father home safely?"

"I'll do what I can," I said. "But I have to tell you—Dmitri isn't exactly the most stable guy I've ever met, even without the daemon bite. Now . . . he's pretty much off the reservation."

"And that is your cross to bear," said Margarita, touching the Orthodox one at her neck. "As it should be." She walked out and slammed the door.

"Yeah," I said. "Nice talking with you, too."

I brushed my hair and pulled it into a low bun—if we were going back to the hotel, it wasn't a question of *if* things would get rough but *when*, and hair flying around for someone to grab onto like a slot-machine lever isn't a real smart move.

Downstairs, I found Kirov sitting on a sagging

velvet sofa, reading a newspaper. He smiled at me when he smelled me. "Good morning, Luna. Did you rest well?"

"Well enough," I said. "Kirov, I need to ask you a favor."

"Of course," he said.

"I need some firepower," I said. "A gun for the human contingent of these gangsters." And for Grigorii and Ekaterina, too, just because they deserved to have someone shoot them. More than once.

"I'll see what I can do." Kirov levered himself off the sofa and folded his paper over his squat stomach. "Do you have a preference for the firearm?"

"Something that makes holes in the people I point it at," I said. "Hollow-point ammunition if you've got it."

"You'll find that the Redbacks have a little of everything." Kirov grinned. "Dmitri asked that you find him when you woke. He's out back, smoking."

I found Dmitri standing in the alley, staring up at the sun balefully. "Sixteen days," he said when I stepped out the door. "That's how long she's been gone, this morning."

"We're getting her back," I said. "I promise."

"You're good at making promises," Dmitri sighed. "Like how you were going to cure me from the daemon infection and stick with me forever. That one was my favorite."

"You can blow me if you think we're going to start that game all over again," I snapped. "Seriously, Dmitri, do you *ever* think before you open your mouth?"

"Do you think before you make promises?" he returned. We were just like the Hamas and the Mossad, going back and forth, equally pissed off and never ready to back down.

"I think plenty," I said. "I think how lucky I am to have gotten rid of you and your alpha-male issues every damn day."

That shut him up. And I immediately felt like the world's biggest bitch for saying it out loud. "Wow," I said. "I'm thinking an 'I'm sorry' isn't gonna cut it here, but . . ."

"Don't say anything else," Dmitri told me. "You did the kindest thing. Now I remember why we never worked in the first place. You and your gods-damned comments."

"I am sticking with you to help you find an innocent little girl who has no business being caught up in this," I hissed. "Not because I feel some obligation for how I treated you. For the record, buster, my *comments* were the least of our problems."

"Yeah," Dmitri said. "You tell yourself that, if it helps."

"It does," I said.

"Denial is definitely your color," Dmitri said.

"Fuck you. Right up the rear shaft."

Kirov came outside then and saved me from having to slap Dmitri hard and repeatedly across the face. How dare he take the high road with me, after what he'd put me through? It wasn't my fault he'd gotten the daemon bite and it wasn't my fault he couldn't be cured. The only chance of that had sunk to the bottom of Siren Bay in order to save Nocturne City from being obliterated by Seamus O'Halloran, and if he expected me to be sorry for that, he could Hex himself.

"Here you are," Kirov said, looking between us. I took the gun out of his grasp, a Walther, the little James Bond gun, powerful and compact.

"Thanks," I told Kirov. To Dmitri, I said, "Come on, Grumpy. Let's go get your daughter."

CHAPTER 18

We went into the hotel the same way we'd gone out—through the service door. This time, though, I wasn't half-starved and disoriented. I was alert, armed, and angry.

"We need to find the office where they keep their business records," I said.

"You really expect a place like this to have records?" Dmitri muttered. "Optimistic, I think."

"Trust me," I said, easing down the hallway, every sense open for anyone who'd object to our presence. "Pimps are even more compulsive about their money than witches are about their spell books. Pimps *and* witches—forget it. They'll have records of every cent that's ever come in and out. Coded, of course, but it'll be there."

"And we break the code how?"

"I'm thinking we hold Grigorii Belikov's head in a toilet until he gives it up. Work for you?"

"Sure does," Dmitri said.

The service elevator was a dank metal box, and my heart thudded as it levered us to the top floor. "There's one more thing," I said. "Once we get the information we need, we have to let these girls out of here."

Dmitri snorted. "Now who's the white knight?"

"I mean it," I said. "If we don't help these women, my involvement ends here. I'm going to the airport and getting on the first plane back to LAX."

"Fine, fine," Dmitri muttered. "Just stay focused. I don't want them to know we're here until it's absolutely necessary."

The doors rolled back and we came face to face with Peter.

"Too late for that," I said. I yanked the Walther out of my belt and held it in his weasel face. "Surprised, comrade?"

Peter's eyes darted toward the girls' suites and I pulled the hammer down. "Don't run. Don't yell. Be a good little gangster and maybe I won't shoot both your kneecaps off purely for what you put me and those other four girls through. *Maybe.*"

Usually, when I was with Dmitri, I relied on him to be the heavy. He enjoyed it, and it meant I took less damage over the course of whatever stupid adventure we had gotten ourselves involved in. I'm not such a feminist that I can't let a guy do the heavy lifting.

But not this time. Peter had fucked with me and he was about to learn exactly how bad of an idea it was. "Turn around," I said. "Hands behind your head."

Peter did as he was told, to his credit, with only a sigh of regret. "Any cameras between here and Grigorii's office?" I said. He grunted, shaking his head *no.*

"Then march, motherfucker. Double time." Peter shuffled ahead of me and Dmitri brought up the rear, his face reading surprise. I ignored him. He'd never seen me get really good and pissed off before, but he was about to.

I can be a real bitch when someone hurts me where I live. Screw with me or my family and all bets are off. I may act like a cop, I may act like a were. You pay your money and you take your chances.

"What will you do?" Peter said. "No way you get out of here again."

"Not the plan," I said. "And incidentally . . ." I drove my foot into the back of his knee hard enough to pop tendons. "Did I say you could talk?"

Peter fell through a door into an office that had once belonged to the manger of the complex—the old paintings and certificates were still on the walls. He rolled, moaning, clutching at the joint. I aimed the pistol between his eyes. "Dmitri, give him the phone."

Dmitri did as he was told, and I held the receiver next to Peter's ear. "Call Grigorii and tell him to come up to the office pronto. You say anything else and I'll blow your brains all over this ugly carpet. Any questions?"

Tears ran down Peter's face, but he punched in a number and spoke into the phone. I looked to Dmitri, who nodded that the thug wasn't talking out of turn. A gun in the face is powerful motivation for a human.

Now I just had to figure out what would work on Grigorii.

Peter cut off the connection. "He said he'll be right up. What are you going to do to me?"

I shrugged. "That's up to the father of a girl you kidnapped and sold." I stepped back, sticking the Walther into my waistband. Dmitri stepped in and leaned over Peter, his fangs growing and his features rippling toward were. Redbacks could phase with or without the moon, and I hoped that we weren't about to be treated to an all-you-can-chew mobster buffet. Blood is hard to clean out of clothing.

Peter started sniffling and shivering, pure panic overtaking him. I heard footsteps outside, smelled that cool non-smell of ice in winter. "Dmitri," I said, positioning myself in the line of sight for anyone coming through the door.

"Damn," Dmitri said. "I was so hoping we'd get some alone time, asshole. This will have to do." He hit Peter in the face and knocked him out. "Sweet dreams."

Dmitri put himself behind the door, and we waited, for a few mile-long heartbeats. Grigorii was speaking to someone, and I recognized the high voice.

"This is your fault, you know," Ekaterina snapped. "If you hadn't been so enamored of that werewolf trash, she never would have played your emotions like a cheap violin and we wouldn't be wasting time looking for her now."

"I know what I'm doing," Grigorii snarled. "I'll find her. Now go back downstairs and mind the till. Peter needs me for something. Probably can't figure out how to check his email again."

Ekaterina's footsteps retreated, and Grigorii twisted the doorknob and stepped in.

His reaction to seeing me alive and well wasn't at all what I expected. He smiled, a slow one that grew from the corners of his lips. "Joanne. You came back to me."

I pointed the Walther, gesturing him into his desk chair. "I just couldn't stay away."

Grigorii slid into his leather chair and cocked his head toward the door. "You can tell your unwashed friend that he doesn't need to hide."

Dmitri shut the door with a bang. "Where is she?"

"Please," I said. "I'll handle this, all right?" I pointed the Walther back at Grigorii. "We're looking for a girl. Masha Sandovsky. One of your thugs kidnapped her from outside of her school."

Grigorii spread his hands. "This name means nothing to me."

"Think fast," I said. "I'm not in the mood to be patient. Or kind."

"I think your information is perhaps faulty, Joanne," said Grigorii. "Maybe your unpleasant friend has led you astray."

Faster than I could react, Dmitri had closed the distance between them and grabbed Grigorii by the back of the neck. "This is my daughter, you son of a bitch, so you have five seconds to tell me where she is before I rip your throat out."

Grigorii swallowed and turned to look at me. "Talk some sense into him, Joanne, before someone gets hurt."

"Sorry," I said. "I'm not my werewolf's keeper."

Grigorii sighed and rotated his gaze back to Dmitri. "Let me go and I will provide you with the information I have."

Dmitri bared his teeth. "I think I'd rather beat it out of you, Belikov."

Grigorii rolled his eyes. "Have it your way."

Dmitri went backward, hit the wall hard enough to dent it and slid down, his eyelids fluttering. "Just a little shock," said Grigorii. "Not much more than what you got in your cage. Elemental magick can be disorienting, though. Let's give him a moment." He ran a hand through his hair. "What do you think of our fair city, Joanne?"

"Hex you," I said. "What did you do to Dmitri?"

"Shocked me," Dmitri said, getting to his feet. "Our boy here is a gods-damned living stun gun, isn't that right, Belikov?"

"I do have some control over electricity, yes." Grigorii shrugged, not seeming bothered in the least that I was holding a gun on him. Then again, I guess when you're the living version of Electro, you don't have to be.

Grigorii rubbed his neck and smoothed down his shirt. "I'll give her the information you're looking for, but only her. You leave the room."

"No way," Dmitri said. "I'm not leaving you two alone."

"Then I'm sure your daughter will enjoy her new life," said Grigorii. "The young ones are profitable. They can get as many as fifteen men a day."

Dmitri roared, and I put myself between Grigorii and his swing. "This is not helping Masha. Wait outside."

He glared at me, black spilling across his pupils, and I cursed under my breath. The daemon was coming out, grabbing hold in moments of stress and anger, taking one more piece of Dmitri away.

"Dmitri," I said, keeping my voice even. "Leave."

"Luna?" he said, blinking. His eyes were back to green. "Did I . . ."

"I'll take care of this," I said, shoving him out the door with more force than was strictly necessary. "You need to wait out there."

I shut the door after him and turned back to Grigorii. "I don't know what you think that accomplished."

"It got you alone," Grigorii said, standing up. "So difficult to talk when some oaf is blundering around." He approached me and reached out his hand. "Put the gun down, Joanne. Let's talk about this and be civilized."

"You don't know the meaning of the word," I said, but I lowered the gun a fraction and didn't flinch when he reached out, slowly, and brushed a midnight strand of hair from in front of my eyes.

"I don't know where the girl is that you're asking about," he said, his fingertips lingering against my cheek. I met his eyes.

"You're lying."

"And how do you know that?" Grigorii said. "You can read my mind, perhaps?" The fingers slid down my jaw, to grip my shoulder and pull me closer. Was he going to bargain with me or make out with me? I felt a tremor of panic in my chest at being so close to him again and fought it down.

"I know that you kidnap girls and sell them," I said. "You and your sister care less about them than about a piece of trash on your shoe, so don't pretend like you're innocent. It doesn't suit you."

"If I am all the things you say," Grigorii said, his other hand traveling over the curve of my hip, "a pimp, a liar, a seller of flesh—then why are you not running from me, far and fast as you can?"

I shoved the Walther into his gut, hard enough to send a breath from his lungs. "You make a better target up close."

Grigorii's lips peeled back in a smile. "I was afraid

that you would spurn my advances." His hand on my skin clamped down and the cold was all over me, like being dipped into a frozen lake naked. Not cold, I realized . . . *shock*. It was dancing in me, just like the silver that had put me down.

My knees buckled and I lost my grip on the gun. Grigorii eased me down to the floor as I fought to breathe, the air whistling in my chest.

"Let me tell you something about my sister," he said. "Our family lived in disgrace after the Romanovs fell, for generations. Ekaterina was bought by a man in our village in Siberia—a filthy, fat man. A whoremonger who took her away and cut her when she tried to escape and come back home. I killed him, hung him up by his ankles like the pig he was, and I'll kill you, too, and anyone else who attempts to step between my family and our livelihood.

"Now, I've only paralyzed you," Grigorii said. "Just a small working to keep you still, but completely reversible. Here are my terms." He pushed my shirt up and caressed one of my breasts. "You allow me to fuck you raw, and I'll let your big friend outside leave unharmed with the information he needs to find his child. Or I will have you both killed. What's your choice?"

I pantomimed trying to talk, although everything above the neck seemed to be working, including my brain, which was clouded with rage to a screaming degree. Grigorii sighed. "Don't struggle. Let me release the working. You'll just burst a blood vessel and then it will be like having my pleasure with a coma patient."

Charming. I'd run into plenty of witches, but not

one who could paralyze with just a touch. Grigorii was extra-special talented. Wasn't I lucky?

The numbness eased, electricity retreating from my nerves, but Grigorii kept his hand on me, holding me down. I wriggled my hand under my body, hoping that he would be otherwise occupied.

"Speak up," Grigorii said. "What choice have you made?"

My hand closed on the Walther where it was pinned under my body and I drew it, scraping a line along my own back. "Get your fucking hands off me."

I struck with the pistol butt, but Grigorii was faster and leaped backward, making me miss his temple. The gun slammed into his nose and he screamed, blood spattering my face with the warmth of spring rain.

Dmitri banged the door open and came in, grabbing Grigorii in a sleeper hold before he could react. "Luna," he said. "Get something to tie him with."

My legs were quivering, and I was still freezing, as if I'd just stood outside naked in a snowstorm, but I jumped up and slammed the door before ripping the phone cord out of the wall.

Dmitri and I tied Grigorii up and Peter, too, just to be on the safe side. "You okay?" Dmitri asked me quietly. "I need to break anything off of him?"

I looked at Grigorii, who stared back at me calmly. He even smiled, blood flowing freely from his mangled nose, over his lips and teeth. "You and I both know that nothing happened you didn't really want, Joanne."

"What's he talking about?" Dmitri snarled. I shook my head.

"Nothing." Grigorii's violation wasn't something I

needed Dmitri riding cavalry on. I didn't want to spend another second in the compound, didn't want to remember what I'd had to do to get away the first time.

There was a laptop sitting closed on the desk, and I booted it up. I was confronted with a blinking login screen. "Password?" I said to Grigorii.

He smirked at me. "Perhaps I'll trade it for a kiss."

Dmitri grabbed the Walther and I grabbed Dmitri, trying to deflect his aim from Grigorii's head. "No!" I snapped. "This is not how we're doing things!" Not that the prick didn't deserve it. My finger lodged against the trigger and the gun spoke, a shot going into the wall next to Grigorii's head. It missed by maybe an inch. He flinched, coughing on plaster dust.

"Password?" I said, wresting the gun from Dmitri's grip.

"That shot has drawn everyone in the building," said Grigorii. "You should be less concerned about the password than about your dramatically shortened lives."

Great job there, Dmitri. "We need to go," I told him.

"Masha . . ." he started.

"We'll find Masha," I said, jerking the laptop's power cord from the wall and shoving the computer into Dmitri's hands. Shouts sounded from down the hall, running footsteps. I knew the cadence of a frantic pursuit all too well, seeing as I was usually on the other end of one.

"What about him?" Dmitri said, jerking his head at Grigorii.

"Yes, white knight," said Grigorii. "What about me? Justice must be served, swift and merciless as a sword blade."

"He talks too damn much, is what," I said to Dmitri. "Now, move your ass. I'm not getting caught here again."

We bolted down the hall, eschewing the elevator for the fire stairs. Outside, into the car, tires squealing as vertigo pulled against my stomach. Dmitri drove for a long time, through twisting back streets, past Orthodox churches with steeples flying like hot-hair balloons against the gray sky, fountain squares that could have been snapshots at high speed on a postcard, old Soviet blocks that had their own square, postmodern beauty.

"We sightseeing?" I asked. Dmitri checked his rearview mirror.

"Making sure that we don't have a tail. The mob is tenacious, even more than American cops." He gave me a pointed look.

"I'm not really in the mood for banter," I said. Lola, Anna, Red, Deedee, even Charlie. "They're all still in that place. Those girls."

"And now we have evidence," Dmitri said. "Isn't that what you live for? The evidence?"

"You know, Grigorii and Ekaterina aren't just going to let us have this," I said. "We can't go back to your pack house."

"Kirov will meet us at a hotel room," he said. "The Redbacks have a few safe houses scattered around."

"And we need someone who can break into this computer," I said.

"I'll see if Kirov knows anyone," he said.

"Trustworthy," I said. "No one weird or fly-by-night. Chances are the Belikovs have some kind of dead man's switch on the hard drive. If we screw up cracking it, the whole thing will wipe."

"Always the optimist," Dmitri said, pulling in to the parking lot of a small hotel.

"I do my best," I told him.

CHAPTER 19

The hotel was a small pocket of civilization in the long parade of urban underbellies that had become my life. It was boutique and old, stuffy and full of velvet and Persian rugs, but it was clean, warm and didn't smell like bodily fluids.

The old man minding the front desk passed over a key without a word, giving me the eye. I gave it right back, until he dropped his eyes down to his Ukrainian-language celebrity magazine. "Come on," Dmitri said.

The elevator was the old-fashioned kind that had a gate and a guy in a monkey suit to press the button for you. "Third floor," Dmitri told him. The gate rolled shut and we started to move, at roughly the speed of a glacier.

"Did that seem easy to you?" I said. Dmitri lifted his shoulder.

"Nothing easy about getting attacked and assaulted by a witch, Luna. But you hit him a good one. He'll live, but he won't be pretty."

I leaned against the gate and rubbed my forehead. "It's just . . . We broke in. We got the jump on him and his goons, and we got his computer. Aside from the gunshot, it was like some movie snatch-and-grab, total smooth sailing. He's a witch, Dmitri. They never give anything away for free."

"Luna, you want to know what I think?"

"Am I gonna hear it, anyway?"

"I think you're overanalyzing things," he said. "We got what we wanted. Now forget about the Belikovs and let's find my daughter so you can go home and I can get her back to her mother."

I sighed, but I let it go. Dmitri would never admit that he was wrong—another one of his charming traits. There had been good ones, too, don't get me wrong, but the stuff that stuck with me was the temper and the stubbornness, the alpha-male attitude that made me feel like I was suffocating when we lived together.

The hotel room was small, European-style, with a sink in the corner and a shared bathroom down the hall. I went to the window and checked the street out of habit. A few cars were parked along the curb, but no one I recognized was on the street.

"I think we're safe," I said to Dmitri. "For now."

Kirov knocked on the door and came in, trailed by a thin girl with lank blonde hair and a laptop case. "This is Jocelyn," said Kirov.

"Yo," Jocelyn said. I cocked my eyebrow at her.

"You're American."

"Canadian," Jocelyn said, slinging her case onto the bed. "Where's the machine you need me to crack?"

"Jocelyn is a freelancer," Kirov explained. "She kindly helps out the pack in exchange for our protection."

"Protection from what?" I asked her.

"I'm not just a programmer," said Jocelyn. "I was a technomancer back home, before some caster witches decided they didn't like my look and chased me out of Toronto. Americans, naturally. I blame your country entirely for me living in this shithole."

"Well, at least she's pleasant," I said to Dmitri. Jocelyn heaved a sigh.

"Do you want me to crack this machine or not?"

Dmitri handed her the laptop. "We need the password, and the files."

Jocelyn sniffed. "Amateur hour. You really got me out of bed for this?" She booted up the machines and attached a USB cable from her laptop to Grigorii's.

"Hmm," she said after a minute. "Maybe we're not dealing with a complete moron. He's got a working on his hard drive."

I blinked. "He enchanted his hard drive?"

"Or had another technomancer do it for him. We're common around here. Must be all the radiation or something."

"Can you crack it?" Dmitri said. He paced, too big for the space, and I grabbed his arm and jerked him into a chair.

Jocelyn sighed, punching in commands on her own. "Give me a few minutes of peace, all right? I need to program a working to crack his security, and offensive spells take time." She started typing, her keyboard the witch's alphabet, and I felt a prickle of magick down my back.

I retreated to the window again, keeping watch. I knew I was being ridiculous, hyper-vigilant, but seeing Grigorii again and feeling his hand against my skin had stirred the primal anger that lived deep in my hindbrain.

"You all right?" Dmitri said at my shoulder. His hands traveled to my neck, massaging. "You look twitchy."

I jerked away from him. "Don't do that."

He frowned. "I'm just trying to keep you calm."

"I am fucking calm," I snarled. "I don't want to be touched, all right?"

"What's the matter with you?" Dmitri said quietly. "If you're cracking up, don't do it in front of someone from my pack. You're embarrassing me."

I looked back at him, saw the black spilling out from his irises, covering the green and white. Turning his eyes into the deep, fathomless oceans of inhumanity that let the daemon look back at me.

"Dmitri," I said quietly. "Look at yourself."

"You're mine," he hissed. "Whether you believe it or not. That man can put his hands on you, but he can never erase my mark."

Something about the voice triggered a memory in me, a daemon staring at me, hungering for me . . . and then backing away.

Good parting, one who wears the mark of Asmodeus.

My jaw set, and I took a step back from Dmitri, only to bang into the window.

"Asmodeus?"

"I warned you, Insoli," he whispered, bending close to my ear. Dmitri's hands reached out and grasped my arm, squeezing hard enough to bruise. "I warned you that we'd see one another again."

I was paralyzed, as much as if Grigorii still had me under his working. The last time I'd seen Asmodeus, the terms had been less than civil. The daemon had saved my life, and I had wiggled out of our bargain in return. Maybe not very sporting of me, but it was a daemon we were talking about, not a homeless orphan.

"Nothing to say, Insoli?" the daemon whispered in Dmitri's voice. His eyes danced, gold flaming up in the depths.

"Leave," I snarled. "Leave him alone. You don't have a fight with Dmitri, you have a fight with me." I shot a look at Kirov and Jocelyn, but they were absorbed in Jocelyn's working. Not that they'd see what I saw. Asmodeus was shy.

"You are so wrong, Insoli," he purred. "So very, very wrong."

I raised my chin. "If you don't leave Dmitri alone, I am going to summon you and exorcise you back into the Dark Ages. You know I will."

He laughed, low in his throat. "You aren't a witch, Luna. You'll kill him if you try and we both know *that* to be the truth."

"Why are you doing this to me?" I demanded. "What is it you want?"

"To see you," he said with a grin, fangs glimmering in the low light. "To tell you that I'll be seeing you again. Sooner than you think."

I opened my mouth to threaten him again, but then Dmitri blinked and his eyes were his own.

"What happened?" he asked. "What did I do?"

"Nothing," I said, easing myself out of his grasp. "Nothing happened at all. You just faded out there for a minute."

He rubbed his forehead. "I've got a bitch of a migraine. Kirov." He walked over to his pack mate and got a pull from Kirov's flask.

I dropped into a chair, gripping the arms to stop my hands from shaking. I had never seen a daemon take possession of a person like that.

Of course it was possible. Dmitri had been standing close enough to kiss me, speaking in the voice of the one daemon who wanted to take a pound of flesh out of my hide.

My panic attack was interrupted by Jocelyn, who snapped her head up. "We're in."

"That was fast," Dmitri said.

"Technomancer who put the wards on this machine wasn't careful," she said. "Left a hole as big as my head in his working. You really want people to stay out, you get someone like me to write a custom spell for your needs."

"We're looking for business records," I said. "Sales, financial transactions, that kind of thing."

"That's your department, peaches," said Jocelyn. "I'm just a locksmith. And I like to be paid promptly."

Kirov drew an envelope out of his pocket and passed it to her. "There you are, my dear."

Jocelyn saluted with the envelope of cash. "Pleasure doing business with you."

"That laptop belongs to some nasty people," I spoke up. "Watch your back, Jocelyn."

"Dude, if the caster witches couldn't catch me, some chain-smoking gangsters who can scribble spells aren't going to be a problem," Jocelyn said with a smirk. "I am that good. Catch you later, Dmitri." She dropped him a wink and walked out.

I snarled. Did every woman in Kiev know him intimately?

Dmitri turned the laptop toward me. "Take a look."

"The records are in English," I said in surprise.

"Not the first language around here," Dmitri said. "Smart, when you think about it."

There were hundreds of spreadsheets on the hard drive, all coded with initials and strings of numbers that meant nothing to me.

"This is absolutely no help," I said. "Look at this."

Dmitri frowned over my shoulder. "Code."

"Well, we knew that was coming," I said. "These notes in the column must be where they took the girls, or who bought them, or some sort of relevant information. You don't just leave gibberish."

The notations were one or two words, nothing overtly threatening.

Bad weather.

Underground.

Charm school.

"And the numbers?" Dmitri said.

I blew out a puff of frustration. "I'm a cop, not a mathematician, Dmitri." I scanned the columns. "Three numbers in one, two in the other," I said. "Locations and girls, I'm guessing, but I can't crack this. I'm not a cryptographer, either."

Kirov pointed at the two-number notation. "Latitude and longitude," he said. "Simple. A way to find a location that anyone knows. All you need for an address is a GPS."

"Perfect," Dmitri said. "Now we just need to crack the names and we'll find Masha."

"But it wouldn't be names," I murmured, thinking of Lola and her insistence that she not know me. "We gave them fake ones, and they never bothered to learn our real ones. How do you keep track of a bunch of women with no names?"

I pressed my finger against the screen. *1-23-140*. Not a birth date. Not a state ID number. No one cared when the girls were born or who they were before. They only cared that they looked good enough to make a buck . . .

"N-1," I said. Dmitri cocked an eyebrow.

"Meaning what?"

"When I get my hair touched up at the salon, N-1 is the color my stylist uses," I said. "One is black hair color in salon speak. And twenty-three, that could be her age, and one-forty—weight." Hair, age, and weight. All that would matter to a man like Grigorii Belikov. All that would matter to his customers.

"Masha has red hair," Dmitri said. "She's fourteen and she weighs, oh, I don't know, one-twenty at the most. Look for that."

I searched for *2-14-120*.

One entry popped up in my search box. Kirov pointed to the location. "That's Kazakhstan."

Dmitri gave a snarl. "Why the fuck take her there?"

I thought the more important question was what were they doing to Masha Sandovsky once she got there. Her notation was unlike any of the other girls. Unlike the innocuous notes, this one was frightening.

Cold storage.

My admittedly disturbing train of thought was interrupted by a screech of tires outside and a moment later, the thud of footsteps in the fire stairs. "Someone's here," Kirov said.

Dmitri snarled and started for the door. "Bastard sons of flea-bitten bitches—I'll *make* them tell me what they did with Masha."

"Wait!" I snapped. "You getting killed isn't going to help this situation."

I slapped the laptop closed and shoved it into my bag along with its power cord. "Kirov, is there another way out of here?"

"Fire stairs," he said. "But they seem to have already covered that . . ."

A pounding started on the door, and then two bullets blew out the lock.

"Window," I said, slinging my bag over my shoulder. I pushed up the ancient sash and swung my leg over the decorative balcony. There were no handholds on the pockmarked brick face of the hotel.

Kirov gave a yell as the first gangster burst into the room and tackled the man, fighting for his gun. "*Dmitri*," I yelled. "Come on!"

"Go," Kirov shouted, having liberated the gun. He got off a few shots, causing the remaining pair of thugs to duck for cover.

This was going to suck. I aimed for the long black sedan that the gangsters had driven up in and let go of the railing, falling three stories down, clutching the laptop bag to my chest.

I landed on my back and crushed the roof of the sedan, setting off a car alarm with a shriek. Dmitri followed suit, landing on the hood.

If anyone in the street thought it was odd that two people had just dropped from a balcony and trashed a car, they didn't let on. For all I knew, this sort of thing happened every day here.

"We need to keep low," Dmitri said, offering me his hand. I took it and pulled myself upright with a groan. Nothing was broken, but I didn't exactly feel like sunshine and roses after that hit.

Dmitri stuck out his arm to hail a cab and gave the driver directions. "Where to?" I asked when he sat back, panting, his face beaded with sweat.

"The train station," he said. "We're going to get Masha."

CHAPTER 20

The train rolled out of the city with a low rumbling, like the sound of a dragon deep in a cave. I slumped against my seat. We'd avoided the Belikovs, but for how long?

Dmitri looked up and down the aisle before settling into the seat next to me. "Long ride. Might as well get comfortable."

I rubbed my temples. "No offense, Dmitri, but you don't exactly give off the comfort vibe."

"You've been acting strange ever since we left the room," Dmitri said. "What are you not telling me?"

The train picked up speed as we left Kiev behind and headed east, and I leaned my forehead against the window. "Just forget it, all right?"

You are wrong, Insoli. So very, very wrong.

"Fine," Dmitri said. "You never let me in. Just build up that shell a little more. It seems to be doing wonders for your personality."

I flipped him off and went back to staring out the window. I didn't mean to fall asleep, but the low brown countryside passing by lulled me into it. My head rolled over onto Dmitri's shoulder, warm and solid, and I let my eyes drift close, breathing in a scent that came back to me in my half-conscious state as a comfort, familiar and real.

The scent of seaweed and bay water, tangy and invasive. Cold wet skin under my cheek, wet hair draped across my neck.

"Alone at last," Lily said. She sat in Dmitri's seat, staring ahead, water dribbling from her hair, her chin, the tips of her fingers. Blood trailed from her chest cavity, the smell of it rotting the air around her. Death coated my tongue, and I forced myself to swallow it down.

I had never seen a real ghost. I never *believed* in ghosts in the same way I believed in daemons and magick. But this wasn't like the dream in my bathtub, and not like my time in the cell.

"It's not a dream at all," I said out loud.

"Correct," Lily said. Her voice was faint, and I had to strain to hear it.

I sucked in a breath and asked the question that they always ask in those ghost movies: "Why me, Lily?"

"I want you to stay alive, for starters," she said. She turned her head slowly and stared at me with her wet, cloudy eyes. "You can't help me if you're dead. No one can help anyone when they're among the dead."

"You didn't answer my question. Why *me*?" I said.

"Because you were the only one who saw me," she said. "You're the only one who *can* see. I'm fading, Lieutenant Wilder. Are you going to let me go?"

"I . . ." I started shivering. I was damp now, as if I were standing in a mist at midnight. "I don't know what you mean, Lily. I can't do anything."

Like a skip in an eight-millimeter film, Lily's hand

lashed out and grabbed my arm. "You better do something," she snarled, lips pulling back, blue with rigor mortis. "Because I'm not leaving."

The train swayed, and I jerked awake, slamming my head on the window. "Ow! Fuck."

Dmitri touched the back of my hand. "You all right?" His touch burned my skin, and I hissed and jerked away. "Luna?" he said, his voice sliding into alarm.

I pushed back my sleeve and looked at my wrist. A small blue handprint was seared into my skin, radiating cold. Dmitri pulled back. "Hex me. What is that thing?"

"It's complicated," I sighed. Dmitri shifted in his seat to look me in the eye.

"I've got time."

"Dmitri, really . . ."

"Look, Luna, you may not be able to deal with my daemon bite, but that doesn't mean I can't be there for you. Tell me what's going on."

I glared. "First of all, has anyone ever told you that you have a really shitty and abrasive way of trying to be helpful?"

Dmitri growled under his breath. "I'm sorry, all right? Go on."

"It's a girl," I said. "A girl that was murdered back in Nocturne City. She's the reason I got into this whole thing with the Belikovs in the first place. I was trying to figure out who killed her." I bit my lip and looked at my feet. The rest sounded too insane to say out loud.

"I'm listening," Dmitri said. He put his hand back over mine, and I didn't pull away. "I'm not going to think you're crazy, Luna."

"I've been having dreams," I said. "About her. Horrible, real, screaming dreams in full color and surround sound. And they're getting worse."

"Hmm," Dmitri said.

"That's it? 'Hmm'? How helpful."

"Hey, listen." He rubbed his thumb in a circle over the back of my hand. "There are plenty of spirits in the old country. My grandmother, gods rest her, had the sight. She could talk to the departed just as easily as I'm talking to you."

"Did any of them ever sear handprints into her flesh?"

Dmitri frowned. "Well, no. That's new."

I sighed and rubbed my free hand over my face. "What's wrong with me, Dmitri?"

"Can't say," he said. "But we'll fix it. Look, you're exhausted. You're under pressure. Maybe your stress is causing some latent talent to surface. Ghost whispering under pressure, or some crap."

I shut my eyes. "Don't even joke about that. Do you know what a nightmare that would be?" The dead reaching for me with their curled-up hands, looking at me from rotted, empty sockets, begging me with maggot-ridden mouths to be their voice, their justice, their vengeance.

"Just a theory," said Dmitri. "I'm going to go get some supper from the dining car. You want anything?"

"Something with caffeine," I said. "I'm not falling asleep again if I can help it. Possibly not ever."

Dmitri leaned over and kissed me on the cheek. "You got it."

I blinked at him as he got up and ambled down the car, going through the folding glass door with a brief surge of wind and the sound of train wheels.

What the hell did Dmitri think he was playing at? His casual kisses and touches were somehow going to win me over, make me forget Will and my life back in Nocturne?

I sighed and pulled Grigorii's laptop out of my bag. Right now, I was just glad of the company, glad that I wasn't alone like I'd been during that horrible week with the Belikovs.

The search of the laptop didn't prove any more fruitful than before, except now, with the train's Wi-Fi and a latitude-longitude widget, I was able to tell where Grigorii had shipped each girl he'd sold. Moscow. Belarus. Bangkok. Pyongyang. The list wasn't encouraging.

I looked at the notation next to Masha's name again. It wasn't a common one—in fact, she looked like one of only two girls sold to the same sort of thing.

Cold storage. What could that possibly imply? I looked at the rest of the list. Criminal codes aren't usually overly complex, because your subordinates have to be able to understand them, and employees of organized crime bosses aren't usually honor students.

I looked at the next notation, for a girl named Olivia. *Wolf pack.* "Wolf pack," I murmured. Wolf packs ran together, slept together.

Hunted together.

Dmitri jostled my elbow as he slid back into his seat. "Ham sandwiches looked okay," he said. "All they had was off-brand soda and some energy drink that translates into 'Ultra Wakeup Juice.' Hope that's all right."

I popped the top of the soda and gulped down a

swallow before I spun the laptop to face Dmitri. "What does *wolf pack* mean to you?"

"Nothing," Dmitri said. "Just like last time."

"Wolf packs are pack hunters," I said. "Look at this location they sent her to. It's just a latitude and longitude. You don't give that unless you're in the middle of nowhere."

I showed him the widget, pulling up a map of the southern corner of Ukraine with the coordinates the Belikovs' records had given me. "Where is that?" I asked Dmitri.

He whistled. "That's the Wolves Land."

"Which is . . . ?" I said, raising my eyebrow.

"It's contaminated land from the Chernobyl fallout," he said. "It's been closed down since 1986—whole towns, all abandoned and empty. It's eerie out there. Olya and I took a ride through, once."

"You and your sister willingly exposed yourself to radiation?" I said. "That explains so much."

"It's not dangerous if you don't stay," he said. "You're saying that *wolf pack* means . . ."

"They hunt the girls," I said. "For sport."

"But not my Masha," said Dmitri.

"Yeah, fortunately," I said. "But we still don't know what *cold storage* means."

The train slowed, and Dmitri tensed. "We're at the border. We'll find out soon enough."

Two hours later, the train left us in a village too small to have a name that I could see, standing on a dusty rail platform under sun that made sweat trickle down my spine like thin fingers on my skin. A rusted sign

peppered with buckshot told us the population and
the number of the rail stop, left over from the Soviets.
Stop 13.

"This doesn't look like a hotbed of mob activity," I
told Dmitri, surveying the low brick buildings and
the few sharp-faced citizens milling on the train platform.

"We'll ask around," he said. "There must be something here, or the Belikovs wouldn't have sold her,
right?" He looked to me, and I sighed.

"Give me Masha's picture," I said. "I'll show it
around. There's a chance whoever bought her let her
be seen."

"I hate the way you say that," Dmitri said. "Bought
her."

"We'll get her back," I said, even though it was beginning to sound hollow even to me.

"Gypsy cab," Dmitri said, pointing at a broken-
down '55 Pontiac sitting by the tracks, dusty as everything else at Stop 13. Dmitri went over and spoke to
the driver, gesturing back and forth. I took the time to
look around and get my bearings.

Stop 13 reminded me of the poor pockets of the
Southwest I'd driven through on a road trip with an
old boyfriend who was a roadie for a crappy country-
rock band. We did an Arizona and New Mexico tour
one summer, hours in a Dodge van under the boiling
pale blue sky. Every so often we'd pass a ghost town,
trailers and shacks, maybe a diner or a filling station
abandoned to time and the elements, skeletal specters
of another era.

Here, the only difference was the few people still
living. A rusted-out Ford pickup pulled by a pair of

donkeys ambled slowly down the main street in front of the tracks. A cat sunned herself on the steps of the ticket booth and hissed when she caught my scent, puffing her tail and skittering under the platform.

"Luna," Dmitri called. He and the gypsy cab's driver had reached an accord. "He says he'll take us to the local motel," said Dmitri. "The family who owns it might know something about Masha."

"What's here?" I asked the cab driver. "Besides nothing, I mean."

"Farmers," he said, his accent thick. "A tire factory."

"How quaint," I muttered. "I wonder if I can find a spot to shop for authentic handicrafts."

The driver knew more English than his accent let on, and he gave a snort, glaring at me in the rearview mirror. We rode the rest of the way to the motel in silence.

More respectable than I expected, the motel was a long low bunker-style abode with a sign bolted to the side and light-up neon letters in the window of the first unit that I assumed meant vacancy.

I shouldered the laptop and my backpack and stepped into the office, triggering a bell. A moment later a woman in a headscarf and a cardigan came rushing from the back room, a huge grin on her face.

"Yes?" she said, clapping her hands together. I just stared—she looked like she was out of an old comedy sketch. Her face was a network of burst veins, her nose was knobby, and the whole image was of someone's kindly grandmother welcoming you to the mother country.

"I . . ." I composed myself and returned her smile. "I need a room."

"Yes?" she said. Perfect. She was the kindly grand-mother who doesn't understand a damn thing you say.

"Dmitri!" I hollered.

He came in, doing the same double-take I did when he laid eyes on the motel owner. He told her we needed a room, with his best charming smile.

"Two beds," I hastened to add. Dmitri paid in cash and exchanged more chatter with the woman in Russian.

"She says there's nothing here except the tire factory," he said. "Nowhere disreputable."

"Disreputable?"

"Hey, that's how she put it," he said. "Come on, she gave us the quiet room, away from the road."

"Yeah," I said. "Thank the gods we'll be away from the constant din of passing donkey trucks."

"Hey, this place is a lot like where Olya and I grew up," Dmitri said as he unlocked our room. "Don't knock it."

"I can see why you got out," I said.

"We didn't have a choice," he said. "My father was killed in a factory accident and my mother sent us to live with the pack elders in Kiev. After that, you know the whole sordid story."

I flicked on the lights and sighed when I saw a single queen bed made up with a spread in a shade of bilious green that I'm fairly sure the FDA had outlawed as a fire hazard in America.

"Dammit, *two* beds," I said. "What's wrong with that old woman?"

"I don't know." Dmitri shrugged. "Guess she's a little hard of hearing."

I slung my bags onto the bed and flopped down. "If this is your cockeyed way of seducing me . . ."

"Sweetheart, if I wanted you, you wouldn't be fighting me," Dmitri said.

I sat up straight, folding my arms. "Oh, is that right, *sweetheart?*"

Dmitri smirked. "That is correct."

"You're an asshole," I said. Dmitri smirked again, setting down his bag and moving toward me.

"Yeah, sweetheart, but I'm your kind of asshole." He pinned my legs against the mattress, leaned forward and inhaled my scent, his breath tickling my ear and behind my neck, something he'd loved to do before.

"Dmitri . . ." I warned. "That's far enough."

"Come on, Luna," he said. "That human can't give you what you want. I can."

"Dmitri, this isn't you," I said. I couldn't see his eyes, but the sibilant echoes in his tone were familiar. "Stop it now, before I have to hurt you."

"I want you to hurt me," he hissed. "Like you hurt me before, because then I can hurt you. I can hold you down and make you scream how sorry you are, over and over again."

The click of the Walther's hammer was the only sound in the small, stuffy motel room. I pressed it into Dmitri's temple, hard enough to leave a mark like a kiss.

"I know how much fun you're having," I said. "But I'm telling you now that you either leave Dmitri out of this game until we find his daughter or I'm going to blow holes all through your shiny new toy."

"You turn me on when you threaten me," Dmitri murmured. "Do you remember how we met? You pointing a gun at me. Begging with that body of yours to be taken down a peg or two."

"I mean it," I said. "I'm not so sentimental that I wouldn't kill a man who's basically dead already just to shut up your incessant yapping, Asmodeus."

I *was* that sentimental, but Asmodeus didn't know that about me. He hadn't exactly seen my soft side.

After an interminable moment, Dmitri released me. I shoved him away and stormed out the door before he came back to himself and I had to explain what had happened, again.

Shoving the Walther into my waistband, I stomped across the parking lot toward the back of the hotel. Asmodeus had a lot of nerve screwing with me this way. I wasn't some plaything on a string that could be jerked back and forth at will.

I was around the corner, out of sight, and I dropped down on the curb, putting my head in my hands.

Biggest mistake of your life, Wilder. How could I have thought that helping Dmitri was the right thing to do? The *sensible* thing? I could be home with Will now, safe, warm, and not trapped in a motel in Kazakhstan with my possessed ex.

Crying caught my attention, from beyond the cluster of trash cans. I stood up, moving toward the sound. "Hello?"

The crying stopped abruptly, and I heard breath and a heartbeat. "Everyone okay back here?" I said, dropping my hand to my gun.

I peered over the cans and saw a pudgy girl with her knees pulled up to her chin, tears running down her reddened face. "What's up?" I asked. "You don't look too happy."

She couldn't have been more than sixteen or seventeen, hair dyed shocking purple at the tips and grown out to mousy blonde roots. I saw pink indentations where piercings had sat on her lips and nose, but no jewelry. Her dress was thin cotton and she was sporting a heavy cardigan, like the woman in the front office.

"I know you can understand me," I said. "I heard you stop crying as soon as I said something."

"I can't talk to you," she hissed. "If I talk, the missus will get me into trouble."

Her accent was thick—Scottish, I thought—and she flinched away when I crouched down beside her. "What's your name? Mine's Luna," I offered, when she didn't say anything.

"Gillian," she finally mumbled. "But the missus just calls me *girl* or some insult in languages I don't understand."

"Where are you from, Gillian?"

"Why are you asking me all of these bloody questions?" She checked a battered watch, bright purple that matched her hair. A child's watch, something you'd buy at the mall to try to look cool.

"Because I'm looking for another girl, the daughter of a . . . a friend, who also came here. If you help me, I'll make sure you get back home."

"Glasgow," she said in answer. "I met a bloke and . . ."

"You woke up in Kiev?" I guessed. The story was getting downright common.

"Stupid," she muttered.

"No," I said, reaching out again and putting a hand

on her shoulder. "You were just trusting, like we all were. Tell me about the missus."

"She's a regular fright, isn't she?" Gillian asked. "Practically runs the village, collects money from the shopkeepers, tells the pickpockets when they can rob the tourists—not that we get many that speak English in this place. Arse-end of the world, this is."

So much for the kindly old grandmother. I should know better—kindly old grandmothers are always wolves. "Have you seen another girl?" I said. "About fourteen, red hair, speaks Ukrainian?"

"Haven't," Gillian said. "I'm just an odd hearth witch—my mother taught me the circle and a bit of casting, but that's all. But apparently over here I'm worth something." She snorted. "Figures. First time in my life I'm worth a damn and I get sold to some crusty old horror to be a servant girl. Like a bloody fairy tale."

I sighed. "Is there anyplace in town that you know of—a brothel, or a tavern, anywhere they'd need a young girl for something less than savory?"

Gillian lifted her shoulder. "Only weird thing in this place is the old laboratory complex."

Laboratory? Oh, this was going to be seven kinds of not good. "What kind of lab?"

"Dunno," Gillian said. "It's some old Soviet heap that they put up when they had control in these parts. Biohazard symbols all over the gate, padlocked and dark—spooky fucking place. I don't go near it." She gave a shiver.

"Okay," I said. *Cold storage.* That could be anything, but a lab experiment was as likely as any other outlandish possibility I could come up with. "Thank you, Gillian."

"Oi," she said. "What about all of your grand promises of a rescue?"

"You're going to come with me," I said, reaching out. "You'll stay with my friend until I find Masha, and then we'll all be leaving here together."

"They took my passport in Kiev," said Gillian. "Can't leave the bloody country, can I?"

"Why don't you let me worry about that?" I said. She let me help her up and we speed-walked back to the motel room, where I unlocked the door. Dmitri jumped out of the chair where he'd been waiting, panic on his face.

"Luna, I . . ."

I held up a hand. "Save it. This is Gillian. She's another one of the Belikovs' pieces of merchandise. She's going to be staying with you."

"With me?" Dmitri folded his arms. "What about Masha?"

"Dmitri," I said, gesturing Gillian to sit on the bed. "After what just happened, do you really think you're fit to be out walking around? Stay here, look after Gillian and I'll be back with Masha soon."

I grabbed my bag and left again before he could object. I was sick of him calling the shots, sick of being pushed around by Asmodeus, sick of Eastern Europe and the whole sordid mess.

I was tired. Too tired to keep marching. I just wanted to turn around and go home. But Masha was still missing, and she was still my responsibility because I'd said I'd help her.

Making promises to victims was something I thought I'd gotten better at, and yet here I was, walking deeper into the nightmare because I was the only one who would go in after her.

CHAPTER 21

The walk to the lab was long and hot, and my tank top was soaked through with sweat by the time I crested the hill outside of the village and looked down into the valley.

The complex wasn't much to look at—three buildings connected by walkways, the entire thing enclosed with barbed-wire fences and warning signs in Russian, bearing the old symbol of the USSR.

It was, as Gillian had said, padlocked and spooky. I shaded my eyes and looked at the road leading in and out. The earth was cracked and dry from lack of rain, and fresh tire tracks were pressed into the roadbed.

Maybe not so abandoned after all. I stopped to take a swig from the water bottle I'd bought at Stop 13 and started down the track. Sometimes the direct approach is best. I dumped a little more of the water down the front of my tank and into my hair to simulate sweat-drenched agony, and walked to the gate.

"Hello?" I called, rattling the mesh. "Hello, is anyone here?"

A long wait passed me by, and I began to think I was wrong, that Masha had been delivered somewhere else and I was a crazy person shouting at an empty lab complex.

Then a buzzer sounded, and the gate rolled back. I stepped inside and started as it shut behind me with a clang.

"Walk to the nearest building," a disembodied voice screeched from a PA speaker. "The yellow door. Push it open and step inside. Do not deviate from my instructions."

"I'm a little lost . . ." I said, keeping up my innocent tourist act. "Can you help me?"

"Walk," the voice ordered sharply. "The yellow door."

So they had eyes on me. I walked, taking in my surroundings as I did in case I had to make an escape later. The buildings were rubbed clean of insignia by wind and rain and everything had that hunkered-down weathered look of old, abandoned places. It was a simple foursquare complex connected by walkways above my head with a central yard made of concrete.

The yellow door led me into a dark room, a desk, a chair and a security grate all I caught before it slammed shut behind me and left me in total darkness, the kind even my eyes couldn't penetrate.

"Hello?" I said again, not needing to fake the tense tone in my voice. "Are you still there?"

There was a buzz and a parade of fluorescent bulbs flickered on, illuminating the holding cage I was in as well as a long gray hallway beyond, accented with pea-green linoleum. Soviet aesthetic at its finest.

"Okay," I said. "I'm no longer amused by this. Either show yourself or I'm leaving."

"You can't leave."

The voice wasn't disembodied, and without the distortion of the PA it was very, very familiar.

Grigorii Belikov stepped from the shadows at the far end of the hallway and paced toward me, his suit navy blue with a lighter pinstripe today, his smirk growing. He had a bandage over his nose, but I gained some small satisfaction from the purple bruise on his face.

"Oh," I said. "Watch me." I turned around and made for the door, which declined to yield under my weight. I gave it a kick, full power, and barely managed to dent it.

"This was once a lab that engineered biological weapons," said Grigorii. "Those doors are meant to keep you in if there is an outbreak." He extended his hand. "Tell me where my records are and I'll let you go, Joanne."

"Hex you," I snarled, backing as far away from him as I could. "What are you even doing here?"

"You stole something of mine," he said. "When that happens, I find the person who took it and get the item back. I'd prefer to do it without a fuss, Joanne."

"You're a slaver," I said. "You don't get to decide what you keep and what you don't."

Grigorii sighed and depressed the button to open the security gate. He came within arm's reach of me and tapped his finger on his chin. "Do you remember what happened the last time we got this close, Joanne? Or is it Luna? Luna Wilder? That were, Kirov, was quite confused by the time I finished with him."

I flinched. Grigorii patted me down and took away my gun. I let him. I hadn't forgotten the punch he packed. "Well? Which is it?"

"Luna," I said. "I seem to remember last time we were close, I smashed your pretty face in, tied you up, and stole enough evidence to put you in a dark and unpleasant Russian prison for seven lifetimes."

Grigorii chuckled. "Do you know who I'm named for, Luna?"

"I have a feeling you're going to tell me." Could I Path Grigorii's energy, if I was ready? There was some magick I couldn't absorb. Could I take the chance, knowing what he'd do to me if I didn't overpower him? Masha and Dmitri were depending on me to get out of this in one piece.

"Grigorii Rasputin," he said. "The advisor to the Romanovs, whom they poisoned, shot, stabbed, beat, castrated and finally drowned. Some say that even with these ministrations, Rasputin did not die but instead used his power to rise again, stronger than before. And that is me as well, Luna. You may think you have drowned the last remainders of my spirit, but I will dog you for a lifetime, like a sentient shadow, until I get what I desire."

"Spooky," I said. I definitely couldn't risk trying to Path his energy now, stuck in this lab as I was. I had to talk my way out of this. "That's supposed to scare me into giving the laptop back?"

"One lives on hope," Grigorii said in the same dry tone. His hand flashed out and he grabbed me by the hair, bending my head back and exposing my neck. "Something else to consider—if you don't give it back, I'll be forced to kill that brute you left back in the village. And the fat sow, too. Such a shame. But this is a dangerous part of the world, and tourists often run into unfortunate trouble."

I swallowed the sudden dry lump in the back of my throat. "You make a good case."

"And your decision?" Grigorii said. I unstrapped my bag and held the laptop.

"One condition."

"You're in no position to bargain, but name it. It might be mildly amusing."

"You let me see Masha Sandovsky after I give this to you."

Grigorii snorted, and it turned into a full-blown laugh. "But of course. That was my intention all along."

Huh. Could have fooled me. "I asked after Sandovsky when the two of you . . . visited me," Grigorii said. He snatched the laptop from my grip with surprising speed. "He's been sniffing around my establishment for a few weeks, and it seems I *did* sell his daughter. Ironic. Most weres know to leave us be, but not him. Particularly dense, that one." He gestured for me to walk ahead of him, and we wound through a maze of corridors, all equally featureless and gray.

"Why are you here?" I asked again. "This is an awfully long way from Kiev just to gloat at me."

"I'm a businessman, Luna," Grigorii said. "And when my business is challenged, I take steps to ensure it doesn't happen again. I told you, Luna. I'm a troubleshooter."

We descended a set of narrow stairs painted with bright red warnings, about falling or running, I imagined. There were doors along this corridor, doors with small round windows and heavy locks that the cop in me knew could only be one thing. "This is a jail," I said.

"A containment facility," Grigorii corrected me. "For

test subjects. And now, for my business interest and the women who serve it."

He looked down to the end of the cell row, where a figure sat at a switchboard. "Sixteen, please."

The door buzzed, and swung open with a *Dr. Caligari*–style creak. I balked reflexively at the darkness inside. Grigorii put his hand on the small of my back, rubbing in circles. Caressing. "Easy, Luna. I won't let anything bad befall you."

I gave a loud growl. "That is really not a good idea, sport."

"As you say," he smiled. He gave me a hard shove and I fell forward into the cell. Grigorii dusted his hands off on a crisp red handkerchief. "Luna, meet your Masha Sandovsky. I'm sure the two of you will become fast friends." He turned his head. "Close sixteen."

The door slammed shut and darkness closed over my head like cold water, but this time I peered into it, trying to see something, anything. I blinked and let my eyes shift, the silver tones jumping out at me, detailing a bench bed with no mattress, a steel toilet bolted to the floor and a hunched figure next to it, her forehead on her knees.

"Masha?" I whispered.

She raised her head a fraction. "Yeah, what of it?"

A swell of relief built in my chest and I inhaled and exhaled the stale air. "Your father sent me. He's been looking for you for a while."

Masha made a derisive sound in the back of her throat. "Dmitri?"

"Do you have another father?"

She blew out a breath. "The dude doesn't show up

for most of my life and then suddenly he's all in my business. Whatever."

"Listen," I said. "You're here because you made some shitty choices and your dad came after you. He's trying, Masha—and I know for a fact that he is going to be really, really fucking glad you're all right."

"That's nice and all," she muttered. "But I'm not getting out of here."

"Not true," I said. "I'm going to take you back to your dad and he's going to take you home."

"You're in this cell same as me," she said. "So, good job there."

I grimaced. "I wasn't expecting Belikov to show up and ambush me."

Masha sighed. "He does that. But hey, at least you know he won't kill you. At least not until you're not useful anymore."

"Meaning what?" I asked her.

Masha lifted her head. "You'll find out. Someone comes every day around this time and . . ." She sighed. "You'll just find out, okay?"

The door clicked open again with a buzz, and I recognized the silhouette immediately. "Mikel," I said. "It's been too long. Threatened anyone who can't fight back lately?"

"Get up," he said. "The both of you."

Masha got up and shuffled into the hall obediently. I followed her, keeping my eyes on Mikel. He smirked at me. "Locked up again. Bad habit with you."

"Before I leave here, I'm going to punch you right in that smirk," I told him.

Mikel led us down the corridor to a set of steel

doors. "Through there," he said. "You know what will happen if you misbehave."

I looked to Masha. "What's he insinuating?"

She sighed heavily as we were buzzed into a small steel hallway with doors at either end. The drains in the floor and the sprinklers overhead spoke to the chamber's old purpose. I shivered. What exactly did we need to be decontaminated from?

"Just sit still and let the doctor examine you," Masha said. "Otherwise, Mr. Belikov gets furious." She touched a scar on her eyebrow. "I tried to fight back. Once."

I thought of what Grigorii must have done to her and winced, my stomach rebelling with a boil of nausea.

The door at the other end of the chamber opened with a clang, and we stepped into a white space, white tiles and white floors, white lights beating down, sterilizing all of the color from the air.

A small dark-haired man with a full gray moustache stood behind a steel table. White lab coat, subdued blue shirt and tie, blue nitrile gloves. "Masha," he said. "And a new girl, how nice." He inclined his bald head at Mikel. "She is a genetic match?"

Mikel shrugged. "That's for you to find out. Belikov just wants her here."

"And you are?" I said to the doctor. Masha went behind a surgical screen and started to undress.

"I am Dr. Emil Gorshkov," he said. "I work with Grigorii. What is your name?"

Mikel frowned. "Less talk, more testing."

Gorshkov raised a hand. "Please. This is my laboratory space. What is your name, girl?"

"Joanne." I didn't want this ever-smiling, bald, cold-eyed doctor to know my real name for reasons I couldn't quite bring clear even in my own head.

"Joanne. Common." He sniffed, his moustache twitching. "Please, undress and put on a gown."

Okay, Luna. Easy. Nothing to be gained by freaking out on the guy and causing a scene. I needed to figure out what was going on here and how the hell I was going to get Masha and me clear without Grigorii killing Dmitri.

"What kind of doctor are you?" I said, stepping behind the screen when Masha exited. White gowns hung in a row, the old kind that wrapped around your waist like in a black-and-white movie set in a mental asylum.

"That's really not your concern," Dr. Gorshkov said. "On the table, Masha. There's a good girl."

I peered around the screen, taking my sweet time getting undressed. Gorshkov turned his back to me, and he rolled an instrument tray over to Masha. "How are you feeling, my dear?"

My dear? He could be anyone's family doctor, checking perfunctorily on his patient as he swabbed her arm with alcohol and grabbed a syringe. Everything was old in this place, like the set of a horror movie. *Dawn of the Former Soviet Werewolf Dead.* All we needed was a shopping mall.

"I'm tired all the time," Masha said. "And I threw up this morning, before you brought that weirdo woman into my cell. I don't like her."

I curled my lip. Either she was trying to throw Belikov and the doctor off the scent, or she was a real brat, even in captivity.

"Gene therapy isn't a walk in the park, Masha," said the doctor. "You are becoming something so much stronger than what you are now. All of my patients were strong, and were rewarded. You must bear these ills with a good attitude or you won't reap the rewards they did."

"It's taking so long," Masha complained. "I feel sick all the time."

"Masha," the doctor sighed. "You are my special child, yes?"

"Yes," she muttered, slouching.

Gorshkov withdrew the syringe and capped it, handing Masha a bandage. "Then trust me when I say that I will tell you everything you need to know about the process and that feeling sick is normal." He patted her cheek. "You are a healthy girl. You'll get through it."

I stepped from behind the curtain. "So I'm guessing this isn't a spa day."

Dr. Gorshkov frowned at me. "Mr. Belikov put you in my care, so I'll thank you to stop with that mouthy manner you have. Sit on the table."

"Did someone say gene therapy?" I said, turning over the possible permutations of what that could mean in my head. None of them made me jump for joy. "What are you doing to us? What changes?"

"*Sit.*" The doctor's eyes darkened, and he took up a new syringe, pointing it at the exam table.

"All right, all right," I said, sitting down. The cold metal made my legs break into goose bumps. "Stab away, Bones," I said. "Hey, can I get you to say 'He's dead, Jim'? The accent would *make* that."

The doctor glared at me as he grabbed my arm, thumped the skin to bring up a vein and jabbed the syringe in. I let out a small yelp. The large-bore needle hurt like a bitch.

"You talk a great deal and don't say anything," he muttered. "Save your breath and keep quiet. Mr. Belikov likes girls who are obedient."

"I could give a flying fuck what Mr. Belikov likes," I muttered. Gorshkov jerked the needle out and didn't offer me a bandage. I grabbed a piece of cotton off the surgical tray and pressed it over the wound. While I was at it, I palmed the small pair of surgical scissors lying next to the gauze pads. Never hurts to be prepared. You can improvise a lot of things with scissors.

The doctor walked my blood over to a centrifuge and set up a vial, spinning it. "We'll type your DNA, and we'll see what you're suitable for." He gestured me to the padded hospital bed, where Masha was sitting and staring at her knees. "You wait over there. No talking. Talking disturbs my concentration."

I went and slumped next to Masha. The gown was too small for me, and it itched in all the nooks and crannies. "Well, he's a bundle of fun."

"I'm not supposed to talk in the exam room," Masha whispered. "Mr. Belikov gets angry."

I reached over to the bed stand and grabbed a prescription pad and a pen. *What is G doing?* I scribbled.

Masha looked at me, at Gorshkov, who was watching the centrifuge spin with the gentle, dopey eyes of a toddler staring at Barney. She grabbed the pad and scribbled back. *Is my dad really @ Stop 13?*

I nodded.

Giving me injections I don't know what of I'm sick all the time.

Gorshkov moved my blood from the centrifuge to a set of test tubes with a pipette, the same process I'd seen at the police academy when we learned about DNA typing and matching.

What is G looking for? I asked Masha.

She bit her lip and wrote. *A perfect match.*

"File cabinets," she said, her voice barely there at all. "Hundreds of them. There are all of these files, medical files. I saw them once when Belikov took me away to . . ." She went quiet, crimson climbing into her cheeks.

I put my hand over hers and gave it a squeeze. Gorshkov's head snapped up, like he could smell insurgency. "No touching! You will sit quietly and behave yourselves."

The next person who told me to behave myself was going to get a foot straight into the ass. "Stick with me," I whispered to Masha. "I won't let them do anything else to you."

She chewed her lip. "Promise?"

I nodded. "Cross my heart and hope to die."

Masha gave me a smile that was almost grateful before she dropped her eyes again.

"No match," Gorshkov announced, his voice sharp with disappointment. "You are useless, Joanne. Mikel, return both of them to holding."

I stood up. "I'm not the girl of your dreams, Doc? Color me crushed."

"Go!" he snapped at me, pointing to the way out through the decontamination chamber. My jaw tightened. I could confront the smug little worm, or I could stick with Masha. I exhaled, forcing myself to stay docile, and followed her out, listening to the door clang shut behind us like a tomb.

CHAPTER 22

When the outside door rolled back, Grigorii was waiting for us. "Oh, look," I said. "It's Prince Charming, the pimp. Be still my heart."

"Mikel, take Masha back to her room," Grigorii said. "Luna and I have an exciting development to discuss." He took me by the arm, like your boyfriend would, gentle and firm.

"Be careful," I said. "You're going to sweep me right off of my feet."

"That's the idea," said Grigorii. He led me away from Masha, until we were in a hospital ward, beds and musty curtains hanging like discarded shrouds.

"Alone at last," Grigorii said, sitting down on one of the beds, the sheets still crisp even though his weight raised a cloud of dust. I sneezed.

"Is this your idea of a romantic getaway?"

"Emil says that you're not a genetic match for my endeavor here," he said. "Which leaves me with a problem, because now I have no way to make a profit from you."

"Yeah, about your endeavor," I said. "What exactly are a geneticist and a gangster up to in this musty old place? Is it aliens? Please say aliens."

Grigorii reached out and tugged at the strings of my hospital gown. "If you'd let me finish, I would say that I'm not sure I want to profit from you."

I tried to tamp down the reflexive twitch at his touch. He noticed it, and dropped his hand. "Why? Do I disgust you?"

"You've got a screw loose," I said. "And you're the bottom scrapings of the magick gene pool. Sorry if I'm not moistening my panties at the thought of getting next to you."

"It's this, or I execute your friend and leave you as an experimental subject for Gorshkov. He's not only a bioengineer, you know. He has . . . other hobbies. We met when he was my customer in Moscow, before I moved to more tolerant climes."

All of my instincts shouted for me to fight, because that's my training—you take control of a situation and if the other person won't give control, you fight for it, make a fuss, cause a scene until you're out of danger. But I'd tried with Grigorii, and he'd almost stopped my heart with a few hundred magick volts. The were paced at the edges of my mind and I let it creep in.

I was only going to get one chance here.

"Can I talk while we do this?" I asked, putting one knee up on the bed and exposing a generous length of thigh. Grigorii's smirk curled to life.

"Go right ahead, my dear. Although I must ask you to please refrain from attacking me again. I'm not into that sort of kink."

"What sort are you into?" I purred. Grigorii's mouth pulled down. I pasted a dopey smile on my face in return. *Easy, Wilder. Don't lay it on too thick.*

"I don't believe in discussing my laundry list of perversions before the actual perversion begins," he said, running his fingers up my leg, grazing against the junction of my thigh.

"So," I said, tugging at the collar of my hospital gown, exposing the top curve of my breasts, "let me see if I'm getting all of this. This is a bioengineering lab. Gorshkov is doing gene therapy on Masha and on more before her. Masha is a were. So I'm thinking that you're doing some evil little experiment to manipulate Masha's were DNA."

I stood back from Grigorii and undid the ties on my gown, letting it pool around my ankles. "How right am I?"

He gave me an admiring nod. "The Soviet regime left behind many interesting projects that someone with vision could use to their benefit. My family has political ties, and a certain ambitious program came to my attention. I hired Gorshkov to implement it." Taking my hand, he drew me close enough to feel his body heat and reached out his free hand for my waist. "Now enough talk. Come to me, Luna," he purred, his tongue flicking out to caress his pale lips.

"You know," I said, running my hand down his jaw in return. His skin felt like wax, stiff and dead. "This is a very perverse way to make me earn my freedom."

"We'll see how you perform," Grigorii said. "And then I'll decide what gets done with you. To you." He guided my hand to his fly. "Get on your knees and take me with your mouth."

I gave him a wink and sank into a crouch. Grigorii's ego was really something—he honestly thought he was completely safe letting a pissy were female at the most sensitive part of his anatomy after I'd already fought him off once.

Idiot.

"Good woman." Grigorii stroked my hair. "They all come in with fire in their eyes, that entitled Western spark in their gaze, and they all break sooner or later and realize that submission is what's best."

I pulled my gown closer with my foot, dropped my hand to feel for the scissors in my sleeve.

"Submission is the only road to survival for people in your situation, my dear," Grigorii continued. "Don't you think I'm right?" He tugged at my scalp. "Tell me you think I'm right."

I looked up at his eyes and drew my lips back to show my fangs. "You know what I think?" I gripped the scissors, the cool metal slipping in the sweat of my palms. "I think you talk too gods-damned much."

Grigorii's face twisted. "I'll teach you to speak to me that way, whore . . ."

He stopped, just froze, letting out a small strangled sound as I buried the scissors in his groin with all of my strength, blood flowing fast, staining the wool of his obscenely expensive suit.

There were no screams, no words, just an expression of pure shock in Grigorii's eyes. I stood up, careful to keep myself away from the blood.

"Good news and bad news, Grigorii," I said, pulling the gown back on. "Good news is, I missed all your major arteries, so you probably won't bleed to death." I tugged the gown's strings tight, up to my throat. I couldn't stand being naked under his paralyzed, accusing gaze for another second. "Bad news is that unlike your buddy Rasputin, I doubt you'll bounce back from this."

Grigorii let out a hiss, a rasping screech of pain, his hands trying to stanch the bleeding, but it was too late. I saw his pupils dilate, black with shock, and his already white skin go cadaver-colored.

I could put a compress on the wound, stop the bleeding long enough for Grigorii to stumble downstairs to Dr. Gorshkov. I could elevate his feet, cover him in a heavy blanket to stave off shock and roll him there myself on one of these beds.

"Please . . ." Grigorii managed. He was on the floor now, a slow dark crimson pool spreading from his wound. I could get him up in a fireman's carry, because he was a small guy and I was strong, and run him back to the lab.

"Please . . ."

I didn't do any of the things I could have, except turn my back and walk out of the hospital ward, my bare feet not making a sound on the linoleum.

And I didn't feel anything when I did.

Once I'd cleared the ward I broke into a run. I had to make a break for it before the doctor figured out what was going on and burned the place to the ground to cover his tracks.

Masha. She was my first priority. Retracing my steps to the holding cells, I came upon the switchboard operator, who stared at me gape-jawed.

I slammed his forehead once into the controls for the cell doors, hard, and he slid out of his chair and curled on the floor with a soft moan. I hit the switch for cell sixteen and jogged down the corridor.

"Masha." I jerked my thumb over my shoulder. "We gotta go."

"Yeah," she mumbled. "There might be a problem there."

"No time for teenage angst, sweetie," I said. "Up and run, now. This is a one-time special offer."

"It's not that," she said. "I'm not feeling so good after that injection . . ." She tried to stand and her stance was drunken, her knees buckling after a few seconds.

"*Crap*," I hissed under my breath and came into the cell, grabbing her by one arm and hauling her against me. "You hold on to me and don't let go, no matter what. Understand?"

"I feel sick," she said, her head lolling against me. "I'm seeing everything double . . ."

"Hey!" I said, grabbing her chin. "I know you're stronger than this, Masha. Your father told me what hell you can give. Now suck it up and walk with me or we're both going to die in here. You want that?"

"No . . ." she moaned.

"Didn't think so. March." We made an odd creature, half-stumbling and half-running down the hall.

It wasn't difficult to find the way back to the door I'd come in, but getting out would be another matter.

We were in sight of the security cage when my grand plan shattered like an ice sculpture in July. A burst of automatic gunfire pocked the wall over my head with divots. Masha slid to the floor with a scream and I followed her, covering her body with mine.

"It's not that easy," said Mikel, walking over to us, his Kalashnikov hanging loosely from his crooked arm. "Haven't you learned by now?"

"You should be less worried about me and more worried about your boss," I said. "He wasn't looking so good when I left him."

Mikel frowned, turning over the possibilities. I was patient. If brains were computers, he'd still be running Windows 98. "Grigorii is a witch," he said finally. "This is just a bluff."

"Steel isn't great for magick-users, and witches can bleed out," I said, my eyes on the rifle. "Just like their hench-thugs."

Mikel glared. "What does that mean?"

I lashed out with my foot and knocked the rifle from his grasp, grabbing it as it slid to the floor. "It means that I meant what I said," I told him. Mikel threw up his hands, but I drove the butt of the Kalashnikov into his face and heard bone snap. I took the clip out of the rifle and dropped it, my heart thudding with the thrill of near-death.

"I told you," I said to Mikel.

He leaped at me again, with surprising fortitude for a plain human who'd just had his face smashed in. Not bright, but sure as hell persistent.

I fell as he grabbed my ankle, and gave a cry as a sharp sting drove through my calf. Mikel had a knife and he was raising it to slash me again.

"Luna!" Masha's small hands grabbed me and pulled me backward, into a small, dark box that smelled like rat poison.

"You can't run from me!" Mikel howled, but a door rolled shut and we began to descend, lights blinking past to show floors as the elevator dropped us into the belly of the lab.

"Where does this go?" I demanded.

"No idea," Masha said. "The lower floors are closed off because they're, like, a safety hazard. No one goes down here except Dr. Gorshkov. It's where the file room is."

"You figured out a lot in two weeks," I said.

"Not much else to do." She shrugged. "Except think about how my mother was probably going insane thinking I'd run off with my boyfriend."

"Your mother was worried sick," I said. Masha snorted.

"Whatever."

"You know, Masha . . ." I started, and then sighed. She coughed, a wet sound that indicated a deep infection, then shrugged at me in the dimness.

"What?"

"I was a lot like you," I said. "And believe me, there's plenty of time to make stupid fuckups about men and partying and your life in general when you're out of the house."

"I can't believe you're giving me a stern pep talk in a condemned elevator while we escape from some freak with a machine gun," she muttered.

"Blow me off if you want," I said. "But if I'd given my mother a little less stress, I wouldn't be a were, and I wouldn't be here, and believe me, sweetie, neither would you."

The elevator ground to a stop and Masha pulled herself to her feet. "Finally."

The door rolled back to dampness, darkness, a slow dripping far in the distance. I felt along the wall and found a panel of switches, which I flipped at random until the lights hissed on. One fizzed and went out immediately, water causing a shower of sparks.

"Comforting," I said. "Reminds me of my office at home."

"Your office is in the basement?" Masha snorted. "Who'd you piss off?"

"Bomb shelter," I corrected. "And too many people to count."

The elevator started to go up again, and I cursed. "Mikel. Come on, we need a place to hide."

We followed the precarious light trail through a maze of corridors, each danker and mustier than the last.

"My dad talked about you," Masha said. "When he came back. Said you were a real bitch and broke his heart over stupid reasons."

"Your dad always did have a way with words," I muttered. My calf was sticky with blood and I stopped to examine it.

"Are you okay?" Masha said anxiously, bending close. I gave her a look and she backed away, the tough teenager face back in place. "I mean, if you croak, who's going to take on that freak with the assault rifle?"

"It's only a flesh wound," I said, giving her a smile. She didn't react. *"Monty Python and the Holy Grail*?" I sighed. "Never mind. Sometimes I forget that you grew up in a country devoid of decadent Western ideas."

"What's next, an 'in Soviet Russia' joke?" she said. "You Americans seem to love those."

"Not bad," I said. "You've got a real mouth on you. I did, too, at your age. Still do. Don't lose it. A big mouth can be your best weapon."

"My mom and dad both tell me I talk too much," Masha said tightly, and clammed up.

I heard the elevator bell sound far behind us, and footsteps. Blood drifted to my nose, along with metal sweat and copper fear. At least now, I had the upper hand even if Mikel had the gun. "In here," I said, gesturing her through a door marked with bright red lettering.

"I dunno," Masha said. "I can't read Kazakh but in Russian it says DANGER—DO NOT ENTER and some other crap I can't make out 'cause it's all faded. That doesn't look promising."

"Trust me," I said. "Come on."

The door led us into a long room, empty of anything at all. I tried the switch and only darkness responded. "Perfect," I said. "Stay behind the door, and stay quiet."

Mikel was calling something out in Ukrainian as he paced down the hallways toward us, singsong and high-pitched.

"Come out, come out, wherever you are," Masha whispered in translation. Mikel's footsteps stopped outside the door, and everything was quiet for a moment except for my heartbeat and Masha's.

And a third, far away in the shadows, thumping strong. A heartbeat that belonged to something I hadn't seen or scented.

Oh, Hex me.

"Masha," I hissed. She goggled at me. "Stay calm," I said. "But you need to know there's someone else in here."

"*What*?" she squeaked.

"I hear you, bitch," Mikel caroled from outside the door. "You think I wouldn't find you? I'll find you and I'll . . ." He shoved the door open and the dim light from the hall barred across the scarred cement floor, laced with creeping mold.

It captured the body in ragged green hiking shorts and a safari vest, crouched in the corner, and it highlighted the needlelike, inch-long fangs rimming the man's mouth when he opened it and let out a snarl that could curdle milk.

Mikel cursed, jumping backward, but it was too late. In a streak, the thing leaped, out the door and onto Mikel's chest, going for the blood on his face from my blow.

There was a crunch. A scream. A sound of tearing ligament and bone.

"Masha," I said. "Move. Now."

"But I don't want to go near that thing!" she wailed.

I grabbed her by the arm and shook her. "Listen! Now is not the time to panic. Stay by me and do what I say and stop crying!"

I was being a real bitch, but we didn't have time to hang around playing with whatever that thing was. I'd seen those fangs before, long as shark's teeth and reaching for my throat. Anton and his strange strength, his eerie movements, his scentless silence as he came upon me, terrified and hiding like prey.

Anton and the thing in the hallway mauling Mikel were the same, except that this one seemed a lot hungrier and a lot more pissed.

"Okay," I said to Masha. "We're going to step out and we're going to run for the elevator. Got it?"

She nodded numbly. "It's too busy feeding on

Mikel to worry about us," I reassured her, and prayed to the bright lady it was true. "Just run, and don't look back."

"O-okay," she stuttered.

"Go!" I shouted, and shoved her through the door. Masha skidded in the blood, righted herself and took off running. I followed her, careful not to trip on Mikel's twitching legs, and thought that I'd managed to evade this latest nightmare when crushing weight landed on my back.

My legs buckled and I went down under the were's weight. He snarled, raking claws through my hair, trying to expose my neck. I drove my elbow backward into his face and rolled out from under him when he reared in pain.

"Luna?" Masha had stopped and was peering around the corner.

"Masha, go!" I screamed. "Your father is in the village! *Run!*"

The were caught me again and I turned around and hit him in the face, hard. That was my job now, my one goal in life. Keep myself between the monster and Masha.

He shook off the blow and returned it, making my jaws snap together and my head ring. He was impossibly strong for his short, squat frame and his eyes were red with burst blood vessels, where they weren't black from pupils dilated in territorial rage.

This was his kingdom, and I was a trespasser. The only way I was getting out alive was to beat him, to be the stronger, dominant were.

Easy, right? He had claws that were obsidian black and sharper than razors. They caught the front of my gown, went through to flesh, scraped red on my sternum.

My feet slicked on Mikel's blood, and I fell, hitting the back of my head hard on the cement. The monster crouched above me, and I knew a death strike when I saw one. I wasn't strong enough as a plain human to put a dent in him, and the decision came easily to me, with none of the overwhelming sense of failure that had accompanied my last partial phase, in Grigorii's brothel.

My fangs grew, my claws sprouted and my spine rippled, giving me the crouch of a predator. I rolled over, coming up in a lunge, feeling my thickened leg muscles launch me to meet the other were in midair. The color bled out of my vision and I snapped at the were's throat, tasting blood.

He pulled me off him like I was a small, annoying toy dog, and threw me. I caught air, and slammed into the wall with a thud that cracked my ribs on the impact side.

I cried out and lost the phase, felt the were slipping away to lick its wounds.

Cracked ribs aren't serious, but they hurt like you're on fire. I curled into the fetal position, struggling to draw breath, to not scream, hot, silent tears soaking my face as the pain blackened my vision.

CHAPTER 23

The thought that I might be dying came through with curious clarity. It didn't bother me too much. Between getting my bell rung by the wall and the blood loss, I was going into shock.

That didn't bother me much, either.

I watched the thing's shadow advance on me, step by step, lips pulling back and nostrils going wide. It was taking its time with the kill. Scenting it.

Then it crouched, and leaped.

I braced myself for a strike that never came. Another shadow intercepted the were in midair, a red wolf the size of a horse that locked its teeth around the creature's throat and slammed it into the ground.

The creature let out a squeal, and then its massive paw came up and raked down the wolf's side, flaying the flesh along its ribs. The wolf let go, and they tangled together for a moment.

Masha screamed from a long way off. *"Daddy!"*

I managed to sit up, ignoring the pain and the dizziness, the cool dampness of my own blood soaking the gown. Dmitri was here. He'd come for me.

Not me. Masha. Who was running at the creature, ready to help her father.

I caught her around the waist before she could get her head taken off, and she screamed and thrashed against me, which didn't do my ribs any favors. "Let me go! We gotta help him!"

"I will!" I shouted. "Getting killed is not gonna do him any favors!"

She went limp at that, and I let her go as a horrible snarl rose from the creature's throat. It was hurt badly—Dmitri's wolf teeth had found a mark in its throat, and its front was a mess of gore.

Dmitri wasn't doing so hot either, though. As they circled and swiped at one another, his back legs tangled and he caught claws across his snout.

"Hey!" I shouted at the creature, clapping my hands. I needed to distract it. Had to. It snarled, but didn't take its eyes off Dmitri, and this time its teeth closed on Dmitri's front leg, pulling him off balance and exposing his belly, claws digging into the soft area behind Dmitri's ribs. Dmitiri howled, and the sound hurt me more than any of the creature's punishment. It was pure animal pain and rage, the last sound something made before it was beaten.

My bare foot came down on a chunk of cement the creature had knocked out of the wall, and I scooped it up and hurled it with all the strength I had left at the thing's head. It cracked against the creature's skull and drew blood, and it turned on me.

"Come on," I growled, spreading my arms. "Try it."

All in all, it looked away for a split second, but it was enough.

Dmitri twisted his spine, his jaws closing on the creature and, with a shake and an echoing *crack*, its neck snapped.

The thing landed bonelessly on top of Dmitri and went still. Blood stained the floor, scent filling the air, and I tried not to choke as I went to my knees in the pool and shoved the thing off Dmitri.

He was phasing back, slowly, unconsciousness or pain turning him from wolf back to man. Masha knelt on his other side, hand pressed over her mouth and eyes enormous. "Is he . . ."

Dmitri groaned, and his eyelids fluttered. "Shit. That could've gone better."

I swallowed hard and tried to keep my voice steady. "You got that right."

"I . . ." He tried to sit up and failed. "I don't want to alarm you here, Luna, but I can't really feel my legs."

I looked down. I'd seen plenty of broken bodies, so it wasn't as bad a shock as it otherwise could have been.

I also couldn't lie to myself about what I was seeing.

A massive set of gashes worked their way across Dmitri's ribs. His abdomen was a mess—I couldn't even say what had been there. The claws had gone in deep, probably down to the spine. Everywhere else was bloody and beaten. Dmitri's arm was sitting at an odd angle, a compound fracture from where the creature had grabbed him. My mind cataloged all this while I felt the blood go out of my head and saw my vision tunnel down.

Dmitri picked up the look on my face. "That bad, huh?"

"Dad . . ." Masha's voice was thin and rattling as paper.

"You're . . ." I gulped. "You're gonna be fine."

Dmitri put his good hand on my arm. His palm

was slicked with the creature's blood. Or his own. It didn't matter. "Don't lie, Luna."

"I . . ." I couldn't make any more words come. This couldn't be happening. He had to be all right. Were healing would come, and he'd be all right. I'd get him out of here, save him like he'd saved me, and he'd still be alive in the morning.

"When you didn't come back I followed you," Dmitri rasped. "And it's a good thing I did. Now you two need to get up and get out of here before anything else comes for you." He squeezed with his good hand. "This is all right, Luna. Don't you think different."

"I'm not leaving you," I managed. I couldn't breathe. It wasn't my ribs. Dmitri had to be all right. He couldn't die because of me.

Dmitri's face softened. "I want you to. Maybe it wasn't true an hour ago, but I want you to leave, Luna. Go. And take care of Masha."

At her name, Masha's eyes spilled over and she sobbed, putting her face against his. "Dad, I don't want you to go."

"Sometimes it doesn't work out that way," he murmured. His voice was getting distant, dreamy. He was slipping. "I love you, baby. All right? You go on now."

Dmitri looked me in the eye as Masha sat back, sobbing. "It was a hell of a ride, Luna. I'm glad . . . I got to see you." A little blood trickled from between his lips, and he coughed. "Now go. Don't make me tell you again."

I held on for just a second longer. "I'm sorry, Dmitri," I said. Sorry for more than this. Sorry it had ever come to this. Just gods-damn sorry for everything.

"Me, too," he whispered, and tried to say something else, but the last of his air went gently out of him, and Dmitri stilled.

"Luna?" Masha swallowed a sob. "What do we do?"

I got to my feet, and for her sake tried to hide the fact I was shaking. Dmitri was gone.

The fact sat in my belly like a stone. Like the creature had reached into my chest, too, and taken something vital away.

I wasn't in love with Dmitri anymore, but he was gone. And he'd done it for me, and for Masha.

I'd been wrong about him. That hurt most of all.

"I don't want to stay here . . ." Masha said, louder. She was panicking. She should be.

Dmitri wanted me to take care of her. He'd let us get away. It was up to me to make sure we did.

"I know," I said. My mind was already compartmentalizing, my cop-brain, my trauma-brain, shoving what had just happened down under layers of numbness that anyone who works in my profession has to develop, or go crazy. "Neither do I." I reached out and pulled her away from Dmitri's body. His eyes were open, and I crouched and shut them.

Then I stood up and turned my back. "We have to do something before we leave, Masha. Can you handle that?"

She nodded. Too slow, dopey. The shock would keep her moving, I hoped, and get us out of here before the full horror of what had happened came back. I hoped it would work for me, too.

"You said there was a file room," I said. "Take me to it." I wasn't shaking anymore. I felt cold, singular, driven in my purpose.

"What's the point?" Masha muttered. "Couldn't stop them. Couldn't stop them from . . ."

"Belikov and his gang made this happen," I said. "We're getting the evidence of what they were up to before we leave here."

I took Masha's hand again. "Come on. Show me where the doctor took you."

She shook her head, trying to sit back down near her father's body.

"Masha," I said. "I know you're strong. You shouldn't have to see this, or remember this, but I need you. You've got to keep it together just a little longer. I'm sorry to ask, but we need these files if we're going to make your dad doing what he did mean anything."

After a moment, she jerked her head at a nearby door. "Here," Masha said, pushing through to the file room, which was an Indiana Jones-esque maze of file cabinets, some on their sides, set at odd angles like slumbering sharp-cornered beasts. Papers blew around my bare ankles in the air stirred by our passage, and dust hung like sunbeams in the stale air.

Only one file drawer had handprints in the layer of grime that coated everything, and I opened the drawer. There were stacks of files, the results of blood tests and DNA typing, which were gibberish to me but that I was sure Dr. Kronen would be very interested in.

"Photographs," Masha said. "Grigorii had pictures that he liked to look at, during. He showed me one."

I dug deeper into the files and found a stack of pictures, each neatly labeled with the date and the code for the subject of the photo.

They were horrific. I worked Homicide for five years and saw plenty of crap that would send a normal person to therapy for the next decade, but these—there was a malice to them, the photographer glorying in the monster he had made. "And what monsters they are," I murmured. I shoved the litany of deformed limbs, lesions, the marks of torture and pain, the fusion of were and human gone wrong, back into a folder. "Let's get out of here," I said to Masha. "And get you home."

CHAPTER 24

The train ride back to Kiev was interminable. Masha slept, the heavy coma sleep of trauma victims who can finally relax and allow themselves to feel safe.

She would need a counselor, medication, possibly for years to deal with the nightmares that would come.

But that wasn't up to me now. I would give her back to her mother and I'd go home. I'd done what Dmitri had asked of me.

Margarita folded Masha into her arms at the train station in Kiev, crying and stroking her hair. She didn't notice I was alone for a minute, but then her face went slack.

I explained, as gently as I could, what had happened. What she would need to do for Masha. I don't think much of it sank in, but by then the numbness that I'd let steal over me was real. I couldn't muster the strength to do more than hug Masha good-bye.

I wasn't needed anymore.

I walked out to the cab line at the front of the station, where I managed to convey to the bemused driver that I needed to go to the United States embassy.

Explaining things to the consul was less trouble

than I expected, possibly because I was dirty, covered in scrapes and sporting two major injuries.

I had to call Bryson to verify my status as a cop and he let out a yell. "Wilder! Fuckin' a! You're all right!"

"As 'all right' as can be expected after two weeks in Kiev," I said. "I'm going to put the consul on the phone, David. Try not to swear at him, all right?"

After I convinced the diplomatic liaison that I was who I said I was, he issued me a temporary passport and I booked a flight back to California. First class. I felt it was the least I deserved after being kidnapped and sold into sexual slavery and then putting a stop to inhuman scientific experiments funded by the Russian mob.

So much for my resolution to cut my spending after my cottage burned down. If that wasn't a sign to downsize, I didn't know what was.

I flew to Munich, and from there to San Francisco, taking a puddle-jumper flight to Nocturne International.

Will was waiting for me at the gate. I had planned to be calm, and stoic, but I practically fell into his arms and buried my face against the lapel of his suit—the gray wool, my favorite. I let the tears come for the first time since I'd been abducted, silent and hot on my face, leaving a trail of moisture and mascara against Will's shirt.

"I'm sorry," I choked. "I made a mess of everything."

"Don't talk," Will whispered, kissing the top of my head, holding me in a viselike grip that his slim frame belied. "Don't say anything. Just let me hold you and convince myself you're really here."

I breathed in Will's scent, soap and aftershave and the sharp prickle of magick underneath, from the curse running in his blood. "It's good to be home," I whispered.

"Good to have you," Will said, finally releasing me. "Jesus, doll, you look like death warmed over."

"Feel like it, too," I said.

"How about a bath and a change of clothes?" Will said. "My loft is closer."

I shouldered the bag with Grigorii Belikov's laptop inside. That, I'd made sure to retrieve before Masha and I left the lab. I only regretted that it wasn't Grigorii and Dr. Gorshkov, in handcuffs. "Fine," I said. "Lead the way."

Will got us back to his condo without breaking any major traffic laws and started a bath for me with the frilly kind of soap for bubbles, before sitting on the toilet lid as I stripped off my clothes painfully. "I'll run a load of laundry," he said. "You should have plenty of stuff to wear from the last time you were over."

"Burn those fucking clothes," I said. "They smell like death."

Will's eyes narrowed at the sight of my ribs, which had grown a spectacular blue-purple bruise, like a cluster of exotic orchids under my skin. "Who did that to you?"

"Something that's dead now," I said honestly. Will passed a hand through his hair, his gesture of nervousness, his tell. I'd missed it so much that I had to restrain myself from kissing him, bruising him in turn.

"I said I wasn't going to ask myself what happened when you were abducted. I said I was going to wait and let you tell me when you were ready."

I paused, in my bra and jeans. "Will . . ."

"I drove myself crazy during the time you were gone," he said. "Thinking about what I knew about the trafficking rings the ATF had been involved in busting, and thinking about you with Dmitri Sandovsky."

That was all it took. I started to cry, my face crumpling up like I was five.

"N-nothing . . ." I started. "Nothing happened . . . He's dead, Will."

"Oh, Christ," Will said, coming to me and pulling me to his chest. "I'm so sorry, Luna. What an asshole thing to say."

I looked at my bloodstained toes, at the Majolica pattern on the tiles on Will's bathroom floor. Memories flooded back, the were sending them to me as vividly as if they were still happening. The crate. The man in my cell after Grigorii had decided to dispose of me. The sound his neck had made, snapping in the small space.

Dmitri's last breath, as his fingers slipped off of my skin.

I've killed people before, good shootings all, and I still always felt the bottomless pit just beyond my toes. Now, I felt nothing. I didn't have remorse. I didn't have anything inside me except a monster and an empty place where everything else used to be.

Will let me go, holding me at arm's length. "Just tell me what to do, Luna."

"I need to be alone," I said, wrapping my arms around me. "It's not you, it's just . . . I haven't had privacy for weeks. Could you . . . ?"

Will nodded, jumping up too quickly, almost tangling in his own legs. "Of course. Of course I can."

He backed out and shut the door, which I locked. Not because I didn't feel safe with Will, but because it was the first time I'd been able to do it since Nikolai Rostov had kidnapped me.

I slipped out of my clothes, kicking them into the corner, and proceeded to scrub every inch of my skin that didn't hurt too much to accept soap and water.

While I scrubbed, I thought. Thinking may not have been my best course of action at the time, but I couldn't stop my mind from unspooling once Will set me on the trail.

I'd killed someone in cold blood, purely for survival, and I didn't feel the least bit guilty about it. He was a rapist who got his rocks off with girls who were too scared or used up to fight back, true, but he was still dead and I was still the instrument of his passing.

What mattered more was that I'd let the were take me again and again, and I hadn't fought it, hadn't tried to bring the beast under the control of my human side like I'd done so successfully for the past year. I'd let the monster run, and I'd enjoyed it.

Will could never know.

That decision settled like a small smooth stone in my gut. I kicked out the plug on the tub and stepped out, wrapping myself up in towels. The steam drifted around me and I scrubbed off the mirror with one palm.

Lily Dubois was standing behind me, reflected in the mirror.

I started, jerking around to find the space behind me empty. When I looked back at the steamy glass, she was still there. "Mirrors used to be made of silver," she said. "My mom told me. Good thing for you they stopped doing that, huh?"

"Lily . . ." I said.

"I told you I wasn't going away," she snarled. "I'm a restless fucking spirit and you're the poor bastard that I'm going to haunt until I get some fucking justice."

This was different than the dreams, than something I could brush off or chalk up to fatigue or fear. I was awake—I had the pruny fingers and toes to show for it.

"Lily . . ." I sighed again, and dropped my gaze from the glass. "I'm listening," I said.

"You want to bring me justice," Lily stated. "And if that's really true, you might want to get off your dumb cop ass and start looking a little closer to home."

I glared at her. "You know what, I don't need that attitude from any snotty teenage girl, especially one who's already dead."

Lily let out a high, musical giggle, then a patch of steam drifted across my vision and she vanished.

Will pounded on the door. "Luna? Luna, who are you talking to?"

"No one," I sighed. "I'll be out in a minute." I got dressed in a pair of my own sweatpants and a jersey from Cedar Hill Community College, then ran a comb through my hair before tying it up. My hair dryer and all of my product was still at my apartment. Will and I hadn't gotten to that stage yet.

He looked up from the dining room table when I came out of the bathroom. "What's this? You jack someone for their laptop in the mother country?"

"It belongs to a guy named Grigorii Belikov," I said.

Will was trying to make nice, make light of our situation, and I wasn't going to point out that he was doing a pretty piss-poor job. I was so starved for normalcy I would have watched him write a grocery list.

"Belikov? How Bond villain," Will muttered.

"He was the ringleader of the operation in Kiev," I said. "Sex slaves, blood sport, selling girls into bondage, all of the good stuff. He and his sister were in charge of the whole thing."

"I can take this down to the Bureau in the morning," Will mused. "Let our tech people have a crack at it. Send what we have to Interpol and hope that they push for prosecution in a country that views interrogation more as a sport than a process." He left the laptop and went into the kitchen. "You hungry? You have to be."

"I am," I said. "But more tired. I'm going to take a nap."

Will nodded. "I'll be here. Just in the next room. I'm not leaving."

I went over to him and wrapped my arms around him, feeling the tears start again. "Thank you," I whispered, "for that."

"Doll," Will said against my hair, "for that, you never have to thank me."

Tucking myself into Will's king-sized bed, I finally let myself relax. I had been holding on to the thought that I hadn't really escaped, that Grigorii or Rostov was going to burst in and wake me up, prove that I was still locked in some dank hole back in Kiev.

The thoughts faded as I drifted off to sleep, but the dreams did not. I'd have them for years, if not forever. You can try to forget, but your dreams never do.

Just something else I was going to have to live with.

* * *

When I woke up, it was because I sensed another body standing over me. I lashed out, found myself pinned by blankets and six-hundred-thread-count sheets, and came upright, panting.

"Easy," Will said. "I didn't mean to wake you."

Sweat had broken out all over me, and my ribs still poked when I breathed in deeply. Bones take a long time to heal, even for a were.

"No, I'm sorry," I said. I was going to have to get a handle on this paranoia sooner rather than later. I was safe. I was home.

"I just needed a tie," Will said. "I'm off to take the laptop to our techs."

"I'm coming with you," I said, throwing back the covers. I could see through the shades that it was morning. "You let me sleep," I said accusingly.

"Fourteen hours," Will agreed, knotting a plum silk tie that set off his eyes. "Figured you needed it, doll, or you'd wake up."

"Just give me a minute to find some real clothes," I said, digging through my side of the closet. A pencil skirt, a blouse that didn't match, and a Ramones T-shirt. Fantastic.

"Luna," Will said gently. "You've just been through a huge trauma and you're pretty banged up. Maybe you should stay in today?"

I inhaled, my reflexive snarl at being told what to do building. Will sighed. "And that sounded like patronizing crap, but I'm worried about you, doll. You're still shaky on your feet."

"Will," I said. "I really don't want to be alone. Can you just let me come to the office?" Admitting that the thought of his empty loft sent shivers through me felt like the worst kind of cowardice, but there it was. Last night, I couldn't wait to get him out of the room and now I was clinging to him like some wide-eyed victim in a bad action movie.

Could I be more pathetic?

"Sure thing," Will said. "I think there's a pair of pants that are yours in the top drawer. Hard to be sure, what with all of my other lady friends . . ."

I felt a smile twitch in spite of my mood. "You're a jackass."

"Yeah, and that's just one of my many endearing qualities." Will slipped on his shoulder rig and suit jacket. I pulled on the pants, which turned out to be a pair of black Dickies I'd used to paint the kitchen in my new apartment that still bore wide swaths of "Summertime Lemonade," and the Ramones shirt. I looked about as far from official as you could get, but I cared about as much as I cared about the feelings of the criminals I'd sent to jail.

Will drove us, his Mustang purring through the early morning streets. The trees were budding and a few flowers were poking their heads out. Spring had started while I'd been away. "You tell Bryson and the SCS you're back yet?" he said. "And your cousin?"

"Holding off on all three until tonight," I said. "I needed a day to just recuperate, get my head straightened out."

Will, to his credit, just nodded and pulled the Mustang into his reserved space in the parking garage underneath the federal building.

We rode the elevator to the ATF's suite with a bunch of FBI agents. My outfit got more than a few glances. The ATF offices are basically a cube farm, with a few offices to the back for senior agents. The ATF, unlike the FBI or the DEA, lets agents pick and run their own cases, each agent an autonomous unit.

The tech room was in the back, a low space crammed with computer equipment and a few shaggy-haired agents poking at it. "Welcome to the mad science lab," Will told me. "Agent Jensen, and our computer specialist, Mr. Pike."

Agent Jensen was tall and skinny, farm-boy blond hair falling in his eyes, while Pike was small, with delicate hands and features suited to working on machines equally delicate. "Pleased to meet you," Jensen said. "Although I have to say, we had a bet running about whether the girl in the photo on Fagin's desk was real or if he downloaded you off the Net."

"She's definitely real," Pike said. "Pay up."

Jensen grumbled and passed him a twenty. I looked at Will with a half-smile. "There's a picture of me on your desk?"

"From when we went down to Berkeley," he said. "When I helped you with that stakeout on the weres who were hooking up with dealers in San Francisco and transporting the stuff back here?"

"Right," I said. Once we'd gotten the pictures we needed, I'd let Bryson and Javier handle the arrests and Will and I had taken a night to explore the city. And now the evidence was in public, for all the world to see.

Dmitri would never have done that. Dmitri would never have the chance.

The stone was back, twice as heavy.

"So, this thing has a European plug," said Pike.

"And it looks like someone's already cracked the hard drive. What exactly am I supposed to do with this piece of crap?"

"Tell me what's on the drive, for starters," Will said. "Luna here risked a lot to get this thing, and the people it belongs to are of the big bad evil variety."

"Got it," said Pike.

"There are a bunch of spreadsheets detailing business transactions between sex traffickers," I said. "But they're in a code. Probably not much use."

"Human trafficking?" said Jensen. "That's an FBI matter, William."

"Well, for now, I'm making it an ATF matter, *Joseph*," Will said. "Can you scan the drive for me or not?"

"Yeah, yeah." Pike waved us off. "Go get coffee or something. I'll be done in half an hour."

Will walked me back to his desk, where a stack of case files was waiting. "Feel like helping me do some light reading?"

"Actually . . ." I said, thinking of the stack of dusty folders I'd brought back from Kazakhstan, "I need to deliver something to the morgue. I'll be back in a few minutes."

"Can I . . ." Will started, but I was already out the door.

CHAPTER 25

The city morgue wasn't a far walk, and it felt good to be outside. The air was starting to warm up, to lose that moist, clingy coolness that it carried in the winter.

I rode the elevator to Dr. Kronen's office, figuring I'd just leave the files for him to look over at his leisure and then go back to Will, but the light was on when I arrived, so I knocked.

"Come in, unless you're here to interrupt me," Kronen called. I poked my head in the door apologetically.

"Sorry, Bart. Guilty as charged."

"Lieutenant Wilder!" he exclaimed. "Good gods, they said you were coming home, but I never expected . . ." He caught hold of himself, smoothing the ends of his tie over his Hobbit-style stomach. "How are you?"

"I think I'm going to be all right," I said, and half-meant it for the first time. "I've got something for you, Doc, if you feel like doing me a solid."

"Anything for you, my dear," he said. "Anything."

It was the first time Kronen had called me *my dear*, and I felt a small smile curl my mouth. "I found these files in a defunct Soviet lab," I said. "They were doing biological experiments, some kind of bioengineering on were DNA. Can you tell me more?"

"These are in Russian," said Dr. Kronen, paging through. "And although I am an accomplished pianist and a fair polo player, reading this is not among my skills."

"Polo?" I said. He waved me off.

"But the test results are the same in any language. They were attempting to manipulate DNA, and the results are disturbing—the cells are turning on the body, destroying it from the inside."

"If this gene therapy actually worked," I said, "what results could one expect?"

"Weres, you say?" Kronen stroked his chin. "Were traits in a human body, I'd gather. Heightened aggression, heightened strength. An undetectable killing machine primed for blood."

"I was afraid you'd say that," I muttered.

"What context were these . . . barbarisms being conducted in?" Kronen said, turning to the pictures.

"A Russian mobster was trying to make his own army of enforcers," I said. "It's surprisingly easy to do with top-secret Soviet research just lying around and kidnapped werewolf tourists as test subjects."

"Barbaric," Kronen said again. "That is the only word I have for this material."

"Thanks, Doc," I said. Just something else to add to the evidence against the Belikovs, if they ever surfaced again. Not that I was holding out a lot of hope on that front.

"I'm very glad to see that you're all right," Kronen said.

"You and me both, Bart," I said. Kronen's phone buzzed, and he held up a finger.

"Excuse me for a moment." He listened, and then held out the extension. "Luna, it's for you."

"Yeah?" I said. "This is Luna Wilder."

"Luna, it's Will." He sounded out of breath, tense and staccato.

"What's wrong? Did something happen?"

"You need to get back here now," he said.

"Will . . ." I started.

"*Now*," he said. "Run."

I hung up and looked at Kronen. "I have to go, Bart. I'm sorry . . ."

"Go." Kronen waved me off. "May I keep these to read?"

"Yeah, sure," I said, already halfway out the door. I took the elevator back to street level and covered the five blocks between the morgue and the federal building at a run. My ribs spasmed, but I didn't care.

"What happened?" I demanded when I burst into the tech-services room. Pike and Jensen looked at me, looked at each other.

"We found something embedded in these spreadsheets," Pike said. "Look, we should really wait for Agent Fagin . . ."

"He's here," Will said, coming in. "Tell Luna what you found."

"Okay," said Pike. "On the surface, this just looks like a bunch of normal data, but the file sizes are huge. So we ran a decryption program, and we got hundreds and hundreds of emails, financial documents, bank account numbers, the works, all hidden as secondary pages in these spreadsheet files."

"Meaning what?" I said.

"The financial transactions go back and forth between Nocturne City and the Belikovs," said Will. "Someone here was backing them, in the trafficking ring and in something else, something to do with bioterrorism."

"Not quite," I said. "More like designer assassins to do whatever dirty work you could think of."

"Really?" Will scratched his chin. "I . . . heard of some crazy shit in Russia during the sixties, but . . . wow. They actually made one of those old programs viable?"

"Unfortunately," I said.

"And we found this email," said Jensen. "When we connected to the server. It was sent from a Web service about twenty hours ago."

"As near as our translator can tell," Will said, reading from a notepad, "it says something along the lines of: *'Project compromised. Family ties must be eliminated. Put him on the road.'* Along with latitude and longitude that lead here, to Nocturne City."

"Oh, gods," I said. "There must be a third one."

"Third what?" Will asked.

"Would you believe a genetically altered were programmed to be a mob hitman?"

Will rubbed his forehead. "With you, sweetheart, I've learned that anything is possible."

"The Belikovs are cleaning house," I said. "I got away, and they're trying to eliminate their backers in the U.S. to keep us from prosecuting them."

Will pointed a finger at Pike. "Find out who's the signatory on the account the payouts originated from," he said.

"Someone named Felix Natchez is the account's owner," said Pike after a moment.

"We may already be too late," Will said. "The assassin's been on the road for almost a day. This Natchez have any priors?"

"He wouldn't," I said softly, feeling like I had just stepped into an express elevator, headed straight down. "He's a cop."

A crooked cop. A cop who had known Lily Dubois . . ."Nathaniel Dubois," I said. Will frowned at me.

"Are you sure?"

"He's in bed with Natchez," I said. "It was Nate Dubois who tried to throw me off his daughter's murder investigation in the first place, with his were thugs. He wanted pack justice, not police work."

"If you're wrong, someone else is going to get murdered," Jensen said.

"A lying, sex-trafficking scumbag," I said. "And anyway, I'm not wrong."

"Call the SCS task force on the local PD for backup," Will said to Jensen. "I'm heading to the Dubois residence."

"Me, too," I said. Will started to object, but I held up my hand. "I'm not letting you go up there alone. If this creature is anything like the one I met in Kazakhstan, your, uh, condition is not going to be a huge benefit. You might be alive, but you'll be in ribbons."

"You sure you're up to it?" Will said, his brow furrowing. Jensen and Pike looked between us, no doubt wondering what *condition* Agent Fagin suffered from.

"I'm sure," I said. "I have to be up to it. I'm the only one who has a chance of stopping him."

"All right," Will said, pulling his holdout pistol from his ankle holster. "Then take this. Can't have you running in there unarmed."

I gave him a small smile. "My hero."

"I try my best," Will said, running for the elevator. I caught up with him at the door.

I prayed that we weren't too late.

And I wondered where on earth I'd find the time to have a wedding.

The Duboises lived just outside of the fashionable part of Cedar Hill, on the back slope that wasn't really Cedar Hill but the part of Garden Hill that wasn't wall-to-wall crackheads, in a refurbished, rambling Craftsman that was still far beyond what I could afford.

Will pulled the Mustang to a crooked stop at the curb and jumped out, eyeing the house. "Doesn't look like a hotbed of mob activity from here."

I pulled my borrowed gun from the waist of my jeans and held it at my side. "I think that's the point."

Will and I mounted the wide porch steps, lined with planter boxes displaying the first flowers of spring, bright reds and pinks, fleshy colors. Bloody colors.

"Mr. Dubois?" Will called, tapping on the door. I was in the second position, my shoulder against the frame, the gun tight in my fist, ready to spring into action should Dubois be waiting on the other side of the door with a shotgun.

There was no answer, and I reached my fist across the fire zone to knock. "Nathaniel, it's Luna Wilder. Can you open the door?"

This time, my ears caught something, far away in another part of the house. A shattering of glass, a faint, strangled scream.

"Will," I said tightly. "He's already here."

Will stepped back, switching positions with me, and pulled his radio off his belt. "Nocturne dispatch, be advised we've detected a disturbance at the Dubois residence and are making entry."

The dispatcher's voice crackled. "Ten-four, Agent Fagin. SCS backup en route. ETA five minutes."

"We don't have five minutes," I said, feeling the sick creep of helplessness in my gut again. I'd been at the mercy of Grigorii Belikov for the past several weeks. No more.

Will gestured to the front door. "Be my guest, doll."

I took a firm stance and planted my right foot against the Duboises' deadbolt. The doorframe splintered and it swung inward, hitting the wall with a crack like a rifle shot. That's the bitch about a hard entry—it always lets the bad guys know you're coming.

The sounds were much louder now, snarls and cries, crashes as a body was tossed from place to place. I touched Will's shoulder. "Upstairs."

"Let me lead," he said. "Just in case they get cute and shoot me."

Will was never macho or alpha about these things—he just stated facts. If he ran into gunfire, he'd get back up. If he was taken down by an enraged genetically modified were, he'd get back up.

I hoped. "I'm right behind you," I said, and Will flicked me a smile.

"That's what I like to hear." Raising his voice from

Will to *Will Fagin, ATF,* he called down the hall, "Federal agent! Whoever's up here, show yourself!"

The hallway had sloped ceilings, like so many of the old houses in Nocturne City, and there were three doors—one on each side and one dead ahead.

The one in front of us was where all the snarling was coming from.

"Help me!" a woman's voice screamed. "I'm in the master bedroom!"

"That's Petra," I said, and Will sprinted ahead, hitting the bedroom door with his shoulder.

We both pulled up short at the scene in the bedroom. Nathaniel Dubois lay facedown, a pool of blood big enough to fill a lake still spreading from under his throat. Dark blood. Arterial blood. The spray was all over the white linens on the king-sized bed, the wall above it and his wife, who cowered in the corner holding a Colt .45 Army pistol on a hunched, dirty, snarling customer that I took to be Belikov's hitwere.

I didn't need to check Nathaniel's pulse to know that he had shuffled loose the mortal coil, so I carefully stepped over his body and drew a bead on the creature.

"Get the fuck away from her."

The were turned on me, flat nostrils flaring. His face was deformed, half in and half out of the phase, hirsute in all the wrong places, his eyes pupiless and gold. He looked like Lon Chaney in *The Wolf Man*, as viewed through the filter of a royally bad acid trip.

"Mine," he snarled, and lashed out at Petra, who screeched and struck at him with the gun.

"Hold still!" Will shouted, tightening his firing stance. "Back away from her!"

"He killed Nate," Petra sobbed. "Nate tried to protect me and that bastard just tore his throat out . . ."

"Petra, it's going to be okay," I said. "I promise you."

The assassin snarled, spittle hanging from his lower lip, and he turned and gave me the smile that I imagine Death gives to you just before your number is up. It was a chilling, animal expression, a grimace of challenge.

"Will . . ." I said, and that was all I got out before the creature went for Petra's throat.

His lunge knocked her pistol upward and it went off with the big *boom* that Colts give, raining plaster and asbestos insulation down on Petra and her attacker. She let out a scream, thrashing beneath him, kicking and scratching like only someone staring their own grisly murder in the face can do.

"I don't have a shot!" Will snapped. "I'll hit her."

"Same here," I said, jamming his pistol into my waistband. Will rotated his gaze a fraction toward me.

"Luna, don't do it."

Really, all of it happened inside five seconds. The creature reared back to tear out Petra's throat, I dropped my firing stance and launched myself at him, catching him high in the chest like a football tackle, tearing him off Petra with my weight, sending the both of us backward.

The big picture window over the Duboises' front porch came up too fast and we fell through it. I felt glass tug at my skin, and the creature and I hit the porch roof with a bone-shaking thud.

He was on top of me, howling, snapping, and I jammed both feet into his gut and heaved with all of my strength. The creature went over my head, scrabbling for purchase, and fell from the roof with a yelp.

I rolled over in time to see him pick himself up from the Duboises' lawn and take off running.

"Hex it," I muttered, looking at the twelve-foot drop. "Well, you've had worse," I said, before I launched myself after him. If he got away, the only evidence of Grigorii Belikov's bioengineering program went with him. So *not* happening on my watch.

Tires squealed and I saw a flash of green metal and chrome before the creature went airborne and crashed down in the street, one leg twisted at an improbable angle.

He struggled up almost immediately, the bone knitting and twisting under the skin before my eyes, like his body was alive, possessed of its own primitive need to hunt and kill.

The driver of the car that hit him jumped out, sweaty, his baby blue tie askew. "Don't you move, asshole!" the driver shouted ineffectually, leveling a Glock.

"Bryson!" I shouted, recognizing my stocky detective and his green Taurus.

"*Wilder?*" he cried. "*Shit.* What the *fuck* is going on here?"

The creature was up now, and he rotated toward Bryson like an alcoholic hones in on an open bar.

"*David!*" I screamed, drawing my own gun. "Get down!"

Bryson ducked behind his car door as the thing started for him at a dead run, and I raised my pistol.

The were grabbed the car door, yanking it half off its hinges, one hand reaching for Bryson through the shattered window and leaving a long line of claw marks in David's blocky forearm.

I squeezed the trigger. One-two-three, *pop-pop-pop*. No hesitation, no wavering, three shots into the center mass, just like they teach you at the academy. I'm not too modest to say that I dropped the creature like a sack of cement.

He fell in the street, boneless, the exit wounds in his back echoes of the flowers on the Duboises' porch.

Bryson shakily pulled himself upright. "Jesus Christ in a motorboat, Wilder," he said. "Jesus *Christ*."

"I know," I said. "I know, but he's dead now. We'll get your arm looked at."

"No, not *that*," Bryson said. "Who the fuck is going to pay for my gods-damned *car*?"

"David . . ." I said, and then shook my head. "Put in a reimbursement request to the department. You *did* total it in the line of duty."

Will came out of the house leading Petra, who was wrapped in his suit jacket. She was sobbing, clinging to Will like he was the life preserver and she was Kate Winslet in *Titanic*.

"David, secure the scene," I said. "I need to take care of this."

"You got it, Wilder," he said, moving to get his camera from the Taurus. "And hey, Wilder?"

I turned back to him. "Yeah, David?"

"It's good to have you back," he said.

"Luna," Will said, "I think we should call a bus for Mrs. Dubois here. She's in a bad way."

"Go ahead," I said. "I'll sit with her."

Will lowered Petra to the front steps and stepped away, using his radio to call for an ambulance.

"This is unreal," Petra said. "First . . . first my Lily and now my husband."

I bit my lip, wondering if now was the time to tell her that Nate had been the financial backer of a homicidal, magick-using mob boss who sold girls like Amway.

She started to sob again. Probably not the time. "Things are going to be all right," I said. "We're going to catch the people responsible."

"What I wouldn't give for five minutes alone with Nikolai Rostov," she snarled. "He's the one who started this poison, who lured my little girl to that awful place, and I'm sure he ratted out my husband."

A finger of cold whispered its way across my neck, raising all of the hairs. "How did you know about Nikolai Rostov?" I said.

She sniffed. "You must have told me."

"No," I said slowly. "I never told anyone except Will and Natalie Lane about going to see Rostov, because I was afraid the FBI would Hex up my case." I faced her. "But you knew."

Petra's eyes darted from me to Will to Bryson, to the two cars that had pulled up behind his and disgorged Batista and Lane. I sighed, rubbing my forehead. The start of a migraine was growling behind my skull. "Nate wasn't the one in charge. It was you."

Petra's nostrils flared. "You have no proof of that."

"Your financials are proof," I said. "I'm sure when we check the bogus account you made Felix Natchez open, your name will be a signatory, and not your husband's. The Russians needed someone to keep the were packs of Nocturne in line while they raped their daughters, and they needed someone with money.

You were in bed with Rostov here, and Belikov overseas." Gods, I hoped not literally.

"This is a very outlandish and amusing story," Petra said coldly. "But I've just lost my husband, so I'm going to go to Agent Fagin and hope he can at least sit with me in silence until my ambulance comes."

I flicked my hand out and grabbed her by the wrist. "Sit down," I said, low. "Don't make me tell you again."

"Why would I kill my own daughter, Lieutenant?" She let out a frantic, braying laugh. "That's utterly ridiculous!"

I lifted one shoulder. "I'm guessing Lily got her fake ID from Ivan Salazko, and when he knew her by sight, she tweaked to what her mommy dearest was involved in. She threatened you, like a good rebellious teen will do, and you had her killed and tried to pin it on her hophead boyfriend."

Petra's face was pale now, a ring of white around her nostrils, and her breath was coming rapidly. I squeezed harder on her wrist, and she let out a small sound. "Funny thing about the Russian mob," I said. "They don't just kill the snitch. They take care of whole families—parents, grandparents, and especially kids. You must know why."

Petra finally dropped her eyes from mine. "So the children won't grow up and begin a vendetta against their parents' killers."

"Right in one," I said. "But you didn't have the stomach to tear out your own daughter's heart, so you had Rostov and Anton, your favorite test subject, do the hands-on work. Am I getting it so far?"

Petra shook her head. "You're just telling stories and I'm listening, Lieutenant."

"I'm guessing this isn't something you fell into," I said. "It takes a long time to develop this kind of stone-cold willingness to kill. What's your maiden name, Petra?"

"Ivanovich," she said numbly. "I guess you'll find that out, anyway." A smile curled around her lips, and her eyes went hard, like beads. There was an utter lack of feeling to the expression, and I knew that she felt nothing about her daughter, or her husband—she'd survived, and that was all that mattered. Animal. Uncomplicated.

"Stand up," I said, hauling her with me. "Petra Ivanovich Dubois, you're under arrest for conspiracy to commit murder—since you didn't have the guts to do it yourself—and I'm sure the U.S. attorney can think of a host of other charges once Interpol catches Ekaterina Belikov."

"Lies, from one criminal turned on another," Petra spat. "You'll never get a conviction, Miss Wilder. I'll be free before the month is out."

"Will," I said. "Mind lending me your cuffs?"

He passed them to me, a frown turning the space between his brows into a valley. "What's going on, Luna?"

"A crusade," said Petra. "A pointless crusade that won't end in anything except humiliation for you, Miss Wilder, and freedom for me."

"Maybe," I said. "But they don't give bail to murder suspects in Las Rojas County, Petra."

"Jail in this country doesn't frighten me," she said. "I saw much worse growing up in Moscow."

"Fair enough," I said. "But like you said yourself, Belikov turned on you. I wonder how long you'll last before someone decides to tie up your loose end. The Russians aren't known for being forgiving, Petra. And then there's your pack, and all the other packs that have lost sisters and mothers and wives to your little smuggling operation. I'd say it'd be a hell of a good betting pool on who gets to you first."

A single shiver passed through her, and she looked at the ground. "They'll give me protection in the jail. You have to protect me."

"Me?" I said, shoving her at Lane, who took her arm firmly. "I don't have to do a damn thing."

"I'll take her to central booking," Lane said. "And SVU will have some questions about her daughter."

"I'd make peace with whatever gods I had," I told Petra. "As of now, you're living on borrowed time."

CHAPTER 26

The crime scene at the Dubois household took an afternoon to clear, and it was dinnertime when Will and I were finally released to clock out of our respective jobs and get something to eat.

"I never would have seen that," Will admitted, when we'd settled into my favorite window booth at the Devere Diner. "Even with my vast experience in the treachery of the fairer sex."

"Oh, is that so?" I said, taking a pull on my chocolate shake. I'd lost weight overseas and I could see all the bones in my hips and elbows and ribs. The skeletal look wasn't real sexy as far as I was concerned, so I was trying to make up for lost time and keep my pants from falling off my ass. "Women are all treacherous bitches, are we?"

"I didn't say it that way, but in certain cases, yes," said Will. "The female is definitely the deadlier of the species. But I never pegged Petra Dubois as a gang leader."

"Belikov is Russian," I said. "She knew him, and they must have started their operation before she moved to the States and met up with her pack-leader husband slash cover story."

Will drained half of his cherry Coke in one gulp. "I kinda feel sorry for the guy. But then again, how blind do you have to be to not notice your wife is a mob boss and a slave trader?"

"Pretty blind," I agreed, playing with my bendy straw. "Or hopelessly in love."

Will rolled his eyes. "You can't expect me to believe that blinded-by-the-light story. I love you, and I've got my eyes wide open."

Our waitress came and left our cheeseburgers—with generous sides of fries—in front of us, but suddenly I'd lost my appetite.

Will was blind, whether he admitted it or not. He couldn't see the change in me, the cold spot in my heart where all of my remorse and desire to keep the monster at bay had vanished. I felt the were in me all the time now, the act of killing under its influence powerful and narcotic.

"You went quiet, doll," Will said. "Something on your mind?"

"Nothing," I said. "I need to pee." I slid out of the booth and booked it to the ladies room at record speed.

Alone in the small space, the smell of mildew, bleach and old tile grout drove any romantic notions I might have had out of my head.

I couldn't marry Will. He didn't know what I was. He would be shocked, horrified, repulsed. He'd leave me.

I ran water into the stained basin and splashed it on my face in an attempt to get a hold on myself. I didn't whine and pout and angst endlessly over men. That wasn't me. But then again, up until a few weeks ago, snapping someone's neck in cold blood and letting my monster rule me wasn't me, either. Hadn't been for fifteen years.

"Gods," I muttered, massaging my temples. "What the fuck am I supposed to do?"

"Stop whining, for starters."

Lily was in the mirror again, and when I spun around she was standing there, her legs trailing off into nothingness, her face pale and misty, shimmering.

"You've got some nerve," I said. "You're the cause of half of this angst and you tell me to quit being emo?"

"When your life is cut short at fourteen, *chica*, you learn to prioritize." Lily sniffed.

"I don't even know if I can stay with Will, or my job, never mind marry him and have a white-picket fucking fence," I muttered. "And Hex it, *why* am I telling someone who isn't even here these things?"

"'Cause I'm listening?" Lily suggested. She sighed, and drifted over to the mirror, running fingers through her hair, licking her pinkie finger and fixing her smeared eyeliner.

"Your mom is in jail," I said. "For what she did to you."

Lily nodded. "I know. Never figured she'd order my death, but there you go. Guess that's why I couldn't shake a leg to the afterlife."

"You can go now. Why are you still here?"

"I'm not staying long," Lily said. "I came to tell you that I wasn't going to, like, haunt your dreams and stuff anymore, and there you are, moaning over some guy who totally won't even care what screwed-up things you did."

"Thanks," I said. "But when you're my age, it's not that simple. I'm not the person Will thinks I am."

"Then *be* that person starting now," said Lily. "The guy wants to marry you, right? He's got to have accepted that you're weird."

"Again," I said with a growl, "thanks. Your dead sarcasm does wonders for my self-esteem."

Lily shrugged and turned away from the mirror. "Whatever. I have to go. It's been real, Lieutenant Wilder."

"Yeah," I said. "Although I'd be lying if I said that I wasn't glad to see the back of you. If I never meet another spirit again, it will be too soon."

"Oh," Lily said, as she faded to little more than a pair of eyes, a pair of hands and a ghostly smile, "I'm not the last you'll meet. Not by a long shot. Not at all."

She was gone before I could ask her what the hell she meant by that statement, and she probably would have just given me attitude, anyway.

Fucking ghosts.

I dried myself off and stepped back into the diner to a snap of dryer, warmer air. Lily tended to make things damp.

Will smiled over the remains of his cheeseburger. "There you are. I was about to send in a search party and some rescue dogs with brandy."

"Sweetie?" I said, taking his free hand. The French fry grease warmed our grip. Will went serious.

"Uh-oh. I know that look. What's gone wrong?"

I took in a deep breath. "I lied to you. There is something going on with me."

Will's gaze softened from panicked to concerned.

For a minute, I pictured that I could tell him what had really happened in Kiev and he wouldn't react with disgust or, worse, pity. It was the pity I really couldn't deal with.

But the feeling only lasted for a second before I brought myself back to the real world, where there are some secrets you just don't share, no matter how understanding your boyfriend appears.

"I see things," I said. "Well, not forever, but lately. I started seeing Lily Dubois. Not dreams, I swear. Really *seeing*."

Will cocked his head. "That's not something you had to be afraid to tell me, Luna."

"I don't know why, or what I did, or why *this* victim, out of the hundreds, decided to start visiting me," I said. "But I don't think it's going away, so I just wanted to warn you."

"Warned," Will said with a smile. "Not running scared. But you should talk to your cousin, figure out why you suddenly have this ability . . ."

I held up a hand. "Later. There's plenty of time for that later, when I'm not eating my first bacon-cheesy slice of heaven in weeks." Sunny had cried on the phone when I called to tell her I was home, but there was time. Time to see her, time to be nicer about her and Mac. Time to be a human being and not a human with a monster digging claws into her back.

Be that person, starting now. For such a bratty kid, she made some damned good sense. I dug into my burger, and Will shifted in his seat, bringing something out of his jacket pocket. "I had hoped for a slightly more romantic way to do this, but . . ."

He popped open the velvet box and I gasped involuntarily at the square-cut diamond and white-gold setting inside. "Oh gods, Will. That's beautiful. And *huge*. Are you on the take?"

His mouth crooked. "No. It's something I've had for a while. I got it in Paris in the 1920s. Just never found the right girl to give it to." He extended the box toward me. "But I have now."

Before I could say anything, Will was down on one knee in the middle of the Devere Diner, in front of the gods and everybody. "Luna Joanne Wilder, I love you and I need you in my life. I don't even care that I had to ask this question twice: Marry me?"

A million things went through my head at that moment, a million in a second and a half. Will would be with me when I phased. He'd see me for what I was.

He'd know what I'd done.

But in that moment, I felt worry wash away like a tide. My life might constantly be in ruins, but the part with Will Fagin was right. Had always been right. *Could* always be right. Was that enough to give my life over to completely?

"Yes," I said, softly. "Yes, Will."

He jumped up and hugged me, and the other diners broke into applause, and the whole thing was a scene I never thought I'd get to play in a thousand years. Not me. Not Luna Wilder, who attracted the wrong kind of men and inevitably screwed everything up, anyway.

"Thank you," Will said quietly. He gave me a wide grin. "I was going to feel like a real ass if you said no. Male ego and all, you know."

"I wouldn't have," I said, looking down at my un-eaten cheeseburger. I still didn't have my appetite back, but for entirely different reasons.

What had I just done? Will loved me and he had absolute faith in me and I'd looked him in the eye and lied that I had the same sort of faith, in him and in myself.

This was going to blow up in my face, just like every other time I'd tried to be normal, to keep the were inside . . .

I took a breath. It wouldn't, this time, because I wouldn't let it. Above all else, I was a survivor, and survivors didn't let the tide drag them down. They kept their heads up, and they forged ahead.

"This is going to be great," Will said. "We'll get married in the fall; I mean, we will if that's all right with you. Just, try to keep Bryson out of the wedding party, okay? Somehow, I think that can only end badly."

He saw the look on my face and trailed off, going serious. "Doll, what's wrong?"

"Will," I said, taking his hands in mine. "There's something I have to tell you."

EPILOGUE

The courtroom in Kiev wasn't ventilated, windows shut up tight, and the air was oppressively thick in the midsummer sun that was beating down on the square outside.

I sat in the witness box, feeling the sweat slide down every piece of skin that didn't already have my blouse stuck to it. Red-faced and soaked. What a great impression on the court.

The translator, a small trim woman with a librarian's bun, black hair and black eyes, looked to the prosecutor and then to me. "Please describe your association with Mr. Belikov."

Grigorii and Ekaterina were at the defendant's table. Ekaterina looked sour as ever, Grigorii green around the gills and skinny, radiating sickness. He had an antibiotic IV hooked up even in the courtroom. Yesterday, his defender had gone into great detail about the infections, the surgeries, the *pain* Grigorii had gone through as a result of my moment with the scissors, as if that somehow excused everything Lola and the parade of other victims had testified to suffering at his hands.

No one in the courtroom besides Ekaterina seemed

particularly moved by his plight. I was just marveling that the slimy bastard had even survived.

"I met Mr. Belikov when I was transported to his compound in Kiev," I said, the translator speaking along with me. "He told me that I was a whore now, and that I would either have sex with the men who chose me or that I'd be beaten and sent to their blood-sport arena to be used as bait."

I paused for the translator to finish and continued, "When I resisted, I was indeed thrown into the arena, where I managed to fight my opponent to a standstill. Then Mr. Belikov sold me to a man who had expressed an interest in having a girl who was injured. That was his turn-on."

"And how did you escape?" the prosecutor asked.

"The man who bought me turned out to be a friend, and he helped me get out of the compound and dressed my wounds so that I wouldn't die of an infection. He saved my life. He died for me."

The prosecutor withdrew and the Belikovs' defender stood up. She was a woman, a hard-ass red-from-the-bottle type who wore too much makeup and was fond of jabbing her finger into my face.

"Isn't it true that this friend was at the time of his demise a convicted criminal?" the translator said.

"In Russia," I said. "And in America. Not here."

"And isn't it true that you offered Mr. Belikov sexual favors in exchange for your release?"

I blinked. Grigorii must have told her about the moment in the lab. "I felt I had no choice," I said. "When you're a woman in a vulnerable position . . ."

"And after Mr. Belikov refused your disease-ridden body, you attacked him?" the translator said. She crinkled her nose, as if having to repeat such obvious grandstanding made her slightly ill.

I locked eyes with the defender. "After *Mr. Belikov* threatened to rape me if I didn't comply, I decided enough was enough and I stabbed him in the groin with a pair of surgical scissors, which is *far* less than he deserved. In my opinion."

The court rippled at that, and the magistrate banged his gavel down. "You're excused," the translator said after a moment. "Thank you."

I left the defense box and decided I needed air. Any kind of air, even the sweltering summer day outside. I needed to be out of sight of the Belikovs' hard gazes and the memories they stirred.

I was back to seeing Dr. Merriman, the police shrink in Nocturne City, and I was here in Ukraine testifying against her advice. She said I had posttraumatic stress, that seeing my captors again would just aggravate it.

I told her that the motherfuckers needed to be put away for good, and that if they somehow walked, I was going to be there to kill Grigorii with my bare hands. That had shut her up.

"Luna?" Will jogged out of the courtroom after me, and I paused on the wide steps to wait for him, breathing the slightly cooler air.

"It got pretty *Law & Order* in there, huh?" I said, trying to keep things light.

After I'd told Will about killing the man in the brothel, about how Dmitri had died, about how I felt like I was one step away from tearing someone's throat out most days, and that I had no hope of holding the were back the way I'd used to, he'd gotten quiet. There had been two or three days of awkward conversation until I'd finally gone home to my own apartment, even though I couldn't sleep and obsessively checked the locks on all of the windows and the front door.

Will hadn't left. He hadn't even asked for the ring back. All of the unsaid words between us were starting to feel like a heavy load on my back.

"I . . . I had no idea," he said. "Luna, even when you told me, you didn't tell me." He didn't reach for me, because we seemed to have forgotten how to be close to each other as my interest in sex waned and my nightmares got worse.

"It happened," I said with a shrug. "And I'd really like to stop talking about it, believe me, but the Belikovs need to go away."

Will shoved his hands into his pockets. He'd had to take unpaid vacation to come with me to the trial, after Interpol had finally tracked down Grigorii and Ekaterina in Thailand, trying to get cheap surgery for Grigorii's disfigurement. They were already reaching out to the locals, Ekaterina having a stake in a dance hall on the outskirts of Bangkok, already running "exotic" girls from the back rooms.

Dr. Gorshkov was still at large, but somehow I had the feeling that without Petra's money and Grigorii's desire to build his own private hit squad of mutant weres, he'd be less than no trouble.

"I'm going to stick with you," Will blurted. I held up my hand to tell him that reassurance wasn't really what I needed, but he pressed on. "Just listen to me. I knew when I proposed that our life wasn't going to be all American dreams and great sex. I knew that we both had our baggage. I'm going to stay. No matter what they did to you, I'll be there. I'll hold you while you sleep and I'll be there when you're ready to be with me again. That's my decision and I'm sticking to it, so please don't try to drive me away anymore. It's getting sort of old."

I felt wetness prick my eyes, salt that wasn't sweat. "I do love you, Will," I said softly.

He gave me a lopsided smile. "I can tell."

Before I could say anything else, about how relieved I was that he wasn't bolting for the hills, I caught a familiar scent. Cloves and sweat, the smell that was his alone.

"Hello, Luna," Dmitri said.

Will cocked an eyebrow. If there was one thing he was good at, it was picking up on weirdness. "You all right?"

"No, I . . ." I stared at Dmitri, at the court reporter who passed through him, lugging a briefcase. "I'm a little dehydrated," I finished lamely.

"Should have said so," Will told me, and went down the steps to a vendor selling water and soda.

"So that's Will," Dmitri said with a smirk. "I thought he'd be taller."

I folded my arms. "You're dead and you're still an ass."

"What can I say?" he told me. "Don't have a lot of time for chitchat."

I knew from Lily that my new mojo didn't work unless the dearly departed in question had serious unfinished business. "What's wrong, Dmitri?" I said, and earned looks from everyone passing by. I ignored them.

"Margarita and Masha are on their way to the

States," Dmitri said. "Maybe Los Angeles, maybe San Francisco . . . somewhere on the West Coast, where the pack will protect them. I need you to look out for them, Luna. You're the only person I can trust to do it."

"I . . ." That hadn't been what I was expecting. "Of course I will, Dmitri. She's your daughter, after all."

Dmitri reached for me, dropped his hand just as his fingers would have passed through my cheek.

"I miss you. Seeing you in Kiev, it just . . . it hammered home what a mistake we made. I wish I'd had time to give it another try."

I gave him a tired smile. "I didn't want to be that woman, Dmitri. You'd always have the daemon in you. You'd always need a pack. I couldn't . . ." I sighed, trying to find the kind words. "That isn't the life I could live."

"So you just move on down the line?" Dmitri demanded hoarsely, cold air prickling around us. "To *Will?*"

"No," I said. "I have moved on, Dmitri." My eyes were hot, stinging, and I looked at my feet. "But I can't forget you, and I'm so sorry it had to end like it did."

Dmitri dropped his own gaze. "I'm not. You know I loved you, Luna. Maybe we couldn't be together, but I'd've done anything for you."

"I know," I said. "I do."

"Good," he said, starting to shimmer like a heat illusion. "I'm done, then. I'm free."

He tried to reach for me once more, but he flickered and disappeared before he could. I swiped a hand over my face, sweat and tears coming away. I barely got out the whisper, "Good-bye, Dmitri."

I turned my back on the spot where he'd stood, and

walked down the steps toward Will, who was holding an Evian water aloft like he'd just won some sort of battle trophy. I had to smile a little. I'd never forget the way Dmitri and I had ended, never stop seeing or feeling it, but I also knew that I'd made the right choice with Will.

The voice stopped me halfway to him, a hiss against the air, hotter than the sun sending zephyrs up from the pavement. A promise of an ending to something I'd set in motion and had no chance of stopping, even now that the man he'd marked was dead. Now I was the only one, the one he was fixed on, the one he would have.

Asmodeus spoke to me, and I could hear him smiling.

"I see you, Insoli. And I'll be with you. Soon enough."

I turned back to him, met those gold eyes looking not out of the face of a man I'd loved, but out of my own face, a copy of my body, looking at me across a vast distance of power.

"You come right ahead," I told the figure of Asmodeus. "I'll be waiting."

"Kittredge knows how to create a believable world, and her fans will enjoy the mix of magic and city grit."

—*Publishers Weekly*

Don't miss these other novels in Caitlin Kittredge's extraordinary Black London series

STREET MAGIC
ISBN: 978-0-312-94361-5

DEMON BOUND
ISBN: 978-0-312-94363-9

Available from St. Martin's Paperbacks